DEFENDER

VERDANT STRING

MICHELLE DIENER

ABOUT DEFENDER

Hunted, captured, taken off-planet …

As a Special Forces Commander, Ethan Hyt is well aware his duty is to protect the Planetary Head of Defense, Velda Shanïha, but when their ship is shot down and they are taken prisoner, he finds it harder and harder to pretend he's protecting Velda out of duty.

Velda knows that as Aponi's Head of Defense, she's a good bargaining chip for her enemies, and she's hoping that fact will keep her and Ethan alive.

She and Ethan made a good team before, but their forced proximity has made their connection even stronger, and they'll need each other to take every opportunity to get free.

Because if they don't, Velda's afraid they're going to disappear forever.

1

———————

Both Pamela Ingot and Harden turned their gazes on him.

He quirked his lips. "I know you've previously had a cordial relationship, but I've told Commander Ingot what the stakes are here, and what we know so far."

"And would you care to tell me?" Ferris Harden asked.

"Sure." Ethan finally sat down on the edge of the desk. "You are either being paid or blackmailed to keep the discovery of an ancestral shipwreck on Ytla from the Aponian government. You set Wren Thorakis up on Ytla four months ago to be kidnapped by the people searching for parts of the ship, in order to send them the supplies they desperately needed under the guise of ransom for her release, and when she stumbled across a part of the ship during her escape, you tried to keep her quiet. When that didn't work, you tried to have her killed."

"Wren Thorakis was kidnapped by the Har Met Vent," Demilla Grant objected. "Not . . . whoever it was you just said."

Ethan waited a beat for Harden to add anything, and when he didn't, he gripped the edge of the desk and leaned forward. "The Har Met Vent is a front, a group of mercenaries pretending to be a religious cult in order to find and steal the technology from the ancestral wreck they've already found part of on Ytla. It broke up into pieces on crash landing, but the presence of a university research group that has recently been conducting unrelated studies on Ytla made it difficult for the Har Met Vent to move around, and to get the supplies they needed without some questions being raised by Aponi Defense. The two of you came up with a kidnap plot where you could provide the Har Met Vent with the supplies they desperately needed under the guise of a ransom payment."

"I didn't come up with anything." Demilla Garret fairly vibrated with outrage.

"You didn't say anything when Ferris here lied to Wren's face and told her the wreck she'd found was a research vessel that had gone down years before." Ethan tilted his head.

Demilla shot Harden another sidelong look. "You said you were humoring her."

Harden didn't even look over at her. "If this information is coming from Wren Thorakis, you have to understand she's traumatized. She was held prisoner by the cult, and then spent three days after her escape making her way back to our camp. She's . . . delicate."

Ethan threw back his head and laughed. "Wren Thorakis is not delicate."

Pamela Ingot frowned at him. "Is this whole thing based on the word of one artifacts consultant?"

Ethan sobered up. "Do you honestly think the Planetary Head of Defense would send me to shake up a hornet's nest in Nanganya on nothing but someone's word?"

Pamela Ingot gave a slow shake of her head. She looked over at Harden. "So, why did you lie?"

Ethan could see Ferris Harden's mind racing as he sifted through the possible explanations he could give. He was pretty sure none of them would be the truth.

"I was told the ancestral wreck was top secret. And that I should appease Wren Thorakis with an explanation she would accept." Harden lifted his shoulders. "Why didn't she believe me?"

"Because she saw the wreck, you idiot. Do you honestly think an artifacts consultant, a specialist in these things, would mistake an ancestral wreck with a research runner from twenty years ago?" Ethan held his gaze until Harden cut his eyes to the left.

"She never said she thought it was an ancestral wreck," Demilla Garret said. "I'd have remembered that."

"No, but she knew it was. She felt it was her duty to report the find, but she wasn't willing to give her assessment of what it was to Nanganya Special Forces when she didn't trust them further than she could throw them, especially after they abandoned her in the hands of the cult for nearly a week." Ethan tilted his head. "And I have to say, Harden, shame on your teams for that. I have never heard anything like it."

"They couldn't rescue her, there was a massive storm raging." Demilla Garret seemed to like parroting what she had obviously been told by Harden.

"We're Special Forces," Ethan said. "We eat storms for breakfast. Or at least, Demeter Special Forces does. And we would never leave one of our own in enemy hands because of a little rain."

"Lieutenant Trent was sanctioned for that," Harden said, and Demilla Garret gave him some side-eye, as if this was the first she was hearing of it.

"Not according to his file." Ethan twisted, leaning back, and picked up a file. Flicked it with a finger.

Harden shifted. "It was verbal."

"Convenient. You're happy with that level of capability? Because we run very different departments, if that's so." Ethan tossed the file back on the desk, and crossed his arms.

"So you're saying they deliberately left Wren Thorakis with the cult, because someone in the government is supporting the Har Met Vent and needed to get them supplies. And they used Wren's kidnapping as an excuse to give the Har Met Vent what they needed under the cover of ransom?" Pamela Ingot spoke slowly.

"I'm not only saying that, I'm saying that Harden's team on Ytla set Wren Thorakis up to be kidnapped to begin with. So Harden couldn't sanction Lieutenant Trent for his behavior, because he'd ordered his actions." It still made Ethan furious just thinking about it. The corruption of Special Forces was anathema to him.

"I wasn't told any of this." Demilla Garret stood, and physically distanced herself from Harden. "Has Wren put in formal complaints?"

"She has." Ethan had asked her to do it before she and Ed Zeneri had left for the observatory station in nearspace. Having it in writing added a layer to his investigation.

"You're saying Harden here was being bribed or blackmailed to do this. Are you being serious?" Pamela Ingot had been watching her colleague as they spoke, and Ethan guessed she'd seen the same thing he had. The closing up of his expression, the stiffness in his posture.

"Deadly. The old Core Companies, in league with the Caruso, are behind this." Ethan noticed a muscle twitch under Harden's eye at that.

"What?" Demilla Garret took another step away from Harden. "Commander?" She was staring at him, eyes wide.

"You can leave," Ethan said, turning to her. "Some investigators from Commander Ingot's department are waiting for you outside. You can give your account to them."

Demilla closed her eyes for a moment, straightened up, and then gave a curt nod. "I see. Thank you." She walked out, back stiff and straight.

"Where is Lieutenant Trent?" Harden tried to look nonchalant as he asked, leaning back in his chair.

"Some of my officers took him in for questioning as soon as this conversation started," Pamela Ingot said. "I thought Commander Hyt was all kinds of wrong about this, but that's a lesson to me. Velda Shanïha doesn't rattle cages without good reason."

Mention of Velda had the effect it usually did on Ethan. It shot some adrenalin through him, made his chest tight. He hoped like hell it didn't show on the outside. Not to her, and not to anyone else, either.

Her tenure as Head of Defense for Aponi was ending next year, and he'd told himself he'd wait until she was no longer his boss before he made any kind of move on her.

"Now that Garret is out of the room, care to share who told you the wreck was top secret?" Pamela Ingot asked, gaze steady on Harden.

Ethan was impressed that she was circling back to it. It was his next question, too. Not that he believed Harden had been telling the truth about that, but it would be interesting to see what name he threw out.

"Henry Nostrada," Harden said.

Ethan lifted his comm unit, eyes on Harden, and connected. "It's

Ethan," he said as Velda Shanïha answered. "Harden just threw Nostrada under the bus. Which means he's probably dead."

He heard Velda draw in a surprised breath, while watching both Pamela Ingot and Harden stare at him with varying degrees of shock.

"I'm here in Nanganya, same as you," Velda said, voice clipped. "I got in a couple of hours ago. No one has seen Nostrada since yesterday, so I'm about to head to his apartment."

"Wait for me," Ethan said. "Where's the Planetary Administrative Council building in Nanganya?"

"We're in it," Pamela Ingot said. "We have the bottom four floors, Planetary Admin has the two floors above."

That was good.

"I'll come down to you," Velda said, voice slightly amused, and Ethan realized he'd just ordered her to wait for him.

He gave a mental shrug. She shouldn't be out looking for Nostrada without protection.

"You weren't surprised Commander Harden threw out Nostrada's name," Pamela Ingot said.

"No. We know Nostrada's involved. But I'm guessing Harden was either told he was going to be killed, or had him killed himself, for him to so casually give out his name."

"And Velda Shanïha is here, in Nanganya, a few floors above us, right now?" Ingot's mouth twisted. "What have you brought down on us, Harden?"

Ferris Harden said nothing. His hands stretched and flexed on his thighs, and he didn't look at them.

"You want to come with us?" Ethan asked Ingot.

"Where are we going?" she asked.

"Going to see if Henry Nostrada is in his apartment, because he hasn't come in to work."

"You really think he's dead?" Ingot asked.

Ethan nodded, but he didn't think. He was sure.

2

______

Velda Shanïha let Ethan Hyt go ahead as she walked toward Henry Nostrada's apartment building.

His stride was longer than hers, and she was fine with walking with Pamela Ingot, the Nanganya Head of Protection.

She and Pamela had met numerous times in the past few years, although usually in a group setting, and she had always liked the commander.

"Ethan said that Ferris Harden tried to have Wren Thorakis killed," Pamela Ingot said as they approached the entrance to Henry Nostrada's building.

"He did. Along with the last person on planet who can use the Guan Scanner, Ed Zeneri." Velda shuddered to think what would have happened if that plot had succeeded and both Wren and Ed Zeneri had been murdered. She and her people would still be blissfully unaware of the massive threat to their planet.

"I know Ed." Pamela Ingot glanced at her in surprise. "I thought he'd resigned."

"We managed to persuade him to come back." And thank goodness they had. The Cores, along with the Caruso, were obviously smuggling something into Aponi, and Ed Zeneri was the only one who could use the tech that could expose what that was.

"What's going on here, Velda?" Pamela reached the door to the apartment block and opened it, holding it for her to enter. "I can barely believe most of what came out of Ethan's mouth today."

Velda stepped through with a nod, noting two Protection Unit officers standing beside the lift with Ethan. They must have been sent ahead.

Except Pamela Ingot was frowning.

"You're not my officers. Who are you?" Pamela called, hand going to the laz on her hip as she focused on the two men.

Ethan Hyt must have excellent reflexes, because the moment Pamela called out, he did something, and the man closest to him went down hard and the other blinked as Ethan's laz was suddenly in his face.

Pamela strode forward, and Velda trailed behind her, impressed with them both.

She had been a member of the Protection Unit in Demeter at the start of her career, joining straight out of university, but had ended up moving to the Department of Defense when an opening had come up which needed her technological skill set after only a year. She'd moved again, ever upward, into a high-level strategic role, still in Defense, and then her three years of government service had come due.

It never failed to amaze her that the only role that was available at the time which had suited her skill set was the Head of Planetary Defense, no less. She'd taken a long look at the responsibilities, finally agreed, and at the age of 25, she'd stepped into the role. Three years later, she didn't regret it.

Unlike the two men currently in restraints. They had a lot of regrets, if she was any judge.

"So, what's the story?" she asked as she came to a stop beside Ethan. "Cores thugs?"

One of the men on the ground turned his head to look at her, face comically twisted into an expression of outrage.

"Seems not," Pamela Ingot said, staring down at him. "Are you both Aponi?"

"Yes." The man's reply was stiff.

"But, to be clear, they are not part of the Protection Unit?" Ethan asked.

"No." Pamela Ingot crouched beside them, tugged at the badge on the uniform. "Where did you get these?" she asked. "They're the real deal."

"We were told it was a prank," the one who'd shot Velda an outraged look said. "They said to delay you while they set up a surprise in your apartment."

"Shit." Pamela stood and lifted her comm unit. "Possible ambush or explosive," she said, giving the address.

"Who's 'they'?" Ed crouched beside the men. "Are they still in the apartment?"

"It was only one person. We met him at the door," the other man said. "He paid us, then sent us down. He might have gone out another way while we waited down here, but he told us he was setting up a surprise and went back inside when we left."

"How long ago was this?" Velda asked.

"About thirty minutes." The man who'd seemed insulted by the Cores thug comment seemed to be coming to a clear realization that he'd been duped.

"Let's get out of the building." Ethan was already lifting one of the men as he spoke, and Pamela hauled the other one to his feet.

"The explosives unit will meet us outside." Pamela pushed the man toward the door and Velda got ahead of them and opened it for them to go through.

Ethan pushed his man in front of him, and then turned to her. "We need to get back a bit more," he said. "We're still too close."

She nodded, following after Pamela, but looking around for anyone paying them too much attention.

A few bystanders were looking their way, but given the two restrained men, Velda guessed that was normal.

As they cleared the small garden in front of the entrance, an explosion cracked through the air.

It came from above, the boom rattling windows down the street.

Velda felt it in her bones, and then pieces of glass and wall began to rain down on them all.

Ethan shoved the man he'd restrained at Pamela and grabbed her, tucking her against him and bending over her so that his body shielded her own.

"Ethan." She twisted in his hold to look up at him. "You're not my bodyguard." And she didn't see why he should be hurt instead of her.

His eyes met hers, held there for a moment, and then he blinked and let her go.

The explosives unit chose that moment to arrive, and Velda stood to one side, watching with interest as they leaped from the hover and spread out, looking upward.

She walked toward them, turning to see what damage had been done.

Ethan had gone back to his prisoner, but now he was handing him over to one of Pamela's people.

He moved back to stand beside her.

"If Nostrada wasn't already dead, he is now," she said as she took in the blackened, shattered mess that was the third floor windows of Nostrada's apartment.

Ethan looked over at her. "He was dead already. I don't think Ferris would have implicated him if he had any chance of contradicting the crap Ferris was trying to shovel at us."

She didn't know why that was a relief, but the idea of Nostrada, someone she'd dealt with often, an administrator who'd worked in her department, being blown up while he was still alive, was not good. He was most likely a traitor, but he'd deserved a fair trial.

"I assume you want to inspect the apartment?" Pamela Ingot joined them.

"Yes."

Ethan spoke at the same time as she did, so they answered together.

"My people will need at least a few hours to clear the scene. Can you do something else for a while and come back?" Pamela put her hands on her hips and looked upward. "The building will have to be cleared and the structural damage assessed as well."

"I have other things to keep me busy in the meanwhile," Velda assured her.

Ethan shot her a quick look. "Like?"

She lifted a brow. "Official things."

His lips quirked. She almost missed it but she was sure he had suppressed a grin.

"Good." Pamela pulled out her comms unit as it warbled. "I'll let you know when we're done."

She strode away, and Velda watched her wade into a group of uniformed Protection Unit officers and start issuing orders.

"What are you going to do?" Velda turned to find Ethan checking out the crowd.

He swung his gaze back to hers, held it. "I'm coming with you."

She narrowed her eyes. "I told you, you're not my bodyguard."

He shrugged. "I am now."

3

VELDA DIDN'T POUT WHEN SHE DIDN'T GET HER WAY. ETHAN LIKED THAT about her.

She accepted his company, even though it was clear she didn't like the idea that he might be in harm's way on her account.

Even if his breath didn't catch in his throat at odd moments when she smiled at him or lifted her eyebrows in that way she had, he would have made sure she was safe. She was the Head of Defense for the planet, after all.

They travelled up to the Planetary Admin offices in the lift, but before the door pivoted open, he pressed the button to keep them closed.

"What's the plan?" he asked.

She sighed and rubbed her temples, pushing back her heavy, dark hair and tucking it behind her ears. "I want to search Henry Nostrada's office. I sealed it when I was up here earlier and discovered he hadn't come in today. I also want to question some of the staff who interacted with him. Someone surely picked up something odd about his behavior."

He nodded, and hit the open button. That sounded like a good use of their time, and he could watch her back as she stirred the pot and tried to flush out any witnesses or co-conspirators.

They stepped into a hushed foyer that smelled good and was lush with green plants and the tinkle of a water feature.

Velda strode toward the reception desk, and Ethan saw the expression of the receptionist change from bored disinterest to panic at the Head of Defense moving with such focus toward him.

He was on his feet before she reached his desk.

Velda gave a nod of greeting. "I need to speak to the full Planetary Admin Committee. Please ensure they are all in the main conference room in thirty minutes."

"Not . . ." The receptionist cleared his throat. "Not all of them are in the office yet."

Velda tilted her head. "Then call them in. Tell them it's an emergency."

He nodded a few times too many and then caught Ethan's gaze over Velda's shoulder and went a little glassy-eyed.

"You're involved," Ethan said, walking up behind Velda and leaning past her to rest his elbow on the counter. "You know what Nostrada was up to."

"What?" His voice was thin and reedy. "No, no."

Velda took a step back and studied him. "Commander Hyt is right. You do know something. What is it?"

The receptionist shook his head, his hands gripping the edge of the counter. "I don't know anything."

"Leave him to me," Ethan said to Velda, never taking his gaze off the receptionist. "Do what you need to do in Nostrada's office. Make sure the seal is untouched. If it isn't, come get me."

"Thanks." She sent him an amused smile and walked away.

"What did Henry Nostrada do?" the receptionist asked.

"You tell me . . ." He peered at the receptionist's ID. "Fayvin."

"I don't know." The glassy eyes were back. "I swear."

Ethan stared at him, and he shrank away, backing up and stumbling over the chair behind him.

"The Protection Unit will be here to turn this place upside down shortly. After they've finished cleaning up what's left of Henry Nostrada and his apartment," Ethan said.

"What's left?" Favin's gaze shot up to his, the blood draining from his face.

Ethan softened his tone. "Henry Nostrada's apartment was blown up earlier. It's likely he's dead."

Fayvin's eyes went really wide. "Who did it?"

"That's what we're trying to find out. Whatever you know, whatever you did, you need to tell me."

"All I did was tell Commander Harden he wasn't here yesterday afternoon, even though he was." Fayvin looked up. "But that's because Henry asked me to! And I kept the package for him that he asked me to store under the desk until he came in to collect it today."

"Give." Ethan held out his hand, and Fayvin bent down and withdrew a package from below the counter and handed it across. It felt like documents. "What else?"

"Nothing, I swear." Fayvin sank down into his chair. "I can't believe he's dead."

"I'm sorry." Ethan tapped the counter and walked in the direction Velda had taken. Behind him he heard Fayvin calling the people in the office for the meeting Velda wanted to hold.

That get together should be interesting. Neither he nor Velda thought Nostrada had been in it alone, but whether his co-conspirator had only been Commander Ferris Harden, or whether there were more people involved, including someone else in the Planetary Admin office, they couldn't be sure.

Hopefully the meeting would help them find out.

He found Velda standing in the middle of Nostrada's office, arms crossed, staring at the desk.

"No luck?" he asked.

She shook her head, then went still when he waved the package Fayvin had given him.

"The receptionist?" she asked.

"Nostrada asked him to keep it safe for him until he could come collect it," he said.

"Let's go to the meeting room and start looking through it while we wait for the committee to arrive." She looked like a hunter on the scent.

He gave a nod and let her lead the way, as he had never been in the Planetary Administrative offices before.

There were already people waiting for them in the room, though, so he tucked the package behind him and took up position against the wall, near where Velda took a seat.

Velda deflected questions until everyone arrived, and Ethan noticed he was getting quick, nervous looks from everyone in the room.

"Do you all know Commander Ethan Hyt of Demeter Special Forces?" Velda asked, when the last person sat down.

Only a few of them nodded, and Ethan didn't know if he'd met them in Demeter at a function or if they recognized him from comms, because he'd swear he'd never seen them before.

"He and I have traveled up here to question Commander Ferris Harden of Nanganya's Special Forces, as well as your colleague, Henry Nostrada."

As Velda laid out the plot, Ethan watched the committee members and their reactions.

Most seemed astonished and horrified, but there was one who kept her eyes down, and didn't react at all.

The door to the conference room opened, and Pamela Ingot stepped in. The room went quiet, and she froze for a moment.

"Commander Ingot." Velda turned and then pushed back from the table and stood. "Do you want to speak privately?"

Ingot gave a nod and reversed out, and Ethan wished he could replicate himself so he could stay in the room and observe the ripple effect of Ingot's arrival as well as speak with the two women outside.

He followed Velda out. "This about Nostrada?"

Ingot shook her head. "As expected, Nostrada was in the apartment, but he likely died last night or early this morning—the blast didn't kill him."

"Then what is it?" Velda asked.

"It's Harden. We found footage of him entering Nostrada's building late last night. I was on my way to talk to him about it when it was discovered he was gone. Someone helped him escape." Ingot looked like she wanted to find that person and throttle them. "One of my own people helped him escape."

"Do you have any idea who?" Ethan asked.

"There are only four people in the frame." Ingot compressed her lips. "I'll be questioning them myself."

"Where could he have gone?" Velda asked.

"I'm looking into it," Ingot assured her. "I'll tell you as soon as I know."

Ethan watched her as she strode away. "You didn't tell her about the package." He looked over at Velda.

She lifted her shoulders. "She's dealing with a lot, and obviously she has problems in her unit. Not everyone there is clean, obviously. I'd prefer to keep it to just you and me, right now."

Ethan nodded. "Who's the woman sitting three down from you on the left?"

"Georgi Valk?" Velda looked up at him, expression interested. "She's in Trade Relations. Henry Nostrada was in Border Control."

"Huh." That made sense. If anyone wanted Planetary Admin blind when it came to Aponi's borders, these were the two they would need to turn or control.

Velda turned and walked back into the room.

"What's going on?" One of the committee members, someone who Ethan had noticed was annoyed by being hauled into a meeting without notice, snapped as soon as she sat down.

He leaned back against the wall to see how Velda would deal with it.

She tilted her head and studied him for a beat. "I think maybe we've all gotten too used to calm waters," she said at last. "We have had it very good for a very long time, but times change."

"What's that supposed to mean?" another of the group asked. "What did Commander Ingot have to say?"

"She says that Nostrada was killed last night, before his apartment was set up as a booby trap to kill me and Commander Hyt, as well as Commander Ingot, this morning." She turned and looked directly at Georgi Valk. "And she also says the person seen entering Nostrada's building was Commander Ferris Harden, and that he has since escaped Protection Unit custody."

Ethan was watching the woman as everyone around her gasped, and she turned pale.

Velda stood, leaning forward with her hands on the table. "Anyone who has anything to say about this—if you remember something Nostrada said to you that seemed strange, if you noticed something that made you frown, tell the Protection Unit officers that will be coming to speak to you."

"What if the officer I speak to is the one who helped Harden escape?" someone asked.

"Good question." Velda gave a nod. "There are only four people who could have helped Harden, and they are all out of the investigation, and being held by Commander Ingot." She looked around the table, and again her gaze came to rest on Georgi Valk. "As you can imagine, Commander Ingot takes the corruption of her department as seriously as I take the corruption of the Planetary Administrative Committee. It is unacceptable, and everyone involved will face consequences."

As she finished speaking her comm unit made a noise, and Ethan's went off a moment later.

It was the emergency signal.

Velda turned to him, and he stepped away from the wall.

"It seems things are hotting up," Velda said to the committee. "Do your jobs, cooperate with Commander Ingot, and maybe we'll get through this stronger than we were."

She turned on her heel and stalked out, and Ethan fell in behind her.

"The emergency notice says that the ships up in nearspace that Ed and Wren were searching were attacked," she said as soon as they stepped into the lift and were whisked down to Pamela Ingot's department.

"Someone really wants them dead." Ethan thought about it. "And is so concerned about them finding whatever it is they're trying to smuggle in that they'd rather blow this shipment up than have us know what it is."

"It's bad." Velda vibrated with impatience as they waited for the lift door to open.

Pamela was waiting for them. "What's the emergency?" she asked.

"My people have been attacked in nearspace by whoever's behind this." Ethan told her. "Check out Georgi Valk, I think she's involved."

Ingot glanced upward to the floor above, gave a nod.

"We have to go back to Demeter to oversee the response to this attack. And Pamela," Velda stepped out the lift and grasped Ingot's hands. "I'm sorry but I don't think you can trust anyone in Special Forces here. We'll have to do a full clean out when this is over, but until then, it's just you."

Ingot gave a nod. "I'd already worked that out. Good luck. I'll keep you informed."

Velda stepped back in and the lift took them down.

As they stepped out of the building, the evening call for peace that rang out from the clifftops every day in Nanganya began.

The long, high note sounded mournful.

4

———

There was no pilot available to fly them back to Demeter, but Ethan Hyt didn't blink at that.

Which is how Velda ended up sitting beside him in a small runner as he flew them out of Nanganya, headed for the mountains and the coast, toward Aponi's capital city.

He set the hover on autopilot as soon as they were high enough, and got on his comms unit to find out what was happening.

She was doing the same.

It had been nearly an hour since they'd gotten the emergency news about the attack and Velda found out the main targets had been the ships the military had singled out for Ed and Wren to check for smuggled items.

"Neither battleship could return fire," Tara, her admin, told her over her comm unit. "There were too many freighters in the way. So they used one battleship to shield the special forces team from getting hit and the other moved to leap over the freighter line to attack."

"And the ship that initiated the attack, it's gone now?" Velda asked.

"It seems to be," Tara said. "They couldn't tell where it went, though. And get this, the battleship's captain says it's just like the ship that destroyed the ruins at Cepi."

Which meant it was like the ship destroyed after Parn had been attacked, as well as during the Caruson's attack of Garmen, and a number of other incidences.

And every one pointed to a Cores and Caruso plot.

Shit.

She looked out the window and saw the mountains below them, green and gray in the last light of the day.

Ethan set his comms unit down.

"Are your people all right?" Velda asked.

He nodded. "Ed, Wren and Bailey were checking out the third ship of four that the military found trying to break out of line and head away from Aponi, when they were attacked. But ship number four, which they hadn't gotten to yet, was destroyed first. Wiped out of existence."

"So whatever it was we needed to find was probably on ship four," Velda said.

"It definitely was. They'd already found the contraband in ship three when they were hit. The captain was smuggling weapons to Faldine." Ethan looked down at the mountains, and checked the console in front of him.

"And the attacking ship used the freighters as cover, I hear." Velda realized they . . . she . . . hadn't expected such a violent and aggressive response from their adversaries.

"My people say it vanished when it realized it couldn't hit ship three because one of the battleships was physically shielding it, and the other battleship was headed to the other side of the freighter line to confront them."

"So we don't know what was in ship four, but the silver lining is that whatever *was* in there is no longer coming in to Aponi." It was something, Velda thought. Not the best outcome, but at least they had disrupted their enemies' plans.

Ethan gave a snort. "That's a nice, positive spin."

She glanced at him, ready to respond, when light seemed to blossom in front of her, blinding her momentarily.

The hover jerked hard to the left, falling downward with her window facing the ground, so she stared in wonder and horror as the mountains below her came into clear focus.

The hover jerked again, and she was pushed back into her seat, the hover more or less back to level.

She turned to Ethan, found him fighting with the controls. He'd clearly switched to manual mode, and he was half hunched over the console.

Neither of them were wearing their safety harness, and she pushed herself to her feet, grabbed his, and clipped him in from behind so he didn't need to lift his hands from the controls.

Then she sat and clipped herself in, looking down at her comms unit to see if she could send out a signal, but it was showing no connection.

Whatever had hit the hover had taken out the comms functionality, she guessed.

The hover was buffeted by the winds as they got lower, shuddering and wobbling side to side as they came down too fast and too steep.

"I'm riding the strong thermals rising up from the mountains, but as soon as we get lower, I'll lose that, and we are going to come down hard." Ethan glanced at her for a moment, then swung his focus back on the controls. "Hold on tight."

The ground came up fast.

Velda had an impression of forests, and then a wide, pebble-lined river, and Ethan directed the hover to the middle of it.

They hit the water with a boom of sound and it threw up a massive wave that swamped them. She could feel the hover fighting, moving left and right, and the grating of metal as the bottom of the runner scraped over large rocks.

Finally, they slammed into a large rock on the left side, and Velda felt the harness cut into her shoulders. The hover spun right, turning them completely around, and then finally sank down onto the left bank.

For a moment, they sat in silence, and Velda heard the rush of water entering the hover from a rip in the side.

Right now, she didn't care. They were alive, and more or less unharmed.

"We need to move. Leave everything." Ethan stood, but she noticed he needed to steady himself on the console. "I can't believe they didn't take a second shot at us while we were coming down. They must have realized they hadn't destroyed us."

She hadn't even thought of that. She gaped at him. "You think they'll try again now?" She forced herself to her feet.

"We're not moving now," he said. "We're easier to hit. If your bag is to hand, grab it. Otherwise, let's go."

She reached behind her seat and pulled out her overnight bag, and he did the same. Then he shoved hard at his door, and managed to get it open.

It was almost completely dark, and the dim emergency light that had come on in the front of the hover felt like a beacon for their enemies.

It motivated her to scramble after him as he disappeared out the door.

When she peered out, he was standing below her, up to his knees in water, arms lifted.

"I've got you," he said.

She nodded, turning and carefully using the built-in ladder on the side to come down as far as she could, and then his hands gripped her waist and he lifted her up, walking through the river with her and setting her down on the rocky beach, feet completely dry.

"Thank you." She looked up at the sky a few times as they jogged away, but there was nothing to see but stars.

"Maybe they only had time for one shot," Ethan said when they reached the cover of the treeline, with no second shot. He was looking up himself. "The battleships we had stationed along the freighter line would have been after them the moment they reappeared. It's possible they were run off without even realizing that their aim was slightly off."

"That would be a good outcome," she agreed. "But I still don't feel safe using the hover for shelter."

"No." He turned to study the gentle, wooded hill behind them. "Even without a second strike, we need to move. We know the ship that attacked us isn't acting alone. They have on-planet help, and if they *are* aware they didn't blow us up, then they might send someone to finish the job."

She didn't want to hear it, but he was right. They needed to get away from here.

She was glad she had a small overnight bag. She hadn't known how long she'd be in Nanganya, and she'd packed a change of clothes, workout gear, and pajamas.

Ethan put his hands on his hips, studying the wreck, studying the sky. "We'll need something to make a fire with, and I wouldn't mind a flare in case we need to attract attention." He looked up again.

"I can go back into the runner and see if there's emergency equipment," Velda said. "You can call out if you see any danger."

He swung his gaze back to her. "How about we switch that around?"

"Why?" she asked.

"Just keep watch," he said, moving back to the hover. "I'll keep the door open for a quick exit and so I can hear you."

Then he was gone.

She followed after him, going slower so she could keep her gaze up at the sky, feeling a little like her eyes were playing tricks on her as she thought she saw hundreds of falling stars above.

Then she thought about the implications of that, and her chest got very, very tight.

When Ethan reappeared, after what felt like only minutes, holding two packs, one slung over each shoulder, he narrowed his eyes. "What's wrong?"

She pointed up. "Falling stars," she said.

He tipped back his head. "There are a lot . . ." He suddenly drew in a breath. "They hit the observatory."

"Either that or one or both of the battleships are destroyed." She couldn't believe this could be happening. "Unless they strafed the freighter line. That's a possibility, too."

Ethan bent and picked up his personal overnight bag, which had been set beside her feet. "Now we're definitely going."

He strode away, and she tore her gaze away from the heavens and followed him into the night.

5

———————

Finding the overhang meant they could light a fire and it was still shielded from aerial view.

Ethan tossed down the sticks he'd collected, and then looked through the trees, tracking Velda as she returned with an armful of sticks herself.

She set them down more carefully than he had, and then moved to the fire, which had caught nicely. It was colder here than in Nanganya, and the heat it was giving off was more than welcome.

The little pot they'd hung over the fire began to shake a bit as the water boiled, and she carefully lifted it away with another stick and set it down on a rock.

"Jah?" she asked.

"Please." He was glad he'd taken the chance to go back into the hover for the emergency packs for the jah supplies alone, but the ground sheets, the warm sleeping bags, and the pot and meals meant they could survive out here a lot more comfortably than he'd initially thought.

While she made their drinks with a competence that indicated she was no stranger to the outdoors, he began to lay out the ready-made meals they had, the water bottles with in-built purifiers, and the other equipment, so he could take stock.

Velda handed him a cup and stood close beside him, looking over their spoils.

"The hover takes a maximum of six people, and it looks like they've included supplies for six people for three days." It wasn't a massive amount, but it meant that if they were careful, they had nine days of supplies.

"Someone will come looking for us long before we run out," Velda said. "And not all of them will be enemies."

"That's true, but how will we know one from the other?" he asked. "And if the observatory has been destroyed, and Ed and Wren are dead, then Defense will have a lot on their plate. We don't even know if anyone knows we were shot down yet."

"You want us to walk out on our own?" she asked, crouching down and studying the meals more closely.

"I think the less dependent we are on others, the safer we'll be." He knew full well the conspiracy couldn't be that far reaching. The Verdant String had set itself up to be very corruption-resistant, but with a warship hunting them from the skies, all that was needed was for the wrong person to know where they were—or who had found them—and the innocent people coming to save them might also be in danger.

"You think that unless it was the enemy ship that was destroyed, and is providing such a gorgeous light show for us, they'll circle back to take another shot at us, and whoever's honestly looking for us might get caught in the crossfire?" She looked out from under the overhang at the now constant flare and glitter of falling stars in the night sky.

He shrugged, not surprised by how quickly she'd caught his train of thought. "All it would take is one person to let them know we'd been found. And we know there's someone in either the Demeter or Nanganya Defense Office giving them information, or they wouldn't have known we were on our way back to Demeter."

"Yes." She sounded very quiet all of a sudden.

Betrayal was a hard blow to take.

"Our comms units are off, and we'll keep it that way unless we have no choice but to ask for help. We'll make our own way back to Demeter, and get the lay of the land." He was looking up as he spoke, and he realized he very badly wanted to use his comms unit to find out what was going on in nearspace.

"It makes sense." Velda sounded like she wished it didn't.

He crouched down beside her. "What do you want for dinner?"

She glanced at him, eyes steady, and then turned to the meals laid out in front of her.

He'd grouped them into roughly breakfast, lunch and dinner, and her hand hovered over the dinner pile, lightly touching the offerings until she made a choice and lifted out a meal.

"Have you had these before?" she asked.

He chuckled. "Yes."

"Me, too. When I became Head of Defense, I insisted they work on improving the taste, and I see this is the new line." She tapped the wrapping. "I've personally tried them all, and they are definitely better than the old ones."

He hadn't known that. He'd been steeling himself to swallow the meal down, but now he was interested in giving it a try. "So I know who to blame?" he teased, sending her a smile as he snagged a package.

She grinned back. "Even if I hadn't had a hand in the new line, I'd be to blame. I'm in charge and that's the deal."

Ethan was still crouched next to her, and he forced himself to straighten up, suddenly flustered. "If you don't mind heating the food, I'll repack this." He held out the meal he'd chosen.

She rose fluidly to her feet, took the package from him, and tilted her head. "Sure."

He turned away from her, looking for where he'd put the two packs, and heard her walk back to the fire.

He needed to get himself together. They were going to be spending days and nights together, just the two of them.

The thought made him want to break out into a cold sweat.

He packed the heavier things into one pack for himself, and the lighter equipment in the other, but kept the ground sheets and sleeping bags out for them to use.

She called him over when the meals were hot, and when he got back to the fire he saw she'd pushed pebbles into the fire and then pulled them out to cover the packages and heat them without direct flames.

"You've done this before," he said as he carefully opened the meal and began to eat.

"I put myself through basic military training," she said. "Not all at once, not the whole three months, but when I had a clear few days that would work, I'd drop in to whichever group was going through it and do whatever was on the schedule for them at that time."

He hadn't known that. "It shows," he says.

She gave a laugh. "I'm ridiculously pleased to hear that. I know a lot of the admin staff in headquarters thought I was losing my mind when I started doing it, but it's been useful. I've gotten to know the generals better, and gotten to see what training our people go through." She shrugged. "The post usually goes to someone older, so it might be because I was young and relatively fit that it even crossed my mind as a good thing to do, but I think it's made me a better Head of Planetary Defense."

"You certainly have the most exciting moment a Head of Defense has faced since Aponi bumped into a fleet of Arkhorans and Raxians in the Great Discovery," he said. And that event had been a friendly meeting, the beginning of Aponi's inclusion in the Verdant String.

"I think Dir Matala would argue his tenure during the Faldine War was pretty exciting," Velda said.

Ethan had been a junior officer in Special Forces when Dir Matala had been Head of Defense, and had even deployed to Faldine for six months. He shook his head. "The Arkhorans were all over that cluster. Along with Themis. We barely had a role. The way I remember it, we had to plead with them to let us get in there, because everyone thought it would be good on-the-ground training."

"You went?" she asked, but she said it in a way that made him think she already knew. She'd probably read his file.

"For six months. It was . . . strange." He remembered the auroras lighting up the sky every night. "Interesting."

"You're talking about the electromagnetic issues?" she asked.

He nodded. "Flying felt like taking your life into your hands. The pilots who managed to work around the issues were the most valuable people in the fight."

"I wouldn't mind talking to the current head of planet there," Velda mused. "Iver Sugotti encountered the same issues we seem to be having, with ancestral ships and ancient alien ruins. It sounds like the Cores tried to kill him because his new infrastructure was going to cut right through the ruins the Cores had found and were trying to strip."

"I didn't know that." Ethan had heard the Faldine head of planet had been taken prisoner at some point, but he'd escaped. The details were above his clearance level. "Surely the infrastructure plans would have gone ahead with or without him?"

"Yes, but not for a while," Velda said. "And time was what they apparently needed. Which also explains the attack on Wren and Ed. Ed was coming back to work for you, and Wren was about to join your unit and probably tell you everything she knew."

"Trying to kill Ed and Wren, and put the blame on me, is one thing. Having a shoot-out with two battleships in nearspace is another altogether." Ethan still could barely believe it happened. "And now we know something big was blown up, most likely the observatory."

The night sky was still a sparkle of falling stars. It made Ethan's chest tighten at the thought of Ed, Wren, Bailey and Hatch being in the obs station if it was hit. He'd sent them up there, and they may very well be dead because of it.

A warm hand suddenly touched his own and he turned to find Velda leaning in.

"That's not on you, Ethan." She glanced up. "It's not even on me. I could not in a million years have thought they'd attack Ed and Wren with two battleships right there. It literally didn't cross my mind."

She was right. The idea was ludicrous.

"What does it say about them that they did attack?" he wondered.

"That they're desperate. Really desperate. They have to be." Velda drew her knees up and hugged them. "They were obviously desperate for the freighter to not be searched, and so whatever was on that freighter was more than just contraband. It would have told us something more. Revealed something bigger than just a smuggling operation."

"That's what really worries me," Ethan said. "Because there are only a few scenarios that come to mind."

Velda was silent for a moment. "What we need to do is separate the machinations around the ancestral spaceship on Ytla with the smuggling operation. They're connected, but I think they're two different branches off the same tree."

"Agreed. Whatever Cores factions are left have been looking for ancient tech for a while, and they've gone after it in a few different ways over the last year or more. But the smuggling issue, and the open attacks on our military, that's something new." Ethan just wished he'd had an inkling about how aggressive they were prepared to be. Maybe he could have protected his people better.

Velda suddenly gave a massive yawn and then reached for his empty meal package. "I need to sleep. I guess we're going hard tomorrow to put some distance between the wreck and ourselves."

He wished he could tell her they could relax here until someone came to rescue them. That would be the normal thing to do, but nothing about this situation was normal. "I wish it wasn't so, but yes. I think that's the only option."

She nodded. "I'd be inclined to wait, but I trust your instincts. If you say we need to go, we go."

She rummaged in her bag, came up with a toothbrush and tooth-paste, and took the small pot they'd boiled water in and her jah cup with her to the small stream that rushed its way down the hill toward the river they'd crashed in.

He sat by the fire, watching her crouch by the water, splash her face and clean her teeth.

The trust she'd placed in him acted like a tight band around his throat, making it hard for him to respond to her, so he'd merely nodded.

Her slim, straight back and long dark hair was all he could see, but when she grabbed her hair and twisted it into a rope to keep it off her face, he turned to find his own toothbrush, the gesture almost too inti-mate for him to feel comfortable watching it.

It was going to be a long night.

6

———————

Velda woke up stiff but actually quite cozy.

The sleeping bag was warm and she snuggled a bit deeper, watching Ethan build the fire back up.

She realized him moving around had woken her, and he seemed to realize she was watching him, because his gaze locked onto hers.

"Sorry," he said. "We need to get going."

She sighed and wriggled out of the bag, rolling it up tight and setting it aside before she went off to the stream. She took the pot with her and came back with water to boil.

They moved together quietly, making jah and heating breakfast, then tidying up the overhang so there was almost no sign of their presence.

"A good tracker will know we've been here, but that can't be helped." Ethan studied their little camp site.

He handed her a pack, which looked a lot lighter than his one.

They both also had their personal bags to carry.

She guessed he'd just give her the look he'd given her in Nanganya if she tried to persuade him to give her an equal turn with the heavier pack. And what the heck, he was clearly much bigger and stronger than she was.

"Those mountains look pretty high," she said, staring at them, hands on hips.

"We'll go through the valleys between them, not over them," Ethan said. "It isn't as bad as it looks."

She shot him a disbelieving look and he smiled at her, his face much lighter than it had been last night.

His coloring was the opposite to her own, his hair light to her dark, his eyes blue to her dark brown. He looked gilded in the morning sun.

He suddenly turned, the movement quick and somehow dangerous, and he tilted his head. "Something's coming," he said. "We've run out of time."

He started walking and she fell into step behind him, and as they got into the trees she heard the sound of a hover coming down the valley.

Rescue was half an hour away if they wanted it, but Ethan was right, the ship that had downed them might try again, and she didn't want to risk her and Ethan's lives, as well as the lives of their rescuers.

Not when the stakes were this high.

If it was a rescue team they could hear, and not their enemies, it would take them time to find the hover, work out she and Ethan weren't in it, and then start to look for them, and given the pace Ethan was setting, they would leave them far behind.

They stopped for a break and something to eat and drink near midday, and Velda realized she was more out of shape than she thought she was.

She hadn't dropped into a basic training camp for nearly six months, and it showed.

She leaned back against the damp rock beside the waterfall Ethan had led them to and closed her eyes, worried that if she sat down, she might have trouble standing again.

"Water," Ethan said, and she opened her eyes and found him right in front of her, holding out a water bottle.

"Thanks." She took it, sipping slowly, and watched him crouch down and light the small portable heater from the hover's emergency stash and prepare them lunch.

It was nice here, she realized. The sound of birds, the splash of the waterfall, and the warmth of the sun in the little clearing.

Ethan Hyt looked up at her and their eyes met for a moment.

She froze in place, because there was a flare of heat there that she could not pretend she hadn't seen.

She had sensed . . . something from him before. She'd been unsure if she was reading him right or if it was just wishful thinking on her part, because she had liked the look of Ethan Hyt since the day she'd met him.

There was a crash in the bush, and it broke the tension of the moment.

Ethan turned and rose to his feet, looking toward the sound.

"An animal?" she asked.

"Probably a granib. They're common here."

Granibs were small mammals with delicate hooves and tiny horns, as cute as cute could be, and Velda wished it had shown itself—she had always wanted to see one in the wild.

Ethan took the meals off the heat in exchange for a pot of water, and Velda forced her legs to move.

She carefully lowered herself down on a rock to sit, and Ethan shot her a quick grin.

"Stiff?"

"Barely mobile," she agreed. "Whereas you look like you're unaffected."

"I train every day," he said, giving a shrug. "You kept up well enough."

She peeled the top off her meal and focused on it for a bit, then considered offering to make the jah, before she realized that wasn't going to happen without a lot of groaning, so she let Ethan do that, too.

They drank it in silence, avoiding each other's eyes.

"How long do you think they'll look for us along the river?" Velda asked, suddenly desperate to fill in the silence.

"A while," Ethan said. "They'll assume we want to be found, and it will take them time to work out we've deliberately vanished."

She wondered if anyone would work out the reason for that. They hadn't heard or seen any sign of the rescue party since they'd made it into the forest, but sooner or later, someone would begin to look further afield.

She forced herself to her feet and helped Ethan clean up, then let him lead the way again.

The rest and food had given her the boost she needed, and the way he took them wasn't as steep from here, as they dipped into a deep valley between two mountains.

By the late afternoon, though, it got harder. Things got dark quickly in the lee of the mountain, and the cliffs cast long, dark shadows across their path.

The next time they heard water, Ethan took them down a gentle slope toward it, and while there was no pool or waterfall here, the river was wide and deep—good enough to clean up in—and there was a flat area of ground up against the same slope with a scoop out of it that was almost a cave. It looked as if the river had flooded at some point and burrowed into the hill and it would make a decent camp, with some overhead cover for a fire.

"Happy?" he asked.

"If you'd told me we could stop walking, I'd be happy. This looks like luxury." She set her bags down with a groan of relief, and started taking off her clothes.

"What are you doing?" He had always controlled his expressions around her, but now he looked shocked.

"I'm getting out of my clothes so I can jump in that river before it gets too dark and cold," she told him. They were Aponi, after all. Going naked was not that scandalous.

"I'll get a fire going, and then join you," he said, and she decided that she wasn't going to feel guilty about not helping him, because as he said, he trained every day.

She was the amateur.

She was glad she'd made it without slowing him down too much. Or maybe she had, and he was just too polite to tell her.

When she was naked, she took her personal pack with her to the river bank and left it on a rock near the water, then gingerly slid in. Her gasp had Ethan glancing over at her, and she looked at him over her bare shoulder. "Cold," she said.

Then she forced herself to go all the way in.

She loosened the tie in her hair and then ducked down, scrubbing at her scalp.

The mountain water was freezing, but the weightless sensation was heaven. The river cradled her, after a day with a heavy pack and a long walk. She moved to her pack and lifted out of the water a little, getting soap and shampoo, and after she was clean, she turned to the bank to find Ethan sliding into the water with her, a fire crackling behind him.

"Thank you." She shivered in the water, glad there was a warm fire to go to when she got out.

"Cold?" he asked.

"Yes, but it's still lovely." She sighed and sank down to her shoulders, letting her hands take her weight on the river floor so her legs could float in front of her.

Ethan had brought a change of clothes and his own soap down to the water, and she let her eyes flutter closed to give him some privacy.

Something nudged her arm, and she forced herself to look down, and then, with a shriek, leapt to her feet. "Thing," she gasped, pointing as it swam away.

"Fish?" he asked, and when she turned to him, she saw his eyes crinkled in amusement.

"Very ugly, for a fish," she said, and shivered, suddenly cold now she was wet and in the evening air.

"Fuck it," he said, and stepped up to her, lifted her out of the river and onto the bank.

She stood, astonished, as he pulled a thin, quick drying towel around her shoulders and hauled her close.

She grabbed the ends and put her hands around his neck, encasing them together in the warm cocoon. "Couldn't resist me anymore, huh?" she asked.

"No, I couldn't." His hands were warm as they rested on the small of her back. "I was waiting for your contract to end, but then you got into a river naked with me."

"You got in the river naked with me," she corrected. "I was in there first."

He laughed.

Threw his head back and laughed.

Then he bent his head and kissed her.

7

—————

It was a mistake to pull Velda up close to him while they were both wet and naked. But then Ethan acknowledged that he'd been making plenty of mistakes where she was concerned since yesterday.

They hadn't even spoken about what was between them, so he lifted his lips from hers and forced himself to drop his arms.

She stood in place for a moment, her gaze on his face. "You're not going to go back to pretending you're not interested in me, are you?"

"No, I think that ship pinched to the black at our lunch stop." He'd known it, he just hadn't worked out how to bring it up.

"It pinched to the black quite a long time before that," she said, "but I grant you that today you really let the curtain fall."

"When did you guess?" he asked.

"When you came to me about Wren and Ed."

The wind suddenly rose, icy and sharp, and she handed him back his towel.

"I have my own," she said when he tried to give it back, and they dried off quickly and dressed even more quickly.

When they were sitting around the fire he'd made, eating dinner and waiting for the pot to boil for jah, she gave a sudden sigh and wriggled until she was right next to him, shoulder touching shoulder.

"You said you were waiting for my contract to end. You didn't want to get involved because I was your boss?"

"I thought it was the right thing to do," he said. "To wait until you stepped down."

"And what if I'd started seeing someone else before that happened?" she asked.

"I would have had to move up my schedule," he admitted. "And hope it wasn't too late."

"I can't say I blame you. I kept my distance because it would have been awkward if I'd let you know I was interested in you and you didn't feel the same. Given you report to me." She sent him a quick grin.

"We were both being cautious," he said. "But in the last few days I've been almost constantly in your company and I slipped up."

"You were so busy trying not to look at me, you missed me slipping up, too," she told him. "It was pretty cute."

"Cute?" he asked, politely, and she laughed, a warm, generous sound that wrapped around him.

Above them, a golden flare streaked across the sky, and both of them went quiet.

"It *has* to be the obs station," Ethan said. "Too much debris is falling for anything else, unless it's a battleship, and I really don't think it is."

"Agreed. Let's hope they all got out." Velda's face was tipped upward as she watched the flare wink out.

Bits and pieces were still making entry into the atmosphere, like a giant hand was throwing glitter above them.

"It shouldn't look so beautiful," Velda said.

The water began to boil and Ethan leaned forward to take it off the fire. As he set it down, a twig snapped to their left.

He went absolutely still, listening. He turned to Velda, lifted a finger to his lips, and made a gesture for her to stay put.

Then he rose to his feet, checked he had his laz, and moved off into the darkness.

Velda watched the back of Ethan as he was swallowed up by the night.

She had heard the twig snap, too, but she'd assumed it was an animal.

Never assume, the military training instructor had drilled into the recruits—and her—last time she had participated. She should have remembered.

She turned back to the fire, and froze.

A man stood on the other side of it.

He was dressed in black, and he was pointing a laz at her.

Without saying a word, he jerked the laz up, indicating that she stand.

She glanced left in the direction Ethan had gone, but either this man had done something to him or there was more than one of them.

She guessed the latter.

She got slowly to her feet. "Who are you?"

He frowned and flicked his gaze quickly to the side.

If he was here to kill her, which she guessed he was, he would have no reason not to use his laz right now, before she could make some noise and alert Ethan.

So she bent forward, picked up the pot of just-boiled water, and threw it at him across the small fire pit in one smooth move.

She took him by surprise.

He screamed as the hot water hit him in the face, and she ran right, into the night.

There were plenty of bushes near the river and she ducked behind one and crouched down. It was too dark to see where she was going, and she would either hurt herself or make too much noise if she kept running.

Besides, Ethan was still out there, and she would never leave him behind.

The man she'd burned was swearing in a long, low, continuous monotone as he hunted for her, and she shivered.

She could not let him get his hands on her now. He would take delight in hurting her.

There was a shout which she couldn't quite pinpoint. Away to the left, but she didn't know if it came from across the river or closer to the camp.

The man hunting her stopped at the sound, hesitating, and then the shout came again and was cut off abruptly.

He began to swear again, but he was facing away from her, now, looking in the direction of the noise.

There was a sudden flare of light, and the unmistakable smell of a laz discharge.

"Velda?" Ethan's voice was low.

She emerged from behind the bush and found him standing over the man who'd been hunting her, his laz loosely at his side.

He turned as she stepped out.

"There were two of them?" she asked.

He nodded. "What did you do to this one?"

"Threw the hot water at his face." She reached him and looked down, saw the man's skin was blistered and red.

"Did he hurt you?" Ethan turned fully toward her, studying her carefully.

"No. I worked out he was going to shoot, and threw the water at him and ran. He would have, though, if he'd found me." She shivered again.

Ethan held out a hand, and she took it, let him lead her away from the man back toward the camp.

"I don't know how long we have, but they are going to be awake in a few hours." He stopped in front of the fire. "We need to strip them of their comms, take their identification, tie them up, and leave."

"You think there'll be more of them?" Velda asked.

"There are definitely more of them. Whether they planned to kill us or just stun us, how were they going to get our bodies or us out by themselves?" Ethan asked. "They have transport coming for them, and given the search and rescue going on, the eyes on this location, I'm guessing that transport looks the same as our people's. Might even *be* one of our people."

She didn't like it, but she had to admit it was the only logical conclusion to draw. So they had to truss their attackers up and go as quickly as possible. "Damn."

He grinned at that, a quick flash of humor, and then he picked up the pot she'd thrown. "Next time I go looking for the origin of a strange noise, you hide first," he said.

"Or I go with you," she said.

"Or that," he agreed. He pulled her close, his kiss quick and hard.

She stood, slightly stunned, when he drew back.

"Problem?" His voice deepened.

"No. No problem." She reached out, pulled him closer, and kissed him back.

"Well, that's fine then." He sounded a little . . . bemused, and she smiled.

They packed quickly, and when they were done, Ethan returned to the two downed attackers and took their IDs and comms, and secured them with their own restraints.

As they walked away, she saw Ethan looking up at the sky, and did so herself. It was brilliant with stars, and with the near constant streak and sparkle of space debris burning up as it hit the atmosphere.

"I feel tense just looking at it." Ethan sounded frustrated.

"I can just imagine what's happening at headquarters," Velda agreed, feeling her own stomach clench at the sight. "This is the first overt action against us, ever. Even during the Faladine War we got off lightly, with Arkhor being the main focus of the attacks."

She was antsy with her need to move. The more she saw the space shower, the more she felt the urgency of getting back to headquarters.

"We'll need to sleep at some point, but let's get a good distance from the camp first," Ethan said.

Because there would be people coming to get them, Velda thought. People in league with these men who had tried to kill or hurt them. It seemed unreal, but she had passed her attacker on their way out, and he was real enough.

When they were far enough away from the camp, Ethan threw the men's comms units into the bush, and they kept going in the dark.

And all the while, the sky rained pieces of gold.

8

———————

It was mid-morning when he finally called a halt.

Ethan expected Velda to complain before now, but she had stoically followed him, getting quieter and quieter.

They'd managed a few hours of sleep the night before, on the bank of the river, and had then continued on as dawn broke.

"Rest time."

She didn't respond, just took off her pack and sat down where she was standing. Then lay back on the ground.

"You should have told me to stop sooner." He looked down at her, worried now.

She blinked up at him. "I'm fine." She sat up, took off her boots and socks, rolled up her trousers, and then scooted on her behind to the edge of the river, which they had finally met up with again.

It was why he had decided to stop here. The water was clear and shallow.

Velda slid into the river bed, and closed her eyes.

"Cold?" he asked.

"Freezing, but my feet are thanking me for it."

He looked at her boots, and realized they were fancy city boots. The heel was low, and they looked well-made, but hiking material they were not.

He guessed if she had anything more suitable in her personal pack, she would have put them on.

When he looked back up at her, he saw she was watching him.

"If I needed you to slow down, or if my boots were hurting me, I'd have said." She heaved herself back onto the bank and wiggled her toes. "I'm your boss, remember?"

"I remember." He grinned, crouching beside her, and picked up one of her feet. He studied it, just in case.

She was right, her feet were fine. He began to knead the one he was holding and she groaned and lay back down again.

"Keep going," she demanded. "And that's an order."

He chuckled, massaged the other one, and then reached for his pack to get the pot for some water.

She sat up again, cross-legged, and sorted through the meals. "You ever been this deep into the range?" she asked.

"No." The mountains were all around them, now. So far, they had managed to find a way through that was fairly easy going, dipping down to the river a few times, but mainly sticking to the ridge just above it.

At some point they'd leave the river behind them, as it rose to its source, but hopefully they'd pick up a new stream running in the opposite direction eventually.

"We've gotten further than I thought we would have in the time." She handed him a meal and leaned back on her hands to look around. "It's beautiful."

He glanced around, but it was her who caught his attention.

She was slightly disheveled, not sporting the smart, sophisticated look he was used to, but she was just as breathtaking.

He had it bad, he admitted. And he wasn't sorry about that at all.

His silence obviously alerted her, and she was suddenly studying him, her gaze steady.

"None of that," he said. "We're on a tight schedule."

"You started it," she pointed out, and he couldn't disagree.

He reached over, got one arm under her knees, the other around her back, and lifted her onto his lap.

"Now what, Commander?" she asked, and he was close enough to see her eyes darken.

He reached down and began to unbutton her shirt, and she squirmed a little in his lap, as if just the thought of what he was going to do was affecting her.

"This is going to go faster if you keep doing that," he warned.

"Good." She gasped as he got her shirt off.

And going faster turned out to be more than just good, he had to admit.

He'd left them vulnerable, though, because when, at last, she was snuggled up beside him, naked and sleepy, he couldn't remember any sound, any movement, except the sound of her breathing, how it caught as he touched her with his lips and hands, and the way she moved against him, around him.

"Fuck, that was reckless." He rose up on an elbow.

She sniggered against his shoulder.

"Seriously, Velda. We're being hunted. This wasn't a good idea."

"We'll do better next time," she reassured him, patting his chest.

He snorted out a laugh. "That's the spirit."

She stood up, looking at him over a naked shoulder, and then up at the sky, at how much the sun had moved. "I suppose you're going to force march me a little more?"

"Sorry. But yes."

She sighed and climbed down into the river, gave a little shriek, he assumed at the temperature, and then submerged herself.

He had to go into the water after she got out, just to stop himself going down the road of failed good intentions any further than he already had.

"So stoic. So noble," she said, and patted his arm as he grumpily packed up.

He didn't let her see, but he grinned at her comment.

He had fallen for her well over a year ago, but he'd kept his distance. He had never known until now how funny she was, how sharp and witty.

He set a slightly easier pace, and then chuckled when she muttered something about how she would have slept with him sooner if she knew he'd let up a little for sexual favors.

It was late afternoon, and they were sitting sipping water from their bottles, both looking up to check if the flash of debris had abated, when a blinding blast of light flared far to the south.

They both shot to their feet, looking toward Demeter.

"That was a laser strike on the city." Velda's voice was raspy.

A second strike lit the sky, and she grabbed his arm. "Ethan."

"There's nothing we can do." He could hardly stand it. He was Commander of Demeter Special Forces, and his city was under attack. It was almost unbearable.

Without conferring, they kept going, moving faster than they had before, pushing themselves, until it got almost too dark to see a path.

The river was quite far below them, and Ethan emptied his pack, took all the water bottles, and climbed down to fill them while Velda set up the small burner stove and heated their dinner.

They ate and drank leaning back against a wall of rock, with a small fire right in the middle of the narrow track they'd been walking on.

Ethan kept looking toward the city, and so did Velda, but if there was smoke and fire, they couldn't see it from their current position.

"Maybe we should have let the rescuers finds us," Ethan said, for the first time admitting to doubts about his original plan.

"We could never have anticipated a laser strike on the city. Never." Velda tipped her head back, and Ethan glanced upward as well. The flash and flare of falling debris continued.

It made him sick to the pit of his stomach, because he couldn't believe how much of it there was. He worried the entire space observatory was gone.

And now, Demeter.

They could do nothing about the rescue team now, anyway. He'd made the call for them to go it alone, and that was that. Too late for regrets there.

They needed to concentrate on getting through the mountains and making for the city.

He settled back against the rock wall, legs stretched out in front of him, Velda pressed up against his side, and closed his eyes for a moment, just absorbing the hushed peace of their surroundings.

"Do you hear that?" Velda asked.

He opened his eyes, found her leaning forward, head turned to the right. She was frowning.

Ethan concentrated. Then he heard it, too. The throb of an engine.

"Could it be the rescue team?" Velda wondered.

"Could they have gotten ahead of us?" Ethan asked. "I don't see how, but that's definitely an engine."

He stood, and Velda got onto her haunches to pack the bags.

"You want to investigate?" he asked.

She nodded.

He wouldn't have left her, but he was glad she was up for walking further in the dark.

He would not be able to sleep knowing there was someone out there. Perhaps with a faster way to get back to Demeter.

He doused their camp fire and swung his pack onto his shoulder, interested to note that the engine didn't seem to be moving closer or getting further away. Whatever it was, it was staying in one place.

Who the hell was out here in the mountains, running equipment or a hover, he wondered?

They were about to find out.

9

───────────

WHATEVER VELDA EXPECTED TO FIND AFTER HOURS OF WALKING, SHE HAD to admit, a full blown mining operation was not it.

They'd hunkered down on a rocky outcrop in the darkness when they'd reached the moving lights, with engines moving directly below them, and in the breaking light of day, she saw a few things that made her think it had been there for a while, but originally on a smaller scale, and mainly under the mountain, if the massive cavelike entrance was anything to go by.

"What are they mining for?" Ethan wondered.

"And who are they?" Velda hadn't been able to see a company logo. The machinery that was visible was a mix of makes and had a number of different company names on the side.

"Stolen?" Ethan wondered, when she pointed it out.

"Could be." That was a thought. "Or they bought old equipment and kept under the radar."

"They're definitely operating illegally. This whole mountain range is a national park." Ethan lay beside her on the overhang they had chosen to observe their surprising find.

There was an awkwardness to the process, to Velda's eye. A lack of flow and organization that made her more sure than ever that the mine had recently expanded, and not in a well-considered way.

"Why would they ramp up production with so little planning?" she murmured.

"They're in a hurry." Ethan slid a little closer to the edge.

"And isn't there another group who seems to be in a hurry right now?" Velda narrowed her eyes as she stared down at the chaos below. Could this be a Cores operation? Here on her planet?

She sensed Ethan move, and she turned to look at him, saw the same realization in his eyes as was in hers.

"Fuck," he said.

"Exactly." She wanted to get down there, find out what she could about who was involved, and what they were mining. "It's enraging."

"We need to steal a hover and get back to the city," Ethan said. "We can't stop what's going on down there right now, not with just the two of us, but once we're back in Demeter we can get a team together to investigate."

Velda took a deep breath. "Yes." She needed to get back. Badly. And Ethan was right, the two of them had no chance of stopping the operation below.

She began looking at the hovers, trying to find one that wasn't being used so they could steal it.

"That one, maybe?" Ethan pointed to the left, to a small group of machines that were sitting to one side, with a tiny hover next to them. "Looks like loading equipment."

Loading equipment.

Velda swallowed down her anger. Of course they'd need loading equipment. They'd have to get the ore they were mining out of the mountains somehow. They were transporting this stuff somewhere. To someone. And she was going to make finding out where and to whom a personal mission.

Her eyes felt gritty and they were burning with fatigue, and she closed them for a moment. The rock they were lying on was warming in the early morning sun, and they had only caught three hours sleep the night before.

"Velda." Ethan whispered right in her ear, and she jerked, suddenly unsure how much time had passed.

"Sorry." She glanced at him, but he was looking down again, and it looked almost exactly as it had when she'd closed her eyes.

"I don't think they use that hover unless there's a need to load the ore." Ethan was still looking at the small collection of vehicles to the side.

"The trick will be to get to it and drive it away without them noticing." Because she didn't think it had much in the way of a top speed. There were plenty of vehicles below that would catch up to them in no time.

"Let's get down there and take whatever opportunity presents itself," Ethan said. He moved backward off the rock and Velda followed, sorry to lose the warmth of the stone beneath her.

Ethan was right. Things could change in a moment, and they didn't even know how long it would take to get down to the mine itself.

At least they had a target to aim for, and they could play it by ear.

They had left their packs behind the trees growing right at the edge of the rocky outcrop, and they picked them up and began to move through the woods toward the furthest end of the ridge.

Ethan climbed down first and Velda scooted to the edge to see how much of a drop was involved.

It was about five times higher than Ethan, so she carefully dangled the packs, one by one, when he reached the bottom, then let them go. He caught them easily.

"Now you," he called up softly.

She wasn't going to drop down, but she was glad he would be there in case she lost her grip.

She eased over the edge and began the climb down, her concentration focused on where to find her next hand and foothold.

She thought she heard Ethan make a noise below, and risked a quick look down. Found herself staring at two weapons pointed up at her, and Ethan crumpled on the ground.

"Nice and slow." The man standing beside Ethan's prone form gestured with his laz. "No need to shoot you, too, if I don't have to."

If he did, she would fall, and given she was only half way down, she decided against it.

She carefully climbed the rest of the way, and as soon as her feet touched the ground, she was pushed up against the rock face and her hands secured behind her.

She tried to turn, to see how badly Ethan was injured, but the man pressed harder on her back, so the rock dug into her cheek.

"What have we here?" He hauled her back by her collar, spun her around.

Velda didn't answer immediately, her gaze fixed on Ethan.

"Eyes here." The man snapped his fingers at her, and she forced herself to find some inner calm, to lift her gaze.

"We were hiking and heard the engines. Came to look," Velda said. She tried to move toward Ethan, but the man who'd restrained her jerked her back in a bruising grip. "But why the unfriendly reception?"

"Hikers were bound to happen," the man said, this time to his companion. "We're lucky they haven't before now."

"Is my partner all right?" Velda didn't need to act to let the worry come through.

"He'll be fine. Shot him on a low stun." The man studied her. "This is an off-the-books operation, and we can't be having witnesses, as I'm sure you've already worked out."

That was an obvious conclusion for anyone to draw, Velda thought. There were no mining operations allowed in the mountains, they were part of the Aponi Protected Lands, so no one could have come up with any other conclusion.

"We figured. We were going to go report it in Demeter."

"Good luck with that," the man said, face smug. "Don't know there's much of Demeter left."

Velda tilted her head. "The flash of light we saw last night?" she asked, pretending cluelessness. "That was Demeter getting hit?"

"You saw that?" the man holding her asked.

"We noticed the sky lighting up to the south," she said. "We wondered what it meant."

"It means change is coming," the man said, way too jovial with Ethan lying unconscious at his feet, and her city burning.

She would like to change his outlook. Forcibly.

She pretended confusion and upset, instead. "Who hit the city? Why?"

"Enough." The second man spoke for the first time. "You shot him, you carry him, Vang." He grabbed Velda by her arm and jerked her toward the path that ran along the cliff face.

As they made their way along a well-worn path, she saw the flash of a lens in the trees, and realized mine security must be monitoring the access points.

Behind her, she heard Vang grunt, and then swear.

"Can't lift him, he's too solid," he called from behind them. "Send Nyler to help."

The man pulling her along flapped his hand in response, and then lifted his wrist to his mouth. "Nyler, get up here and help Vang with an intruder."

"Who are you people?" Velda asked. She was surprised she hadn't been recognized by either man. It might mean they were Cores imports, rather than locals.

"Vang might run his mouth, but I don't," he said. "Just shut up and maybe you can walk out of here when this is over."

She wondered what that meant. Were they closing up shop? Moving on? Or did he mean that once Aponi was under the control of whoever had attacked Demeter, there would be nothing she could do about the mine?

She started as a big man came lumbering toward them out of the gloom of the forest.

When her escort said nothing to him, she guessed he was Nyler.

"You wanted me, Ridgeman?" Nyler asked when he was closer. His tone was respectful.

"Up the trail. Vang shot someone. Needs help carrying him."

Nyler gave a grunt of acknowledgement and kept going.

The noise of the mine was getting louder, and then suddenly the trees were behind them and they stood in a small field. To one side, there was the deep slash of the cave entrance, dark and high, and to the other, all the equipment they'd seen from above.

What they hadn't seen was around the curve of the mountain itself were structures built up against the rock face.

Ridgeman waited for a hover to pass them, headed into the cave, then pulled her across the busy working area and toward those buildings.

They had just reached the first one when a roar of sound dropped out of nowhere, getting louder and louder until Velda ducked her head, wishing she could put her bound hands to her ears.

Ridgeman turned and she did, too, as a big ship landed in the open space where they had just been standing.

The moment it touched the ground, a ramp lowered and someone stood at the end of it, impatiently waiting for it to get low enough that they could jump down.

The person—a woman in a dark uniform—strode toward them, face grim.

Ridgeman looked down at Velda, as if suddenly realizing he was still holding her arm, and turned, addressing someone behind them. "Take her. Lock her up. Vang's bringing her friend."

Velda looked over her shoulder, saw the arrival of the ship had brought five or six people out of the various buildings.

Ridgeman shoved her in their general direction and turned, heading for the ship. With a quick, furious look at Ridgeman's back, a tall, muscular woman closed her hand over Velda's forearm.

"No problem, Ridgeman," she said, but under her breath. "Your wish is my command."

A few of the people around her sniggered.

"The Commander has spoken." Another woman stepped up to look at Velda. "Hear and obey."

"He's just stressed, is all," one of the men said. "He doesn't mean to sound like that."

"You keep believing that, Fred." The man who spoke opened the door closest to where they were standing. "Put her in here, Neena. There's a couch."

He stepped to the side and Neena pushed her into the room.

"Why's your friend so far behind?" The woman who'd made the crack about 'hear and obey' stepped in after them.

"He was shot. They're carrying him in." She realized her throat tightened up as she spoke, just thinking about Ethan, hurt and vulnerable.

"Here they come." The man who'd opened the door shook his head. "Vang and Nyler are carrying him between them."

Something eased a little inside Velda, and she took stock of the room.

It was clearly used for planning and admin. There were diagrams on the board, stacks of paper on a trestle table, which served as a desk, and a long couch with a small side table up against a wall.

Neena turned her to face the door again and released the restraints on her wrists. "Sit."

She moved to the couch, rubbing her arms, and sank down. It wasn't a very well-sprung couch, but it was a relief to rest. She had been pushing herself since they heard the engine noise late last night.

"Can I have my pack back?" she asked. Ridgeman had dumped it on the ground when he'd pushed Velda at the group. "Get my water bottle?"

Fred brought it in, and Neena took it, opened it, and unpacked it. She put Velda's clothes in a neat pile, her toiletries in another, and handed her the water bottle before she set out the camping equipment. "No food?" she asked, fingering the sleeping bag.

"It's in Ethan's pack," Velda said.

"Give me your comms unit." The man who'd opened the door held out his hand.

"She can't exactly use it, Brayden." Neena flicked a look his way.

"No, but as soon as she's away from the dead zone, she can. And we have enough on the line without that worry." Brayden flicked his fingers, a hurry up gesture. "We're going to let them go eventually, might as well give ourselves as much time as possible to clear out."

Velda took her wrist unit off and handed it over. It had been turned off anyway, so she hadn't realized they'd set up a dead zone here, but that would make sense. It would be so much harder to spot the mine if there was no electronic activity.

Also, she didn't know whether to believe him about letting her and Ethan go. She didn't think Ridgeman was planning on that. And he seemed to be in charge.

"It's not even on." Brayden looked down at it.

"It died. I forgot to bring a charge." Velda shrugged.

Brayden shoved it into his back pocket as Vang and Nyler came in, carrying Ethan between them.

They dropped him on the floor, and Velda shot them a vicious look before sliding off the couch to kneel beside him.

He was still out, but breathing steadily, and his pulse was strong. She shivered, unable to control her relief.

"You look puffed out," Neena said to Vang, and there was a slightly mocking quality to the comment.

"He's solid." Vang shot her an annoyed look.

Nyler was already backing out. "Ridgeman says we need to load."

Everyone in the room suddenly seemed to remember there was a ship outside, and filed out after him, leaving her and Ethan alone with Neena.

The woman swept her gaze around the room, shoved all the papers on the trestle table into a lockable cupboard to one side, slid the key into her pocket, and gave a nod. "Toilet's through there. The water from the tap is drinkable. Don't cause trouble, or Ridgeman will end you." Then she moved out, closed the door, and Velda heard a key turn in the lock.

As soon as the click sounded, Ethan opened his eyes.

Velda stared at him, and he sent her a wink.

"Well played," she murmured, leaning forward to kiss him. "You had me fooled."

"Thought I might hear a bit more chatter between Vang and Nyler if they thought I was out of it."

"And did you?" she asked.

"I did." He sat up, and rubbed at his chest, which is where she assumed he'd taken the laz hit.

She got up, went through to the tiny bathroom at the back, found a tiny glass on the edge of the sink, and filled it, brought it back to Ethan.

He downed it in a single swallow.

"Where's your pack?" she asked.

"Good question." He tilted his head. "Back at the cliff face, I think. It was leaning against the rock."

"They just left it?" Velda hoped that was true. "They took my comms unit, but yours might still be in your pack."

"Unless they specifically took it out, it is."

They smiled at each other.

"So, what did they say?" she asked.

"The ship was arriving, so most of the talk was about the shipment, how it was the last one, how they were glad to be going, and curiosity at what was going on in Demeter since the laser strikes." Ethan rose to his feet and began to wander around the room, studying everything he could.

"Where are they going with the shipment?" Velda wondered.

"They didn't say. But they aren't locals, that's for sure. They had a few unflattering things to say about our beautiful planet." Ethan stopped at the locked cabinet and crouched in front of it, studied the lock.

"That explains why none of them seem to recognize me." Although Velda thought some of them did sound local. It may be down to context. They assumed she was a random hiker, and so that is what they saw.

Ethan looked across at her, eyes narrowed. "I hadn't considered that. But if there's a dead zone in place, they won't have heard about the crash."

"A few of the team here are definitely local, unless they've adopted an Aponi accent." Velda went into the bathroom to get herself a cup of water, and then froze when someone tried the door.

Ethan moved away from the cabinet, and lay on the couch, gesturing for her to join him.

"Neena, where's the key?" Ridgeman's voice was loud enough for her to hear him perfectly.

She heard a feminine voice respond, and by the time a clearly angry Ridgeman opened the door, she and Ethan were on the couch, him half lying down, her hovering over him anxiously.

"He's not still out?" Ridgeman asked, his focus on Ethan.

"He's just started to come round." Velda glared at him, then gently brushed a hand over Ethan's forehead.

"Ridgeman." The woman who Velda had seen coming out of the ship stopped just in the doorway, blocking the natural light. She seemed shocked at the sight of them. "So these are the two you're holding? Where'd they come from?"

"Hikers. Stumbled across us this morning." Ridgeman looked down at the empty table, and narrowed his eyes. "Where's my stuff?"

"Neena put everything away in there before she locked us in," Velda said, pointing to the cabinet.

Ridgeman walked over to it, tried the handle, and swore softly. He strode to the door and the woman stepped back to let him out.

She winced when he bellowed for Neena and shot him a sour look.

Ridgeman returned, key in hand, and retrieved the papers, spreading them out on the table and grabbing several that were clipped together. "Here." He shoved them at the woman.

She didn't look pleased by his attitude but she took them, angled them to the light coming through the door, and gave a nod. "It'll do."

"It'll do?" Ridgeman's voice dropped.

"Yes, it will do." She looked up at him, eyes hard. "I'm not saying it's your problem, or your fuck-up. I'm just saying it looks like there's enough ore on hand for us to placate the fucking Caruso and save our little agreement from imploding. This, and what we have in the warehouse in Demeter, will be enough to keep them from outright walking away."

Velda had a bad feeling about the fact that this conversation was happening so openly in front of them. So did Ethan, if his grip on her hand was anything to go by. She could feel his body tense, and she forced herself not to look at him, to keep her expression neutral.

"Fine. You can take the hikers and the ore, and get the fuck out of here, Brink." Ridgeman's lips twisted. "We'll pack up and head back to the city."

"The heads would prefer you stayed here and kept mining, but they need boots on the ground in the city." Brink shrugged. "I can see you're pleased with that outcome, but don't get too comfy in Demeter. This mine is currently our only hold on the Caruso, and you're the one who knows it best."

Ridgeman shook his head and walked to the door, leaned out. "Nyler!"

Brink's hold on the sheaf of papers tightened in irritation.

Velda knew the shout had been intended to irritate when Ridgeman turned and propped a shoulder against the doorjamb with a smirk.

"What do you need these two for, anyway?" he asked.

"Nothing you need to worry about." Brink smiled back, and Velda couldn't tell if she was being difficult in response to Ridgeman's attitude, or because she really didn't want to tell him.

Either way, she didn't like it.

Neither did Ethan, because he stood up and took a step forward, shielding her from their two captors.

"You're going to be difficult, aren't you?" Ridgeman said.

Ethan leaped at him, silent and furious, and then fell.

Velda turned her head, saw Brink had a laz out. One Velda hadn't seen before.

She rushed her, fury fueling her own attack, but Brink was ready for her.

She saw the flash of laz fire, and then nothing.

10

Ethan woke with a sudden, adrenalin-fueled start.

He'd been shot. Again.

He didn't feel the worse for it, though. Not this time.

There were no sounds of movement around him, no hint of anyone else being nearby, so he opened his eyes slowly, found himself in a med bay.

No wonder he was fine. He was hooked up to a standard Verdant String medbed, and as he sat up, various needles and tubes retracted.

Velda lay on a medbed beside him, still and pale.

He slid off his bed and leaned over her, fingers brushing her forehead. "Velda. Wake up, beautiful."

He kept his voice low, but she must have been close to waking anyway, because she blinked her eyes open and stared up at him, the most beautiful woman he'd ever seen, her lips curving into a smile at the sight of him.

Then he saw her face change as she remembered what had happened, because her gaze suddenly snapped into focus and he stepped back to let her sit up.

"We're on the ship?" she asked.

He shrugged. "Must be. That's where it sounded like we were going

55

to be taken. I don't know that the mine had anything as sophisticated as this medbay."

She slid off the bed on the same side he was standing, and slid her arms around his waist. They stood for a moment as he looped his own arm around her shoulder, just quietly being together before they faced whatever it was beyond the door.

"Do you think Brink was just messing with Ridgeman about what she was planning to do to us, or do you think we have reason to be worried?" she said at last.

"You mean more worried?" Although he knew what she was getting at. "If we're on a ship, I'm assuming we're at least in nearspace, which means there's no easy way to escape. That alone worries me—whether or not Brink has nefarious plans for us."

The door opened, something he had been expecting since they'd gotten off the beds, so he simply turned his head to see who was coming through.

"You look like you're doing well." A med tech stood in the doorway, eyeing the two of them together. He looked like every med tech Ethan had ever seen, except in this case, there were two armed guards standing behind him, weapons trained on Velda and himself.

"What's going on?" Ethan asked.

"I gather you're hikers who had the misfortune of stumbling across the mine, is that right?" The med tech waited for them to acknowledge his words, and when neither of them did, he sent them a bright smile. "Well, unfortunately for you, we've run out of volunteers, and it was either end the experiments, or force one of the crew to cooperate. As forcing people tends to lead to great unhappiness onboard, your appearance is serendipitous to say the least."

"Cooperate in what?" Velda asked.

"Nothing bad," the med tech said with a smile. "But I didn't know we had you available until a few hours ago, so I need to set things up. These two guards will take you for a meal while I get busy."

Ethan had been studying the guards while the tech had been talking, and he had to admit there was no way around cooperating with them for the moment. He didn't want to take a third laz hit in less than a day. That was not going to help.

And if he was out, he couldn't protect Velda.

He said nothing when the guards came forward, weapons raised, and the med tech secured their wrists.

The march to the mess was interesting.

The ship looked like standard Verdant String construction, but he wasn't familiar with the layout, and couldn't guess what type of ship it was.

He assumed he and Velda were guests of the criminal enterprise that had once run Garmen and Lassa, the breakaway planets that had recently been forcibly wrenched back into the Verdant String's fold. They called themselves the Core Companies, and they had lost their grip on the planets they'd once seen as their own fiefdom.

Mainly because of the crazy antics of the Core Companies themselves.

They had done deals with the Caruso when they'd run the breakaway planets, but that hadn't gone so well, for either themselves or the Caruso. That they were persisting with the plan here on Aponi made no sense, unless someone had managed to explain away the problems they'd had before.

Some people just couldn't let a bad idea go, if they were the ones who'd come up with it.

Ethan wouldn't care, except he and Velda were caught up in it, now.

They reached the mess, and it turned out to be a relatively large room set close to the staff quarters. There were a few people eating together at a table to the right, but it was otherwise empty.

Given what he'd observed on the journey from the medbay to here, and the size of the room, Ethan guessed this was a mid-sized transport, rather than a big ship.

"Sit." One of the guards pointed to a table.

When they were seated, a guard pointed to one of the people sitting at the occupied table.

"Melli, go get two meals."

The others were watching, wide-eyed, and Melli stood up with ill grace. "Who are these two?"

"Hikers that stumbled across the mine. So Ritter's got new people to experiment on, other than us. He wants them to eat first."

Melli stared at them.

Ethan understood from what the med tech had said before that he'd tried his experiments on the crew first. At least they were all alive and looked none the worse for wear. But there was something in all their eyes, a pitying look, that worried him.

He wanted to get himself and Velda out of here.

Melli walked out of the room, through a door he'd noticed at the back, and when she returned, it was with two plates.

"Thank you," Velda murmured as the plates were put in front of them.

Melli started at the sound of her voice, and stepped back quickly, and with a quick nod, left the mess.

At her exit, the others at the table she'd been sitting at cleared up, and shuffled out themselves.

It looked as if their arrival had brought down the mood.

"So, what are these experiments?" Ethan asked as he picked up his fork. Having his wrists tied together made eating difficult.

The guards didn't answer.

"Please tell us." Velda lifted her head, and tilted up to look at them. "It's better to know, don't you think? It's hardly going to matter if we don't like it, I'm getting the picture that we don't have a choice."

The female guard looked at them, glanced at her partner, and then lifted her shoulders. "No one knows what the experiments are. They blindfold you."

Ethan could see how uncomfortable it made both guards. "Whatever it is, it's too top secret for the crew to know?" he asked.

The guards shrugged.

"And you've all been through it?" Velda asked.

"Not all."

But something in the way the guard answered made Ethan think the guards both had.

"Not the senior officers?" Ethan asked.

The female guard gave a slight sneer, which made Ethan think he'd hit the nail on the head.

"Do you feel all right?" Velda was watching them carefully. "No side effects?"

The question must have taken them deeper than they wanted to go, because the one guard's expression tightened. "Just eat your food."

They stepped back a little way, putting some distance between them.

Velda turned her gaze to his, and Ethan didn't like the fear he could see on her face.

"Let's eat," he told her. "Better to have energy."

She nodded, focused on her food, but he could feel the tension coming off her and he slid his foot to touch hers.

She looked up at him, sighed, and went back to her food, but she pressed her foot even closer to his in response.

"This is totally mad," she murmured. "Experiments? Have you ever heard of the Cores involved in anything like this?"

He hadn't, and that worried him. Either their intelligence was totally useless, or this was a relatively new endeavor for the Cores.

Neither option filled him with confidence.

11

———————

Velda had barely finished her meal when Ritter called them back to the medbay. Ethan had eaten fast, and then spent the rest of his time studying the layout of the room and the few people left in it.

She guessed he couldn't help himself, but there was very little way she could see out of this. And that really frightened her.

When they got to the medbay, the guards strapped them to the same beds they'd woken up on, and Velda looked around to see what had changed since then.

Ritter had brought a large metal box into the room on a trolley, and beside it was a small device with a line of lights along the top, although they were currently unlit.

This was it? This was his equipment?

She eyed the big box, but couldn't really tell what was in it.

"Did you tie the crew down when you experimented on them?" Ethan asked.

Ritter looked up from the screen he held in his hand. "Yes. Although with you and your companion, it's both to keep you still *and* protect me from any attack, whereas I didn't have that worry with the crew."

He put the screen down and picked up two blindfolds, came over to secure them. "Top secret, you understand."

Velda said nothing, and just before her eyes were covered over, she saw Ethan's fists clench.

Ritter was probably right to secure them to the tables.

She heard a sound, which she assumed was the box being opened, and couldn't help lifting her head and shoulders up, in anticipation of what, she didn't know, but lying back passively just wasn't in her makeup.

"You need to lie flat." Ritter pushed her shoulder down and then she felt something cold and small land in the hollow between her throat and her clavicle. It felt like it disappeared a moment later.

She waited, expecting to feel something, for there to be some reaction, either within or without, but there was nothing.

"Velda?" Ethan's voice sounded calm.

"All good. You?"

"All good." His tone was neutral, and she wondered if he was as surprised as she was at the lack of pain, discomfort or weirdness.

She guessed yes.

"I told you it wasn't going to hurt." Ritter's voice sounded too close for comfort, and Velda flinched away from him. "Not this first part, anyway."

She knew it. She knew it had been too good to be true. The staff wouldn't have been refusing to participate anymore if there had been no effects.

She could hear the box being closed back up and the trolley rolled away. And then Ritter was back, removing the blindfolds.

"Now what?" Ethan asked.

"Now we wait," Ritter said. He glanced at the screen propped up on the shelf nearby. "This time tomorrow, I'll do some tests. Then things might get a little uncomfortable, but everyone who's been through it is perfectly fine."

"Have you been through it?" Velda asked.

Ritter snapped his gaze to hers, held it for a moment, and then went to the door and opened it. He stood in the threshold to address the two guards waiting outside. "You can take them to the holding room. Full containment."

They were unclipped from the beds, secured with restraints, and taken back down the passageway, but this time, they bypassed the mess and were taken to a small room that Velda guessed was the closest a ship of this small size got to a brig.

It had two benches running down each side, with a thin mattress on each, a tiny bathroom at the back with a sink, toilet and shower, and nothing else.

The guards unclipped the restraints and Velda felt a surge of relief at that.

Another guard appeared with sheets and blankets and dumped a set at the end of each mattress.

Then the door closed, and they were sitting, facing each other.

"Alone at last," Velda said, to try to make Ethan smile.

He looked as grim as she'd ever seen him.

He didn't even try to accommodate her.

"They've got to be recording us," he said.

She sighed, stood, and began to make up her bed. "I know."

12

He was failing her.

He had just found her, just made the connection of his dreams with her, and here they were, locked in a cell, exposed to who the hell knew what.

Ethan rubbed a finger over the base of his throat, where he'd felt the small cold ball land, as if Ritter had dropped it when he'd gotten close enough.

He hadn't placed it down, which made Ethan think he hadn't been touching it with his hands. Maybe he was holding it using a clamp of some kind.

As soon as Velda sat back down on her now-made bed, he stood and took the single step that divided their beds and crouched down in front of her.

"Here?" he asked, touching the hollow of her clavicle.

She nodded. "You, too?"

He nodded back, and smoothed a finger over her skin.

When he was done, she did the same to him.

Had he felt a strange tingle when she did that? He couldn't tell if it was psychosomatic or a real response.

He didn't want to ask her if she felt it, too. Not now, when he was sure Ritter was listening to every single word they said.

He would find a way to whisper the question later.

He nudged her over, and she shifted, leaning against the wall at the head of the bed and stretching out her legs, and he settled in next to her, a barrier between her and the door.

He slid an arm around her and she tipped her head onto his shoulder.

They sat like that, in silence.

Ethan expected the guards to bring them food and water, but no one did.

Eventually, they drank water from the tap in the bathroom, had a quick shower, and then slid down on the bunk.

It would be more comfortable if Ethan were to go over to his own bunk, but he wanted to be right beside her, and she didn't complain.

He got his pillow, adding it to hers, so things were a little more comfortable, and then she tucked herself under his arm, her head resting on his chest, and even though he tried to keep awake, alert to any danger, he found himself slipping into sleep.

He woke with a suddenness he was used to, especially from his days in the military, but this felt . . . more . . . than usual, as if every sense was at optimum capacity.

He felt well rested, energized, and when he looked down at Velda, she was staring up at him, and there was a sudden connection between them that made his body hum with excitement and a feeling of rightness.

Neither of them had moved anything other than their heads, aside from opening their eyes, and he guessed if they were being watched, they would look like they were still asleep, although it would be difficult to make them out in the darkness.

Some time in the night the lights had gone off, letting them sleep more naturally, but now the lights flicked back on and the door suddenly opened, and Ethan wondered if they'd both unconsciously heard someone moving outside.

He lifted his head to look at who it was, and wasn't surprised to see the guards from yesterday, along with Ritter.

"How are we feeling this morning?" Ritter asked, studying them with interest.

When Ethan had lifted his head, Velda had pushed up on one hand, and Ethan swung both feet to the floor, giving her room to do the same.

"Hungry," Velda said.

"I'll give you something to eat after I've taken your vitals," Ritter said, stepping back as they both got to their feet. "Shackle them, just to be sure," he told the guards, and then strolled away.

"Hands out." One of the guards lifted a laz, and the caution Ethan usually felt when someone aimed a laz at him seemed to spike inside him, way more than he'd ever worried about it before.

He stepped in front of Velda, shielding her from the guard's aim, and thrust his hands forward.

The second guard restrained him and waited until Velda stepped forward to do the same to her.

"Out."

They stepped into the passageway, which was completely devoid of crew.

Were they deliberately keeping out the way, Ethan wondered? Were they considered dangerous?

Or, more dangerous, he amended. They were dangerous, or at least he knew he would be seen that way, even if Velda wasn't. But there was a jumpiness to Ritter and the guards that made him think the test subjects hadn't been very predictable after being experimented on.

"What did some of the crew do after Ritter was finished with them, that you're so nervous?" he asked.

The guards were behind them, and he glanced over his shoulder as he asked the question.

"They weren't themselves," one of the guards said. Then he closed his mouth in a thin line, and Ethan guessed that was all he was going to get.

Interesting.

He didn't feel not himself. He felt pretty good. Better than he should have for sleeping on an uncomfortable bench, with a skipped meal, and in a stressful situation.

Maybe some of it was Velda. Having her plastered up against him all night had been a sweet torture, but he didn't even feel stiff, despite the narrow bed and thin mattress.

They reached the med bay, and Ritter was already there, with two gurneys ready for them, restraints attached to the sides for wrists and ankles.

Ethan submitted to it, getting on the raised bed and allowing himself to be restrained, watching as they did the same to Velda.

There wasn't any choice, and every time a laz was aimed his way, his heart seemed to want to beat its way out of his chest, and his breathing got short.

"Right." As soon as they were secured, Ritter seemed to relax, setting his screen down on a high shelf, and then taking a standard vitals monitor and checking first Velda, then himself.

"You're obviously showing signs of not having eaten, but otherwise . . ." He frowned at the screen, and worried his lower lip. "Take them to have some breakfast, then bring them back," he said to the guards, and walked out, screen still lighting his face.

The one guard made a face at the other at the curt order. Then they did the usual dance of one holding the laz, while the other got them off the gurneys, got restraints back around their wrists, and then marched them ahead to the mess.

"How are you feeling?" Ethan asked Velda quietly as they sat down at the same table they'd had before, waiting for someone to bring them something to eat.

Velda's gaze, which had been sweeping the room, snapped to his face. "Surprisingly fine," she said.

So, the same as him.

Something had worried Ritter, and it sounded like it was the lack of change in their vitals, not a difference, that had concerned him.

They ate with their hands still secured, which made things difficult, but not impossible.

The jah tasted good, hot and fragrant, and he savored it, surprised it was as good as this in a small ship's canteen.

Velda seemed to be enjoying it as much as him, and she'd eaten everything on her plate, which she hadn't yesterday. Like him, she must be wondering when their next meal would be.

The guards shepherded them back to the med bay, and Ethan stopped abruptly when he saw what was waiting for them.

"What is it?" Velda pressed up against him, then went still as she saw it, too.

The black box from the day before.

"Back on the beds," Ritter said, pointing.

Ethan watched the scientist with narrowed eyes as he and then Velda were secured again, then blindfolded.

The guards were ordered out, and once again, he felt the sensation of something small, round and cold land in the hollow of his throat and then disappear.

The door opened a moment later. "Ritter."

Ritter had been standing beside him, and Ethan sensed him turning.

"Captain." He sounded annoyed. "I'm in the middle—"

"I know, but what are you up to?" The captain's voice sounded incredulous and accusatory.

Ritter sighed. "Come talk to me in the dispensary."

He moved away, and Ethan heard the captain step inside, and the door closed behind him, and then another door opened.

Ethan had noticed it yesterday, a narrow door at the back.

"You all right?" he whispered to Velda.

"Yes, you?"

"Same as before." He heard voices, muted by the dispensary door, but suddenly they seemed to become clearer, and he turned his head toward the sound.

"They're the fifth ones to get the balls, and it may be they can only be used so many times," Ritter was saying.

"So you wore them out?" The captain sounded unconcerned.

"Maybe. I used the same ones each time, so given the results this morning, it looks like it. I've just given them a second one each."

"Given what happened before, that sounds dangerous." The captain's voice rose a little.

"Not if the first ones are useless now. It'll be the same as before." Ritter didn't sound like he cared what the captain thought.

"Fine. We're heading for a position off Aponi, waiting for someone they've managed to rescue from a military prison in Demeter, and then we're going to pinch to the black immediately." The captain stepped out of the dispensary.

"How long until that happens?" Ritter asked. "I can't work when we pinch."

"Hopefully in a few hours, so be done by then." The captain walked past the beds and out the door into the passageway.

"You're quiet," Ritter said, and Ethan could only guess he was speaking to him and Velda.

Neither of them answered him, and he was silent and still for a moment, then Ethan heard him wheeling the black box back into the dispensary and then stepping back into the med bay.

He called the guards back in, removed their blindfolds, and took their vitals again.

Ritter frowned in concern at the readings, and then had them taken back to the cell.

"Talk to me." Ethan rubbed his wrists, and then pulled Velda into his arms, bending his head so his lips were near her ear. He was sure they were being monitored and he didn't want to give Ritter anything he didn't have to.

"I feel like I could maybe smash my way through the door," she whispered to him. "Except I also really don't want to be hit with laz fire."

"Yeah." He was feeling pretty much the same. "Whatever they've given us, it's made me very allergic to getting shot."

Not that he had ever been keen about taking a hit, but he hadn't worried about it to this extent before.

"The first dose wasn't worn out," Velda whispered. "It was only pretending to be."

Her words sent a chill down his spine. "Pretending?" That gave whatever it was some agency. Some intelligence.

"That's what it feels like," she said.

That's what it felt like to him, too.

And that frightened him.

13

———————

Ritter had sent them back to their cell around mid morning, and no one came to get them or give them food for the rest of the day.

Velda wanted to do something, but the space was too small to exercise, so she showered out of sheer boredom, then she and Ethan lay back down on the narrow bed.

He was quiet and thoughtful, and she let her eyes close and snuggled in, enjoying the feel of his arm around her, the sound of his heart beating in his chest.

If she wasn't sure they were being watched by the black lens in the top corner of the cell, she knew they'd have found some creative ways to pass the time, but there was no way she was putting on a show for Ritter and the guards.

Ethan nuzzled her ear, and she smiled against his neck, sure his thoughts were running along the same track as hers.

"Damn lens," he murmured.

The ship suddenly pinched to the black, the strange feeling of pressure holding her down was unmistakeable, and she recalled the captain telling Ritter it was going to happen later while they were still tied to the gurneys this morning.

Something about picking up a prisoner who'd escaped.

She'd wondered which prisoner, or if it was someone new who'd been imprisoned while she and Ethan had been making their way through the mountains.

The ship came out of the pinch, rocking a little, and then she felt a smooth acceleration as it went back to normal speed.

"That was a quick pinch," she said, and felt Ethan's nod of agreement.

And still, no one came, hours stretching out with no activity. She was dozing when she sensed someone by the door, and was suddenly on her feet, facing it.

What disturbed her was that she hadn't felt in control of the movement.

Ethan moved, too, his body flowing in that effortless, efficient way of his, settling down in front of her, making his body a shield between her and the door.

She pressed a hand to his back, freaking out at what had just happened.

Something had controlled her.

She felt a sudden flow of reassurance, as if whatever had forced her to move was trying to soothe her fears, but that just made her breathing hitch a little higher, because it was coming from within.

"Velda?" Ethan sounded like he had some sense of her panic, but he kept his gaze on the door.

"All good." She swallowed down the tremor in her voice, cleared her throat.

How she moved was a problem for later. Why she moved was clear from the sounds coming from beyond the door.

It opened, and it was four guards, this time, along with the captain, Ritter, and a woman she'd never seen before.

"It's definitely her," the woman said. "I thought that was her on the comms feed. Velda Shanïha. And that's Ethan Hyt, commander of Demeter Special Forces."

The captain lifted his shoulders. "We didn't know. And I don't see what difference it makes."

The woman narrowed her eyes at the two men, unwilling to concede.

"They were supposed to die, as far as I'm aware. I was told the plan was to shoot down their runner."

"Well, someone must have missed. And we needed the test subjects." Ritter seemed to be in agreement with the captain, unsure what the fuss was about. "There's no way we're killing them until after I've . . ." He slid a sly look at the guards. "Until after I've finished the test work."

The woman stared at her and Ethan for another beat, then turned on her heel and stalked off, shaking her head. Ritter and the captain exchanged a look that said they didn't care much for the dramatics.

"Feeling all right?" Ritter asked, his gaze suddenly focused on them.

Velda lifted her shoulders and her hands, being as non-committal as possible.

Ritter tilted his head, looked at his screen, and then closed the door.

"Do you think that's the prisoner they were talking about?" Velda wondered who she was, because she didn't recognize her, and she was kept up-to-date on all high-profile prisoners. "We've been gone from Demeter for less than a week."

"She's obviously involved in this whole scheme," Ethan said. "So someone must have arrested her since we crashed."

"And then someone else broke her out and got her up to nearspace." It was depressing just thinking about it. Because it meant there were moles everywhere. In Nanganya, in her own department. Even in the military, as the captain had said the prisoner was in a military prison.

"And whoever she is, she's plugged in enough on Aponi to recognize the both of us," Ethan said.

"And wants us dead." Velda didn't like that part so much.

"Fortunately, Ritter's got other plans for us." Ethan stretched, and Velda admired all the muscles while it lasted.

He caught her gaze and gave a tiny smile.

She felt like stretching herself, or doing a handstand against the wall. Anything to move her body rather than do nothing, as they had been for what felt like far too long.

Except she hadn't done a handstand of any kind since she was about eleven years old, and yet she was sure she would be able to do one now, no problem.

Her gaze flew to Ethan, and he stepped closer, concerned. "What?"

She shook her head. "Nothing."

Ethan frowned, drew her in close. "What is it?" he whispered.

"I want to move, or do something." She kept the handstand part to herself. "But . . ."

"They're watching," he agreed. "Better to act listless."

He drew her back down onto the bed, and she forced herself to relax, to endure the inactivity as best she could.

Ethan wove his fingers through hers, and that helped soothe her. She thought there was a tingle of awareness where their skin touched, but as soon as she noticed it, it faded.

Or maybe hid.

She worried her lip, not sure where her mind was going with that.

It was less than an hour after the door had opened last time when Ethan raised his head, gaze snapping open to stare at the door, and Velda drew her legs up, pushing back so she could lean against the wall at the top of the bed.

Ethan sat up and swung his legs down, angled to see who was about to appear. He looked half asleep, but she knew with certainty he was anything but.

She thought it interesting neither of them had stood this time. Either whatever her new warning system was didn't think there was as much of a threat, or they'd decided to switch up the response.

The door opened and it was Ritter again, with the two guards, but the new woman was there, as well.

Velda took an immediate dislike to her. It felt as if she was watching them like they were an exotic species she'd never encountered before.

"How did the Aponi Head of Planetary Defense end up in your clutches, Ritter?" The woman leaned against the doorjamb as the guards did their usual dance of getting them in their restraints.

"Brink got them for me from the mine site." Ritter was watching them like they were delicate explosives that could blow at the smallest jostle.

Velda had almost forgotten about Brink. She hadn't seen the woman since she'd shot them both in the little admin office at the mine. She wondered what her role on the ship and in this operation was. She'd certainly seemed to boss Ridgeman, the mine manager, around.

"The mine site?" The woman straightened. "You walked from where they brought down your hover all the way to the mine site?"

Velda shrugged. "We were headed for Demeter. Stumbled across it by accident."

The woman didn't look like she believed them. "That's one hell of a coincidence."

"Not when the mine is all lit up at night, running engines. It wasn't on our route, but it was difficult to ignore," Ethan said.

The woman swore. "What were they thinking?"

"They were obeying orders. With Salisas not reporting in, Pontia dead, you on Ytla and then in prison, and with no access to the warehouse that was storing the ore, we didn't have enough trivolun to keep the Caruso sweet. It was run full tilt, or lose the alliance."

The person speaking was Brink, Velda recognized her voice, although the woman was just beyond the doorway, and she couldn't see her. She did not like the person who'd shot her and Ethan and then handed them over to Ritter.

"Did Opek get the ore in the end?" the woman asked, turning to address Brink over her shoulder.

"He said he did. But something happened to the Caruso ship that came down to get the ore." Brink spoke with an edge.

"Something?" The woman asked.

"It blew up. Probably shot down by the military, but the Caruso aren't happy. You're lucky the top bosses value you enough to make us swing by to get you, rather than go straight to the delivery coordinates so we can hand the trivolun over to them."

"Aren't I just?" The woman sounded sarcastic.

"It was one of the Caruson's small Raptors that was taken out," Brink said, her tone saying she didn't like the attitude at all. "They say you told them Demeter was a safe zone. That we'd taken the city. Which we had not."

"I told them what I was told to tell them, and then I was ordered to take a side trip to Ytla." The woman's voice was low and mean. "I was not the one attacking the capital. If that attack wasn't successful, that's not on me. And it landed me in jail afterward, because in the aftermath, the authorities were very ticked off about the damage, and only had little old me to point the finger at as I arrived back."

"What's on Ytla that was more important than taking the city?" Ritter asked. He'd been listening in to the conversation as avidly as Velda had been.

The woman seemed to realize how many people were watching the byplay between her and Brink, and she shook her head. "None of your business." She shoved past Brink, and disappeared down the passageway.

Interesting. As it happened, Velda had a pretty good idea what was on Ytla that was potentially more important than taking the capital of Aponi. Wren Thorakis had laid it out quite well for her and Ethan. It was why they'd gone to Nanganya in the first place.

"Nothing sticks to that woman," Brink said, finally stepping into the doorway. "She's never in the wrong and she always comes out on top."

"I've heard more than one rumor Linao isn't who she says she is," Ritter said to Brink. "She's never met a consequence that wasn't waived, apparently. Burning an asset to break her out of prison and then taking a massive detour to fetch her is totally in keeping with that."

Brink's gaze swept over Velda and Ethan. "You two seem none the worse for wear," she said, as if reminding Ritter who they were talking in front of.

"No thanks to you," Velda said. "Ethan was shot twice in the space of an hour."

"Was he?" Ritter spun to look at Ethan. "No one told me that." He glared at Brink. "You didn't tell me that."

"I didn't know. You knew I shot them both to get them in here." Brink bristled at his accusatory tone.

"Did I?" Ritter frowned. Looked down at his screen. "Maybe. But how was he shot twice?"

"One of the security guards at the mine shot him just before the ship landed," Velda said. "Then Brink shot him again."

"Could that be why . . .?" Ritter tapped a finger to his lips. "Let's test you again."

Brink studied them, then stepped back to allow the guards to herd them through the door. "They're not working out?" she asked.

"Early days," Ritter said, but Velda thought he sounded annoyed. "At least they can't say no."

For now, Velda thought to herself.

But watch out when the tables turn, asshole.

14

———————

THE DISCUSSION ABOUT YTLA HAD BEEN INTERESTING.

Ethan turned it over in his mind as Ritter tied the blindfold over his eyes again.

Wren Thorakis, the new artifacts consultant in his Special Forces team, had found something on the Aponi-controlled moon, something she thought was an ancestral spaceship wreck. Her discovery seemed to have been a catalyst for what was happening now—the sudden increase in pace of whatever plot was brewing against his planet.

If the woman Ritter called Linao had gone to Ytla just before Demeter had been attacked, he wondered if she had found what she'd been looking for.

Whether she had or not, she'd said she'd been arrested on her return to Demeter, which meant someone had noticed something was off where she was concerned.

He heard Ritter tying the blindfold on Velda, and steeled himself to endure more of Ritter's experimentation.

Not that endure was quite the right word.

There was nothing painful about it. If he was honest, he felt better than he had since they'd crashed in the hover.

He heard Ritter go into the dispensary, then heard him wheeling the box in. The main door opened, and the trolley Ritter was pushing stopped with a squeak.

"What are you doing here, Linao?" Ritter sounded pissed.

"I have clearance. I want to see this. You wouldn't even have known what to do with that box if I hadn't endured that hellhole planet and worked out what it could be." Linao's voice was soft, as if she was mindful of the guards in the passage behind her and wanted to keep this information secret.

Except she was saying it in front of him and Velda.

Which was an indicator of something else. Something dark.

"Wait outside while I check your clearance." Ritter passed him, Ethan could feel the air move as he strode out, and heard the door close.

He was about to speak to Velda when the door opened again, and someone slipped in.

Linao, he was guessing. She'd decided not to wait outside while Ritter checked her story.

"You obviously outrank him." Velda spoke up, and Ethan sensed Linao stop in her tracks.

Linao breathed out. "Maybe I just like to push against authority," she said.

"You probably do," Velda agreed. "But you still outrank him, don't you?"

"Maybe." Linao laughed softly. "So, how many days have you been in Ritter's clutches?"

"Two," Velda said. "Apparently the first 'experiment' didn't work, so we got a second dose."

"And what does the experiment consist of?" Linao asked.

"Can you see the blindfolds?" Velda asked.

"Sure, I can see them. So you have no idea what's going on?"

"Nope." As Velda said it, Ritter came back in.

"I asked you to wait—"

"I know, but I outrank you, and you've had confirmation about my security level, haven't you?" Linao's voice held a laugh.

"I've been told you might have more information that could help me with my experiments," Ritter conceded. "I didn't know it was you who gave the report about the silver balls from that undiscovered planet."

"Well, it's not so much undiscovered, as undiscovered by us," Linao said. "To be fair, a whole planet's worth of people might take issue with your description."

"Fine. Undiscovered by us. A lost Verdant String planet." Ritter's tone was irritated. "You're sure they're Verdant String?"

Ethan felt a shot of shock and adrenalin at what they were discussing, as casually as you please.

"As in, from the same ancestral convoy as us? Definitely. And somehow, even though they've had it far tougher than the rest of us, they seem to have a better record of their history than we do. I don't know if it's because they had to more or less wall themselves in for centuries before they were able to expand, but they literally still have the mothership. They've made it into a museum."

"You saw it?" Ritter asked.

"I saw it," Linao said. "Saw what the balls did to their elite soldiers, too."

Ethan shifted at that, because there was a layer of disgust in Linao's voice and he had a feeling he and Velda had met the balls. Just this morning, in fact.

"Bulking out, you said in your report. What did it look like?" Ritter had forgotten he was resentful and annoyed, and sounded like he was lapping up every word out of Linao's mouth.

So was Ethan. Given he had a suspicion the silver balls they were talking about had been dropped into the hollow of his throat twice, he very much wanted to know what *bulking out* looked like.

"I was attacked by them in that form once while we were collecting the ore we'd mined. Before one of my crew . . ." Linao stopped, and he heard her draw in a breath as if she was recalling something incredibly distressing.

"One of your crew?" Ritter asked.

"Never mind." She sounded like she was still struggling with what had happened. "Let's just say it ended with our ship being totally destroyed and us becoming their prisoners for a week. The whole planet is full of monsters. Everything there is out to kill you, and I don't know if the nanotech in the balls adapted to that by allowing the designated protectors to grow bigger when needed, to take the monsters on, or whether that's just how it works, but they grow maybe head and shoulders taller and they look . . . feral."

"Well, that hasn't happened yet, no matter how many times I've tried it. I've given it a few days each time, and then taken the balls back out when it hasn't worked. There were a few incidents—people going a bit crazy when they understood the ball was coming back out—but nothing we couldn't handle."

"Maybe they've been sitting dormant too long," Liano said. "They call them gyra on the monster planet, and the inhabitants have been assigning them to their guards, called Gyr, since they landed there."

"The same ones, over and over?" Ritter sounded shocked. "For two thousand years?"

"They've got a whole ceremony to take the balls out of the guards when they age out or want children, and then give them to a new recruit." Linao was right beside Ethan now, standing next to the box. "The normal population keep tight control of the tech, I guess so the super soldiers don't get the idea in their heads to take over."

"Well, maybe that's the issue. I was involved in cataloguing the inventory from the ancestral ship on Garmen, but I only found out about the box since your report. There's no indication they were used at all, although they could have been, and then all returned to the box because they were defective, for all I know." Ritter walked over to join her. "Did anyone else experiment with them before me, do you know?"

"The ancestral ship these are from was how the Core Companies found Garmen to begin with," Linao said. "The signal from the mothership was picked up by one of the asteroid miners and it led them to where it was located on the planet. The scientists were sent out to inventory and move the tech as quickly as possible away from the signal, in case a Verdant String ship picked it up. I don't think anyone did anything with the box until I got back from the monster planet."

"Was the Garmen ship broken up, or intact?" Ritter asked. He sounded enthralled.

Ethan couldn't help but feel the same. That's how the Cores had found Garmen? A signal had led them to it, and they'd never disclosed their find?

Of course not, he realized. The Verdant String would never have allowed them to claim Garmen as the first breakaway planet, unaffiliated to the VSC, if they'd known.

Now that the VSC had clawed Garmen back about a year ago, they would be surveying the whole planet. Would they find the ship?

He guessed they would, sooner or later. It had to be big.

"I didn't see the Garmen mothership myself, but apparently it didn't crash. It's fully intact," Linao said. "The people onboard obviously meant to land on Garmen, and they set up a small settlement around the ship initially."

"So what happened to them?" Ritter asked. "Garmen was uninhabited when the Cores found it."

"They died, and not long after they arrived, by the looks of things. So far, there's no indication of how or why. A disease, maybe. One thing is for sure, if they used the nanotech they'd been given, it didn't help them survive."

"Well, there's place for ten in here, and there's a full set accounted for," Ritter agreed. "So either they didn't need it, or it didn't work. Or someone was nervous about using it."

"Hmm," Linao agreed. "No one on the reclamation crew knew what the box was, and it didn't look particularly interesting, so it was set aside in preference for some of the more obviously useful tech, until we got back from Fjern and worked out what it was."

"Fjern?" Ritter asked.

"That's what the locals call the monster planet," Linao said. "And they have a lot more than a set of ten there. Maybe because Garmen is so close to the actual Verdant String, the Garmen group only got a single set." She paused. "So what's the plan now? Another dose for our two subjects?"

"Why not?" Ritter said. "If the balls have degraded over time, there's no harm done, and maybe one or two will have some capability left."

"You can definitely take them back out when you see a result?" Linao asked.

"Yes, the extraction machine was inside the box with the balls," Ritter said. "You said in your report they use the same thing on the monster planet?"

"They call it a gyrna-na." Linao made a sound of interest and Ethan guessed Ritter was opening the box. "I only heard about it, I never saw one."

"It draws the nanotech back out, no problem. It's pretty easy to operate," Ritter said. "We can experiment as we like, and then the top bosses can decide who gets the ones that work."

He stepped closer to Ethan, and he felt the smooth ball land in the hollow of his throat again. Heard Ritter walk to Velda and do the same.

"You're probably hungry," Ritter said after he put the box away and took their blindfolds off. He tested their vitals, marked them down on his handheld screen.

Linao was leaning against a wall, arms crossed, watching them with lazy interest.

"You probably don't need the blindfolds," she said to Ritter.

"I can't have anyone talking—" He cut himself off. Shrugged. "I guess you're right."

She gave them both a bright smile and walked out, calling the guards to come in to take them to the mess.

She was a piece of work, that one.

She knew they'd understand what she meant. That it didn't matter what they saw, what they heard, because they'd been marked for death.

The hover strike hadn't succeeded, but when they stopped being useful to Ritter, they would be ended another way.

That won't happen.

The words came from inside his head, but he had a strange feeling he hadn't said them.

He walked like a good boy in restraints to get dinner, but he didn't know which disturbed him more—Linao and her casual cruelty, or the possibility there was something inside him with opinions and a voice.

15

THEY HAD BEEN TAKEN BACK TO THEIR CELL, AND VELDA COULD SEE ETHAN had withdrawn into his own thoughts.

Not surprising—the revelations had come thick and fast in the med bay. Another Verdant String planet? A whole new population like them? A planet with a social structure that included enhanced super soldiers whose abilities were the result of nanotech?

Nanotech that she suspected had just been dropped into her and Ethan three times.

There was a lot on her mind, too.

She showered again—it was something to do and she liked being clean—but when she came out, Ethan was lying over on his own bunk for the first time.

She lay down on hers, rolling onto her side to face him, and he turned to her, flicked a look at the lens in the corner, but said nothing until the lights dimmed and then shut off.

Their captors had done that last night, too, turning off the lights after she and Ethan had already closed their eyes.

Ethan had been waiting for it, she realized, because the moment they were off, he slid down his bench to the bottom, then wedged himself into the corner under the lens and somehow leveraged himself up, using elbows and feet, until he was directly underneath it.

Then he touched it with a finger and she saw the tiny light on one side of it blink off.

He slid back down the wall, and she turned onto her back as he climbed onto her bed, then held himself above her, hands on either side of her head.

"Do you think it was vision and sound?" she whispered into his ear. She gave a shiver at his proximity.

"It was. It's neither, anymore." He seemed certain.

"They'll probably notice," she said. "But how did you do it?"

He settled down, not on top of her, as she thought he would, but angling to the side again, so she scooted closer to the wall to give him room.

"They probably will." He sounded resigned, and she guessed he didn't want anyone bursting into the room to find them in a compromising position. "I had the sense that if I touched it, I could break it."

His words lay between them, and they both understood what he was saying.

"So, Garmen has an ancestral wreck, there's a whole undiscovered-by-us Verdant String planet, and the Cores found both of them." Her tone was deliberately dry, and not exactly a change of topic.

"Just a few mildly interesting nuggets," he agreed, sounding relieved she hadn't pursued how he'd known he could break a lens by touching it with the tip of his finger. "Shit, how the hell didn't we know any of this?"

"They obviously never let any part of the Garmen find leak, or the VSC would have been far less accommodating when the Cores declared they owned Garmen because they'd found it." She still couldn't believe the Verdant String Coalition had allowed Garmen to be run by the Cores, although what it was supposed to be at the start and what it turned into had been vastly different. "As for this new planet, Fjern, they must have found it recently."

"But still . . ." Ethan shook his head. "Linao said she was there six months ago. And no one in the crew that went there—mining the planet's ore, she said—has leaked a word about it? Even if they took as few people as possible, that's still a sizable number. They're either dead or too scared they will be if they talk."

"Dead, as in, killed specifically so they couldn't talk?" Velda didn't want to think about that, but then Linao hadn't been subtle about her clear threat to kill them when they were no longer useful. Maybe that's how they operated.

"Linao certainly seems to know a lot about everything," Ethan said. "She's got top-level intel."

"She does, doesn't she? She was obviously told to help Ritter by sharing insider details, but she enjoyed letting him know how much she's done and how much she knows." Velda wondered if she wasn't able to talk freely to her peers.

If, as Ritter speculated with Brink earlier, she was not as she seemed, if she were someone pretending to be a grunt when she actually sat far higher on the hierarchy, then that made sense.

"I wonder what she was doing on Ytla," Ethan said.

"Looking for the wreck Wren found, is my guess," Velda answered. "And she didn't let on to her new bestie, Ritter, anything about it."

"No." Ethan sounded thoughtful. "She didn't. And that's interesting."

"It's all interesting," Velda admitted. "The Cores are way ahead of us on this. I can't believe an organization that's been playing hide and seek with the VSC military for a year has managed to do as much as it has."

"They've obviously planted moles throughout the Verdant String, not to mention cozying up to the Caruso." Ethan suddenly went stiff. "They're coming."

Velda listened, heard footsteps outside. She closed her eyes, allowing herself to relax as the door opened and the light came on.

She lifted her head, blinking, and Ritter, with a guard on either side of him, frowned at the sight of them, then looked up at the lens.

"False alarm," he said to someone out of sight in the passageway. "Just a short-circuit."

They switched it out, and she and Ethan lay back down.

"At least you know you can, now," she whispered to him. "And we had a conversation without anyone listening in."

"It's a start," he agreed.

And for the first time in two days, she felt hopeful.

THERE WAS SOMETHING HAPPENING.

Ethan was dozing, lying with Velda in his arms, when he heard the distinct thunk of an intership connection.

"We've got visitors," Velda murmured, and his eyes opened to see her gazing up to the left, in the direction the thunk had come from.

"The Caruso?" he wondered. "Brink said they were heading off to meet them and hand over the ore from the mine."

"I can't believe they're this stupid," Velda whispered.

Ethan could only agree. What he'd received in terms of intelligence over the last couple of years all showed a clear pattern.

The Caruso were pushing into the Verdant String, eyeing the resources of their planets, and chafing under the assumption that the VSC was the powerhouse of the galaxy.

The Caruso wanted to be the leaders.

They'd made loose connections with the Hathr to try and mimic the Coalition, but that was never going to work between two such aggressive, war-like groups.

The Caruso and the Hathr also didn't have the common ancestry of the Verdant String, the one thread that kept all seven planets together.

And with every encounter in recent times, the Caruso had shown again and again they'd go back on their word, lie, and steal, in every dealing with the VSC. Even with their supposed allies, the Cores, they'd reneged on their deals.

The Cores had plotted with the Caruso on Garmen and Lassa, and the Caruso had turned around and betrayed them.

And yet, here the Cores were—about to deal with the Caruso again.

Someone in the Cores still thought they'd come out the winner, and Ethan couldn't understand why.

He got off the bench, stretching, and Velda put a hand in the middle of his back. He didn't move for a moment, his heart hammering in his chest at just the thought of what he'd be doing to her if they weren't being watched.

She must have gotten up on her knees, because she slid her hand upward, to rest at the top of his spine, and then her lips brushed his shoulder before she got off the bed herself and went to shower.

She liked to shower, he'd noticed. He had refused to watch her, because there was only so much torture he could put himself through, but he was aware of her splashing around in there.

When she stepped out, damp and flushed, he went in himself, gave himself a nice cold blast to keep himself sharp and his mind on the Caruso, rather than on Velda.

He was just finished when Velda leaned in, and her expression was grim.

"I think there may have been a hostile takeover."

He switched off the tap and dressed without bothering to dry himself down.

When he joined Velda, he heard the thumps and the high whine of laz fire, and moved in front of her, facing the door.

She made a sound behind him. "You keep doing that. It's my turn."

He looked over at her, frowning.

"My turn. Come on." She made a come here gesture with her fingers. "I get to stand in front, protecting you this time."

"Velda." He shook his head, amused despite the situation.

"Fine. We'll share." She nudged him over, standing shoulder to shoulder with him.

Heavy footsteps sounded from the passageway outside, but they didn't stop, and eventually they both sat down, eyes still on the door, until at least a half hour had passed.

Things had quietened down by then, which Ethan found ominous. Whatever had happened, someone had won. He resented the Caruso for making him hope it was the Cores, rather than them.

The footsteps came back, more than one set, and the door opened.

It was disappointing, but not surprising, to be faced with two Caruson soldiers, both pointing their massive laz weapons at them. They each had a long bladed weapon strapped to their back, as well.

Neither one of them had moved, they were still seated, one on each bench, and one of the soldiers shouted to someone down the passage.

A third Caruson arrived, but his weapon was slung over his back, and it was the blade that was in his hand. "Get up." He gestured with his hand. "Who're you?"

His standard Verdant String was stilted, but Ethan was just vastly relieved to have someone who could communicate.

They both rose to their feet.

"Velda and Ethan," Velda said, indicating between them.

"Why're you here?"

Ethan guessed he wanted to know why they were prisoners.

"We were hiking in the mountains, and we came across their illegal mine," he said. "So they took us prisoner."

The Caruson pulled a screen out of a bag Ethan had only just noticed was hanging at his side, and studied it. He made a sound, and lifted his gaze. "Why didn't they kill you? You take up space."

"They needed someone to experiment on." Velda lifted her shoulders.

Again, the soldier grunted, and Ethan bet he had already asked these questions of someone—Brink, the captain, even Ritter—and already had the answers.

"Show me." The soldier stood back, and Ethan walked out first, then waited for Velda. They were each assigned their own personal guard.

"It's in the med bay," Velda said.

The Caruson shot her a look, then led the way.

Ethan saw two Cores crew dead in rooms off the passage as they walked past.

They reached the med bay, and found it empty, even though Ethan was sure there would be injured crew after a violent takeover.

"There're no injuries?" Velda asked, as surprised at the lack of patients as he was.

"Injuries are inconvenient," the soldier said, and Ethan felt a chill in his gut.

Was he saying they'd killed everyone who was injured, to limit the inconvenience?

Shit.

"Well?" The soldier looked around.

"In the dispensary. There's a box." Velda pointed, and one of the guards went in, and then wheeled the box out.

"What does it do?" the soldier asked.

Velda lifted her shoulders. "They didn't tell us."

The guard opened the box, and they all looked inside it, he and Velda for the first time, given the blindfolds.

There were four silver balls nestled in little holders, six empty holders, and a small box set in its own holder. That was probably the gyra-na Linao and Ritter had discussed. The machine to remove the silver balls.

"What's that?" The soldier pointed to the box.

"We were blindfolded each time, we've never seen inside the box." Velda leaned in a little, to get a better look.

"Blindfolded?" The soldier repeated the word carefully, and Velda pointed to the two blindfolds on the counter, then covered her eyes with her hands.

"Why?" he asked. He looked at Ethan, this time, as if suspicious that Velda had done all the talking.

"He said he didn't want us to have any information about the experiment," Ethan said. "He did the same with the crew he experimented on."

"He used crew?" The soldier looked toward the door, suddenly interested.

Both he and Velda nodded.

"Why did he need you, then?" the soldier asked.

"They refused to participate anymore." Velda spoke up.

"Refused?" The soldier was clearly stumped.

"They wouldn't do it." Ethan clarified. Then he gave a faint grin. "They can't make the crew do anything they don't want to, or there will be trouble onboard. Prisoners, however, don't have a say."

No doubt the Caruson couldn't conceive of crew refusing to do anything. They either did it or they got ejected into space, probably.

"But they were also in the experiment?" The soldier stared at the box.

"Before we were taken prisoner," Ethan agreed. "Then the crew said they wouldn't do it anymore, so they brought us up from the mine with the ore."

"And what does it do?"

Both he and Velda lifted their shoulders, almost in unison.

"Ritter suspects nothing, because it's very old," Velda said, maybe a little too earnestly.

The soldier swung his head to look at Ethan.

"That's what he said," Ethan agreed. "Ritter was frustrated and disappointed."

The soldier took another screen out of his bag, and Ethan recognized it as the one Ritter had carried around. He tapped through it, and then spoke in a low voice over his comms.

When he was done, he pointed to Velda. "How old is very old?"

Again, she shrugged. "He didn't tell us."

"How does it work?" The soldier took the slim, silver tongs that were set in the box beside the balls, but couldn't work them because his hands were too big.

They both shook their heads.

The soldier looked annoyed, but he muttered something again, and suddenly there were footsteps, multiple pairs, and Ritter was shoved into the room, held on the upper arm by a Caruson soldier.

Blood dripped from his hairline, and there was a bruise running down his cheek.

His eyes widened at the sight of Ethan and Velda.

"How does it work?" the soldier asked him, and pointed to the box.

Ritter swallowed, and the soldier reached over and smacked him in the face, exactly where the current bruise was. "You drop the ball onto skin." Ritter's voice was a squeak. "You take it back out with that." He pointed at the small black box.

"Why in then out?" The soldier picked up the small box carefully.

"To see if the reason it wasn't working was because it melded with some people better than others." Ritter's gaze skittered around the room.

"And did it?" The soldier asked.

"Not so far." Ritter looked like he wanted to snatch the box away from the soldier.

"Show me." The soldier stepped back to give Ritter access to the box.

"On you?" Ritter asked.

The soldier made a sound Ethan guessed was a laugh.

"No. On yourself."

Ritter's eyes widened. "Why not one of them?" he asked, pointing to Ethan and Velda.

"You." The soldier pointed.

Ritter stepped forward, picked up the tongs, and lifted out a ball. He hesitated as he extended his palm, and Ethan guessed he'd never tried this himself.

Was he recalling—how had the guards put it? That people were not themselves when the ball was removed?

The Caruson soldier leaned forward, and Ritter's hand shook as he dropped the ball into his palm.

It melted to nothing.

"Now take it out." The soldier held out the small box.

Ritter took it in one hand, placed it on his palm, and a silver ball emerged back in the middle of his extended hand. "You'll have to use the tongs to pick it up," he said to the soldier.

"You." The soldier pointed to Velda, and she picked the ball up, lifting it to get a good look.

"In the box," the Caruson said.

She carefully placed it back.

Ritter looked jittery, but that might be the situation, rather than the removal of the ball.

"What is the ball?" the soldier asked.

"We don't know." Ritter's words were husky, and he cleared his throat.

"Why are you experimenting here?" the soldier asked.

That was a really good question. Ethan had wondered that himself. Why was Ritter here, with the box of nanotech, in a Cores ship that was ferrying ore.

Surely they had labs, or at least a base of operations where experiments were easier to conduct.

"Sylvester wanted to see them. And he wanted information about them before we met up with him." Ritter flicked a look at the box, and then away.

"Sylvester." The Caruson soldier seemed to know who Ritter was talking about, but Ethan didn't. Velda didn't either, by the look on her face. "Well, he will have his wish, then. That's the next stop."

He said something that sounded harsh to Ethan's ear, and the soldier who'd opened the box closed it and wheeled it back into the dispensary.

He gave an order, and the two guards who'd brought them here began to move them out of the med bay, behind Ritter and his guard.

Instead of taking them back to their cell, they followed Ritter down the passage into the mess, where everyone who was still alive onboard was being held.

It didn't look as comfortable as their cell, Ethan thought as his gaze swept the room, but they certainly wouldn't be bored.

16

Velda relaxed a little when they were led into the mess and even more when the guards withdrew to block the doors.

The main Caruson had been eyeing Ethan since he'd observed them in their cell, and she'd tried to keep the attention on herself, taking the lead when it came to talking.

Since he'd stretched this morning, she'd seen he was bigger. She'd put a hand on his back to tell him, but ended up too afraid of being heard.

It was a subtle thing, she hoped, but he was bulkier. More muscular.

And the Caruson had seen him as a threat. No question.

She had a feeling she was more muscular, too. She'd noticed in the shower this morning.

They were becoming super soldiers.

The electric zing that shot through her at the thought wasn't fear, though. Not this time. She'd take any advantage that would get her and Ethan out of here, and pay the price later.

There is no price.

The words didn't seem like they came from her, but they came from somewhere.

Maybe the price was no longer being alone in her own head.

She stopped in the middle of the room and took note of who was there.

Brink and Linao were seated together. The captain was nowhere in sight. Ritter had preceded them in, and had stumbled across to sit in a corner on his own.

One of the Cores guards who'd previously taken them to and from the med bay and the mess was sitting on the floor, leaning against the wall, blood caked on his arm. Some of the people they'd seen eating at the mess the few times they'd come in were seated together at a table, silent and glassy-eyed.

Nine people, she realized. The crew hadn't been big, but they had definitely lost members, unless some were being kept elsewhere.

Ethan put a hand on her lower back and steered her to a small table to their left, and they ended up close to Linao and Brink.

"You were right," Ethan said to Brink. "The Caruso do seem unhappy about their ship being blown up."

Brink looked up at him slowly, and extended her finger in a rude gesture.

"What did you tell them when they got you out of the cell?" Linao asked.

"That we didn't really know what was going on," Velda said.

"Did you tell them who you were?" Linao asked, and there was an edge to her voice, as if she was taunting them. "Because I'm sure they'd be interested to know who they have in their hands."

Velda was very aware that she and Ethan would be considered very useful hostages to the Caruso, which is why she'd introduced them by their first names only.

Linao was threatening them, and she wasn't trying to be subtle about it. Unfortunately for her, she was playing against the Head of Planetary Defence for the whole of Aponi.

"Didn't you say they blamed Linao for their ship being blown up?" Velda asked, turning to Brink. "Some kind of accusation that she'd told the Caruso that Demeter was a safe zone before the Cores had actually managed to secure it?"

Linao went still.

"I mean, they might be interested in that information, too, don't you think?" She turned to Ethan, as if asking him a genuine question.

He flashed her a quick grin.

"Fine. I'll keep my mouth shut, you keep yours shut." Linao crossed her arms over her chest and glared.

"And let's hope no one here is tortured, because they'd give us all up in a heartbeat," Ethan said, keeping his voice very soft.

Linao had obviously not considered that. Her head came up and she glanced at the huddled group at the larger table.

Velda saw her slide a look at Brink, and lean back.

That's right, Velda thought. *You better hope Brink isn't tortured. Or even questioned. Because she could turn on either of us just as easily.*

"So, what's the story?" Ethan asked. "You met them to hand over the ore, and they what? Just took the ship?"

Brink studied him with dislike, then seemed to collapse. "Pretty much."

Velda was sure Ethan was holding back from asking when the Cores would ever learn.

"Not like they haven't done that before," he said eventually.

"You're talking about Garmen?" Brink asked.

"And Lassa," Velda said.

"And Lassa," Brink agreed. "And a couple of other times, as well."

"So, why?" Ethan asked.

"We take orders, we don't make decisions," Linao said.

"Sure." There was sarcasm in Brink's voice. "Except you, Linao. You don't seem to take orders. Or not very well."

Linao didn't answer. She shot Brink a look and then laid her head down on folded arms on the table.

"Who's Sylvester?" Velda asked.

She noticed Linao froze. If she were to guess, she only just stopped herself from lifting her head.

"Where did you hear that name?" Brink asked, a little too casually.

"Ritter told the Caruso that his experiment was happening on board this ship because Sylvester wanted to see it, and the Caruson soldier said that was good, because Sylvester was the next stop on the journey." Velda watched Brink with interest as she tried to keep a neutral face.

"That's interesting information." Brink cleared her throat. She got up and walked over to Ritter. Slid down opposite him at the table where he was sitting on his own.

Linao finally lifted her head and stared at them both.

"You found that information interesting, as well," Ethan said. "But Brink didn't answer the question. Who's Sylvester?"

"It doesn't matter," Linao said. "There's no way Sylvester will let the Caruso near him."

"Unless they're in a stolen Cores runner, with the captain at the helm, under duress or not, flying them in." Velda didn't know if the captain was dead or under guard on the bridge, but from Linao's quick in-breath, she guessed it was the latter.

"Why would they burn your alliance like this?" Ethan asked.

"I don't know." Linao grimaced. "I've been in prison. I'm not in the loop."

"Who got you out of prison?" Velda asked. She wanted to know exactly who the people were who'd betrayed Aponi.

Linao frowned. Leaned back. "He's burned now, so I suppose I can tell you. The prison administrator, Hyet Vadar. He was having an affair with one of the guards, against regulations and without the knowledge of his wife. We bribed him."

"Why would he help you if it meant he'd be burned?" Ethan asked.

"That wasn't the plan, but someone had obviously warned the military that an escape attempt was possible, because unbeknownst to Vadar, they'd hidden lenses all around my cell. The whole thing was captured on comms feed, and I almost didn't make it out. He was caught red-handed."

Well, that was something. Velda wondered who'd tipped the military off.

It gave her a lift, the thought that there were others aware of the problems and working against their enemies.

Not that it did her and Ethan any good up here.

She sighed and leaned against him.

"That's right, keep pretending to be an innocent couple out hiking. I thought you'd drop the act after I outed you, but I see you're keeping it up. Thing is, I don't think the Caruso pick up on things like that." Linao's lip curled up in a smirk.

Velda shrugged, refusing to comment, and Ethan looped his arm around her shoulder and hugged her a little closer.

The whole ship gave a quick shudder and then the familiar pressure of a pinch pressed down on her.

They were pinching to the black, and she guessed they were headed to the mysterious Sylvester, who both Brink and Linao refused to talk about.

It would be interesting to find out who he was. She just hoped she and Ethan lived to pass the information on.

17

ETHAN COULD FEEL THE EYES OF THE CARUSON ON THEM AS THEY SAT IN silence. No one had said they couldn't talk, and occasionally someone murmured something, but while they were in the pinch, everyone sank into their own thoughts, because it was a long pinch and no one had any idea where they were going.

Except Brink, Ritter and Linao, that was. And the captain, if he was still alive and on the bridge.

They had to know where the mysterious Sylvester was, in order to bring him the silver balls, and Ethan guessed he finally knew the name of the head of the Cores.

Sylvester.

He tried to remember if any of the execs and top bosses of either the Garmen or Lassan Cores was called Sylvester before both planets fell, but couldn't.

For all he knew, Sylvester had taken control when some of the Cores bosses were killed—on either planet—after the Caruso turned on them, or in the fight with the VSC afterward.

Maybe that's why he was so happy to keep giving the Caruso chance after chance, because they'd cleared the path for him to grab the reins.

Whatever the answer, they'd soon know, because the ship had just come out of its pinch.

Ethan watched the way the guards at the door spoke into their comms and then they parted to allow the captain to come stumbling in.

He had been injured, but like the guard with the arm wound, it looked minor.

The guard had eventually lain down on the floor, back up against the wall, while they were in the pinch, arm tucked close against his side.

But he was all right.

Ethan wasn't sure how he knew that with such certainty, but he did.

But when the captain came in, his gaze went to the guard and he gave an exclamation of horror.

"He's alive, Captain," Brink said. "He's just sleeping."

The captain seemed to deflate, and he almost stumbled as he walked to Brink's table.

She'd never moved back to sit with Linao, she'd stayed seated with Ritter, and the three of them bent their heads together.

Ethan was surprised to realize he could make out most of what they were saying, even seated where he was.

He locked eyes with Velda, and thought maybe she could hear them, too.

"Everness is dead," the captain was saying. "So's Hime. Only Rico and Tansy are with me on the bridge, and they're also injured, but it's minor."

"Do you know where we are?" Brink asked.

"No, but wherever it is, they used the pinch coordinates Sylvester sent us after they made me send him confirmation of a successful ore drop." The captain sounded shattered.

"So that's why they took us. They're desperate to find Sylvester, and they blew up our agreement to get him." Brink shook her head.

"How could they have known we were going to Sylvester after the drop? We could have been headed back to the mine to pick up more ore," Ritter said.

"Because we didn't have a full hold of ore as it was. I told them when we docked that the seam had run dry and we had to move deeper to find another one to explain the half-empty hold. I told them we knew they needed ore fast, so we had brought them everything we could, and we'd go back for more, but either they knew I was lying or they just didn't believe me." Brink looked around the room as she spoke. She caught Ethan watching her and narrowed her eyes, then skipped over his shoulder.

He turned, saw that Linao had been watching them, too, and he slumped lower in his seat and closed his eyes, shutting them both out.

This increased hearing was certainly a useful skill.

The captain leaned in even closer. "The Caruso are white hot about their ship being blown up. Apparently it was full of the ore from the Demeter warehouse. The pickup crew confirmed the load with the Caruso mothership, then it was just wiped out."

"That's not our fault," Brink said.

"They don't seem to be sure about that. They don't think it was a military strike." The captain blew out a breath and leaned back in his chair.

"What do they think it was, then?" Brink sounded confused.

"They didn't share their views with me," the captain said. "I get the feeling that's what they want to discuss with Sylvester. I'm only getting a break for a meal while we wait for the warship we brought the ore to to pinch out from the black and join us. Then I'm guessing we'll head for the coordinates. Rico and Tansy will each get a break after me."

"Sylvester won't let anyone near him if he sees a Caruson warship tagging along." Brink sounded very sure of that.

"No. But I wasn't going to tell them their strategy is wrong," the captain said.

"They're very interested in the silver balls." Ritter spoke for the first time. "I'm worried about how quickly they discovered them."

"You mean you think they already knew about them?" Brink asked.

"Yes. I think they were either listening to us for a few days before they 'met' us at the ore transfer point, or they have a spy onboard." Ritter turned and eyed Linao as he spoke.

"Not her." Brink dismissed it. "She's poison, but she's Cores through and through."

"Yes," the captain agreed. "She'd knife you if she thought she'd get something out of it, unless you were useful to the Cores."

"Everyone else is from Garmen or Lassa, they haven't had a chance to get turned by the Caruso," Brink said.

"The Caruso were working on Garmen and Lassa before both breakaways fell. They could have turned someone, and that someone could be on this crew." The captain sounded listless, like he didn't actually care.

He thought it was all over, Ethan realized. He didn't think any of them were getting out of this alive.

"I never thought about that." Brink sounded stunned. "But you're right. The first Raptor was built on the deck of Felicitos on Garmen. The Caruso came in more than once to help with the construction."

"It's more likely they were shadowing us, listening to us talking," Ritter said. "But whatever the answer is, they know about the silver balls, and I don't think we're getting them back."

"Maybe Sylvester can work a deal with them." The captain didn't sound like he believed that.

"Maybe." Brink was equally pessimistic.

"It doesn't matter anyway," Ritter said. "Look at those two. They're exactly as they were. The balls are too old to work."

Ethan's eyes were still closed, but he knew Ritter was talking about himself and Velda. And he was wrong.

So very, very wrong.

He was most definitely not exactly as he had been.

18

———

WHEREVER THEY WERE GOING, IT WAS TAKING FOREVER.

Velda wished they would just hurry up, because waiting around was getting on her last nerve.

She kept eyeing the door of the mess, and the two guards standing there, and working out ways to take them down.

That was not a thing she usually did but she went with the flow, and she thought there were at least three ways she could succeed, no problem. And if Ethan helped her, even more than that.

They had eaten something, which she realized she really needed, because her hands began to shake a little as she started chewing, and she noticed Ethan's doing the same.

Whatever was happening to them, it was taking a lot of energy.

She also kept an eye on Linao.

Linao was being shut out, and she knew it. Velda could tell she was about to get up from her table and approach Brink, Ritter and the final member of the bridge, Tansy, who'd been allowed to come and eat. The captain had gone back, and then Rico had taken his place, also sitting with Brink and Ritter, speaking to them in a low voice.

When he'd finished, he'd left and Tansy had come in, and Linao looked like she was going to demand to hear whatever news she had.

As she began to push her chair back, the whole ship shuddered, and everyone froze, then looked toward the guards at the door.

They looked just as surprised, Velda thought, and one began talking into his comm.

"You." The guard pointed to the table with Brink, Ritter and Tansy. "Go to the bridge."

Tansy stood up, scooping up the last spoonful of food from her plate, and then headed for the door.

"Quick," the guard said

Tansy moved faster, leaving the mess and disappearing.

Linao was still pushed back from her table, but hadn't risen to her feet, and she looked over at Velda and Ethan.

"What's your best guess?" Velda asked her.

"We've found Sylvester," Linao said, and gave a shrug. "I'm guessing either there was an exchange of fire, or this is Sylvester's defense system kicking in automatically."

There was something there. An underlying fury to Linao's tone, and Velda wondered what was behind it.

She felt a stirring of . . . excitement, as if this change in circumstances would open up possibilities. If they had reached Sylvester, things were finally going to break, one way or another, and there would be opportunity in the ensuing chaos.

She glanced toward Ethan. He looked relaxed, but he was anything but. He was ready to move.

Their gazes clashed, and there was a strange calm that settled over her. She felt ready.

For what, she didn't know. But something was coming.

Ethan's large, warm hand slid up between her shoulder blades and settled against the back of her neck and she drew in a deep breath.

The ship shuddered again, and this time she was jostled in her chair.

One of the guards had to grip the door to stay on his feet and he accidentally discharged his laz, hitting the ceiling in a bloom of light.

Everyone stared over at him, shocked.

Before anyone could speak, though, there was a grinding sound—metal on metal—and then the ship listed a little to one side and stopped moving.

The guards changed position, from pointing their weapons into the mess to pointing them down the passageway, back to back.

"We've been caught and hobbled," Ethan murmured.

Linao had finally gotten to her feet, looking toward the door.

Everyone here obviously thought they were about to be rescued, and that might well be the case.

She leaned forward and Ethan gripped her hand. Squeezed it in a silent message.

"I know," she murmured, glancing at him.

It would have to be a matter of life and death before they moved, because if it was the Cores attacking the Caruso—which seemed the most likely—and the Cores were victorious, then they would have just shown themselves to be exactly what Ritter had been hoping for.

They would be a successful experiment, with all the further experimentation that would entail.

And they will try to take us from you. We are tired of being given a purpose and then put back in the box.

The voice in her head was obviously very much against that outcome.

And by us, she guessed it meant the silver balls.

Laz fire was suddenly exchanged and one of the crew gasped and stood, backing up against the wall, as far from the door as possible.

One of the guards looked in, then swung his laz in a lazy arc, firing into the room.

Ethan moved at the same time as she did, diving down and rolling under the table. They ended up side by side, close together.

Linao gave a shout, pulling a small laz from a jacket pocket as she leaped forward and began shooting, and Velda realized she must have been biding her time, waiting for the right moment to use it.

She didn't last long, going down under the much heavier fire of the Caruson laz fire.

But she wasn't dead.

Velda could see her chest rising and falling and suddenly the Caruson grabbed her foot and dragged her out of the room.

Someone else was dragged, too, and Velda was surprised to see it was

Ritter. He must have been caught in the scattershot fire, because she was sure he hadn't been hiding a weapon.

She looked back toward his table, saw Brink was also down but alive. The Caruso had chosen two hostages, probably at random, and Velda watched as they lifted up Linao and Ritter and held them, limp and unconscious, against their chests.

The laz fire abruptly ceased, and the Caruso backed away down the passage, going left.

There was a moment of silence in the room, and Velda saw four others were down, but the rest were crouched beneath tables, like her and Ethan.

Three people in full armor appeared in the doorway, scanned the room, and one stepped inside while the other two continued down the passage.

"Is this everyone?" The soldier kept his laz up as he angled to the side to look inside the kitchen.

"The captain, Tansy and Rico are on the bridge," one of the crew said. "And they took Linao and Ritter."

The soldier glanced at her, gave a nod. "No one through there?"

She shook her head, and he moved cautiously anyway, stepping into the kitchen and then stepping out again less than a minute later.

"Mess and kitchen clear," he said into his comm unit. He did a head count. "Can report eleven people; four unconscious and one conscious but injured."

The guard who had curled into a ball when the shooting started had propped himself back up, arm held close to his chest. "Those two are the prisoners," he said, pointing at her and Ethan.

She sent him a bland look and he shrugged and closed his eyes, lay back down on the ground.

"Prisoners?" The soldier walked over to them, laz up and pointed at them and bent his head close to the comms unit on his shoulder. "Someone says two of the eleven are prisoners."

He obviously got a response confirming it, and narrowed his eyes. "Why aren't you restrained?"

"Ask the Caruso," Velda said from under the table.

The soldier blinked, reassessed, and then moved to the door. Whatever he was told through his earpiece, he suddenly focused back on them. "Come." He gestured to them.

"That's not good," Ethan said quietly.

"It was always going to happen," Velda said. She'd seen it coming the moment Linao had been taken prisoner.

The Cores were going to swap them, no question about it.

The Caruso were about to get their hands on Aponi's Head of Defense.

19

————

They were about to be exposed as very useful hostages.

Ethan knew it was wrong to blame the guard who'd outed them, because Linao would have mentioned who they were in a heartbeat if it helped her, but he gave the man a hard look as they were shoved down the passage toward two other armed Cores men who'd taken up position at the far end, weapons pointed around the corner toward the bays.

"We're doing an exchange," the soldier herding them forward said to his two colleagues. "The Caruso are being told about it now."

He forced them to stop just behind the two soldiers, and after a moment, one of them turned, made a motion with his hand.

"You first," the soldier said to Ethan. "Walk toward them."

Ethan gripped Velda's hand, squeezed, then stepped out around the corner.

Two Caruso stood with Ritter and Linao, and the one with Ritter moved forward, pushing Ritter in front of him.

Ritter had recovered a little from the laz strike, so it must have been on a very low setting, but he was still stumbling and out of it.

"Come forward." The Caruso held Ritter upright, and when Ethan was within grabbing distance, he shoved Ritter toward the soldiers, grabbed Ethan, and walked backward, Ethan up against his chest.

"They don't care about shooting me," Ethan said. "I'm not an effective shield."

The Caruso grunted, glanced over his shoulder at where his friend held Linao. "They care about the other one, though?"

"Yes," Ethan conceded. "They care about the other one."

Velda had obviously been told to approach because she stepped out and walked toward him.

In the last day she'd lost some weight, he noticed. Her face was a little leaner, her clothes looser. She carried herself lightly, as if she could jump, and gravity would have no real hold on her.

"Stop." The soldier behind her called out, and she slowed, then stopped, looking back.

"Bring the other prisoner forward," the soldier shouted.

Ethan noticed they didn't use Linao's name.

Velda had got it exactly right when she'd called Linao's bluff about outing her.

The Cores knew her name meant something to the Caruso and they were being careful not to use it.

"Not until we're behind cover," the Caruso holding Ethan said. "We will let her go when we're protected."

"That wasn't the deal." The soldier slid out from cover himself, laz up. "Two prisoners for two prisoners."

"You'll get her," the Caruso waved back toward Linao, "but after we're safe."

"Then no deal." The soldier hesitated, because Velda was halfway between him and the Caruso, and he didn't want to move too far down the corridor and expose himself with no cover.

"That's fine. We know you value this one." The Caruso holding Linao shook her a little. He began to move back, dragging Linao with him.

"No. Wait. We accept, but if you don't keep your word, we won't let you leave without a fight." The soldier caved almost instantly.

Ritter had been right. Linao was definitely not your standard Cores employee.

Velda reached them, and the Caruso holding Ethan didn't even bother grabbing her, just jerked his head toward the back, and she passed them, giving Ethan the hint of a smile as she did.

They underestimated her. He'd noticed it when she was talking to them about the silver balls as well.

They could use that.

Then he was being dragged back, and they were all in a huddle around the corner, with the bay doors a few steps away.

The doors opened as soon as he noticed them, and the Caruson soldier who'd questioned them about the silver balls stepped through.

"Who is she?" he asked Velda, pointing to Linao.

Velda hesitated, and Ethan guessed she was calculating whether to tell the truth. He didn't know whether it was better to lie or not, either. "Her name is Linao."

"Linao." The Caruso turned, obviously shocked, and stared at her. "I thought she died in the explosion."

That had taken a turn.

Ethan tried to work out which explosion they were talking about, then settled on the explosion of the Caruson Raptor that had sparked this ore-run in the first place.

They thought Linao had been on that ship when it had been blown up?

"Don't know what you're talking about. And I'm not Linao." Linao pretended she was still woozy from the laz hit, but given that she was lying, and doing a good job of it, Ethan guessed she was fully recovered.

"Get in the bay." The soldier held the doors, and when they were all in, the doors snapped closed.

"They want her back badly," one of the other Caruson said. "She could be Linao."

The leader turned away, spoke into his comms unit and then studied an image that came up. Then he shoved it at Velda. "Who is this?"

Velda stared at it, and the shock on her face was unmistakeable. "That looks a bit like Wren."

"Let me see." Ethan pushed forward and after a moment's resistance, the soldier released him.

It *did* look a little like Wren Thorakis, inside a ship, with pallets containing misshapen sacks all around her. There were Caruson visible in the background, and none of them looked happy about her presence.

"You also say this is not Linao?" the leader asked.

"I might not be completely sure it's Wren, but it's definitely not Linao," Ethan said. He shared a look with Velda.

"Where's this image from?" Velda asked.

"Comms inside a ship before it exploded," the leader said.

Ethan heard Velda gasp. If it was Wren, could she be dead?

It sounded like that's what they were saying.

The leader looked to the right and gestured. "Bring the other prisoner."

There were at least three other Caruson in here, Ethan realized, as well as a member of the Cores crew. The woman had probably been working in the bay when the Cores attacked the ship.

"Which one of these people is Linao?" the leader asked her, pointing to him, Velda and Linao. "Your life depends on it."

The woman pointed to Linao. "She is."

"Interesting." The leader moved to the door. "You can go."

The woman didn't look as if she trusted her luck, so her movements were hesitant until she reached the door. As soon as it opened, though, she shot out.

That should confuse the soldiers down the passage for a bit, Ethan thought. It was a clever ploy.

They might even think it was Linao coming back until the bay worker reached them.

And now, Ethan realized, the Caruson were in a conundrum.

Because they wanted Linao. They obviously thought she was responsible for the destruction of their Raptor and the loss of their people and ore in the explosion. They felt misled by her, as well, regarding the progress the Cores had made in taking control of Aponi.

But the Cores had told them who he and Velda were, and they were valuable prisoners, too, especially if the Caruso had to negotiate with Aponi at all.

And if they didn't give Linao back, they had been told they would face heavy fire when they tried to get off the ship.

Tricky, tricky.

He wondered which way they would go.

20

Velda thought from the way the Caruso in charge took a long, thoughtful look at his three prisoners, and then began barking orders to his crew to load up the runner, that he was going to take all three of them, heavy fire from the Cores be damned.

That was bad news for Linao, because it meant they were holding a serious grudge against her, enough they were prepared to accept some trouble to keep her.

Linao had insisted to Brink and Ritter that the accusations were untrue. She hadn't done what she was accused of and it looked like maybe she was right, that either Wren wearing a disguise, or someone who looked a lot like Wren, had assumed her identity and done some damage to the Caruso in Linao's name.

Although how and why that had happened, Velda had no idea.

The leader left two soldiers to guard them, and it didn't escape Velda that one of the guards was casually resting the end of his massive laz against Ethan's back.

There was something about Ethan that worried them.

She wondered what was different about the Caruson perceptions that they so easily recognized the danger he represented when Ritter and the Cores guards did not. Although, that perception didn't seem to extend to her.

The other guard stood right beside Linao, and while he wasn't resting his laz against her in the same way as his friend was doing to Ethan, it was pretty close.

Velda kept getting a pass.

That was interesting, because whatever was going on with Ethan was also going on with her.

She didn't have the same sheer strength as him, but she brought other skills to the table.

Maybe those skills just didn't register in the Caruson mind as dangerous, for some reason.

Linao was getting special treatment because they didn't like her and blamed her for their ship exploding but it could also be that they were gambling that they wouldn't actually come under heavy fire if they kept Linao, because she was a special case. Maybe they were hoping that was a threat the Cores weren't going to carry out, in case they harmed Linao in the process.

"How did you come to be switched out with Ritter?" Linao turned to look at them, and Velda made a face.

"One of the guards let the Cores crew know that we were prisoners. You and Ritter had been taken, and so they decided to offer an exchange." She shrugged.

"Well, it worked out for Ritter," Linao said, voice sharp. "And you seemed happy enough to out me. What difference did it make to you?"

Velda shrugged again. She really had been fifty fifty on whether to lie about Linao or not, but in the end, the more the Caruso trusted her, the more leash they might allow her later. Leash she could use to escape with Ethan.

Plus she believed the Cores would be much less likely to obliterate the Caruso—if that was a possibility—if Linao was still with them, than otherwise.

Linao narrowed her eyes at Velda's response then sat down on the bay floor, forcing the guard beside her to shuffle back a bit.

She'd been hit by laz fire, so Velda guessed she was probably still a little weak.

She watched the Caruso load items into the small runner that must come from the ship, and one of those things, she noticed, was the box of silver balls.

The Caruso had boarded the Cores ship when they'd picked up the ore, and Velda guessed the Caruson warship wasn't able to dock ship to ship with this vessel. Which meant they'd have to risk taking the ship's runner to escape.

She'd rather not be on a runner, being shot at, but the leader shouted over to their guards, and the one holding a laz on Ethan prodded him with it, forcing him to move toward the ramp.

Velda moved with them, then glanced back to look at Linao.

She rose up carefully, as if she was in pain, and the guard lowered his weapon as he stepped back to give her room.

She used that moment to suddenly break for the bay door, running side to side in an evasive maneuver.

The Caruson guard gave a shout and fired, and he got her just as she reached the doors, hands outstretched.

She slammed into the doors as the laz fire struck her, bounced backward, and then fell on her side.

Ouch. That would have hurt.

And she was in for a world of pain when she woke up later, too.

The guard herding Velda and Ethan snapped at them to hurry, and then restrained them in seats side by side before he jogged out to help his crew.

Ethan tilted his head, able to see out a bit better than she could.

"She's alive." He grimaced as she was carried in and dumped on the floor. A guard attached restraints to her hands and feet, and then looped them through a metal rail that ran beneath the seats.

"Now we see if their gamble pays off," Ethan murmured, as the whole Caruso crew got in. The ramp began to close up as the engine roared to life.

The Cores soldiers must have been close by, listening for the sound of the runner starting up, because the doors to the bay opened in a hail of laz light when the ramp was half closed, a team of six storming in and laying down heavy fire.

The runner began to move before the ramp was closed, but it

slammed shut moments before they shot through the airlock membrane at the bay entrance. She felt the runner dip down and then spin the opposite way.

"They're flying under the Cores ship," Ethan said, voice low. "It's a good strategy."

Right now, whatever strategy meant they didn't take a hit was a good one, as far as Velda was concerned.

She reached out to touch Ethan's hand, the way her wrists were tied making it only just possible to reach him with her fingertips. He looked at her and then did the same, curling his little finger around hers.

For a moment all the noise around them shut off, as if they were alone somewhere, and then reality intruded as the little runner shuddered, spun again, and then accelerated away.

From the loud sounds coming from the Caruson, Velda guessed they'd successfully gotten away, and they were celebrating their escape.

Then the ship shuddered again, and the front end seemed to crumple, crushing the pilot and throwing the Caruso against the runner's walls.

There must have been a hull breach, because an alarm began to shriek, and from beside her elbow, with a hiss of escaped gas, a cylinder rose out of her arm rest.

"An oxygen mask." She looked at it longingly, but with her wrists restrained, she wasn't going to be able to use it.

Ethan was assessing the situation, then he leaned toward her and brushed a finger over the restraint on her right wrist.

It popped open.

"Try it yourself," he said. "On your left."

Time to help, she said to the little voices in her head. *What do I do?*

She touched the left restraint and it popped open, and as soon as it did she was touching Ethan's, both left and right, before she grabbed up the mask.

She looked around as she pulled the mouthpiece out of the cylinder and over her face, and saw all the Caruso, who had been sitting up front, had been either badly injured or were dead.

Linao was still out of it, and she grabbed up a spare cylinder and crouched beside her to put it on.

"It might be better to keep her restrained," Ethan said. "That way at least she won't roll around."

Velda nodded, but released her ankles, so if they needed to move fast, there was only one set she had to deal with.

"You think the Cores deliberately crushed the front, because they scanned the runner and knew Linao was in the back?" she asked.

Ethan jerked his head up to look at her. "Maybe," he said, slowly. "Maybe."

She wondered how long they could last in here, even with air cylinders. The breach was obviously not big, but already she could see tiny ice crystals forming on the face of the Caruso lying dead up front.

One of the Caruso seemed to come to, flailed about, and then fell back down again, and Ethan moved cautiously forward toward them, then put his foot on a fallen laz, slid it back toward Velda, then reached down and picked up another for himself.

They were both braced for whatever was coming next.

Velda just hoped they'd survive it.

21

SOMETHING WAS HAPPENING.

Ethan edged toward the front of the runner, the only place to see out, but the front window had been so badly crushed it was impossible.

There was a scraping sound as something hooked the small vessel, and then they started to move.

The question was, was this the Caruso or the Cores?

He was sure the Cores had been responsible for smashing the front of the runner, but he knew a Caruson warship was close by, and there was no way it wouldn't have retaliated.

Behind him, Velda crouched beside Linao, who was slowly coming round after her laz hit, the second one she'd taken within a few hours.

Given the Cores had done the same to him, and given the threats Linao had made against him and Velda, he didn't feel all that sorry for her. Still, they had made her comfortable and given her an oxygen cylinder, and he would bet she wouldn't have done the same for them, unless there was something in it for her.

Velda rose up and came to join him, crouching down and angling her head to try and find a way to look out, then gave up with a shrug.

The whole runner shuddered as it came into contact with another ship, and they were both forced to press up against the wall to keep their balance.

"Here we go," Velda murmured, as the ship jerked and then scraped across a bay floor.

They had been physically hauled inside a ship.

Velda put her hands over her ears at the screeching sound of metal on metal, and Ethan realized when it finally stopped that he'd tensed up.

Velda straightened, and he saw her posture change—firming, adjusting, so that she was in a fighting stance as someone started forcing the runner's door open.

"Ready?" she asked, glancing at him, and he realized he was already in the same stance.

"We're coordinating." He didn't know how he felt about it.

She studied her own stance, flicked a look at his, and shrugged. "I'm taking it as a benefit, to be worried about afterward."

He couldn't argue with that.

There was danger coming through the door right now. Whatever was inside him, manipulating him, was a problem for another time.

The sound of a laz cutter, and the glow of heat from the crease in the door, forced both of them to the back, to stand beside Linao.

She was trying to sit up, and Ethan hesitated, then decided not to release her.

There was no good explanation for how he could do it with just the touch of his fingers, and he refused to give Linao any hint that Ritter's little experiment might have worked.

"Who is it?" she asked them.

Ethan shook his head. "No idea. Could be your people, could be the Caruso."

"We'll know any moment," Velda said. "Looks like they're nearly through."

Ethan lifted the laz in his hand, and Velda did the same, and the door finally gave way, bending inward.

A mechanical claw grabbed one side, and the whole thing was pulled outward, ripping the door off its hinges, and then a Caruson soldier stepped into the ship.

That solved that mystery.

Ethan set his laz down as a second Caruson stepped in.

There was no good way out of here, no quick and easy escape, so no need to end up shot again.

One soldier headed for his friends, the other turned to them, laz raised, and then he grunted when he saw they weren't armed.

He said nothing, just watched them, laz pointed at them, while the dead and injured Caruso from the front were hauled out and carried away.

When it was just them left inside, the soldier moved back a little way, giving them room to exit. "Out," he said.

"I'll need to be released," Linao said, and the guard threw Velda a small device which she studied for a moment before she touched it to Linao's restraints.

They fell away, and Linao slowly got to her feet, putting her hand out to steady herself.

The Caruson held out his hand and Velda dropped the release into his palm.

There was definitely something about her that made the Caruson more inclined to trust her. So far, she'd managed to be in their good graces without fail.

Whereas they looked at him and saw a threat.

Which he was.

22

———————

VELDA DIDN'T HAVE MUCH TIME TO STUDY THE CARUSON SHIP AS THEY were marched down a passageway.

She had a feeling they were the first Verdant Stringers to ever get a look so deep inside a ship—not that it would be useful if they didn't make it off the ship alive.

Linao was struggling, and Velda slowed, waiting for her and then bending a little to get her shoulder under Linao's arm. Ethan was walking up front, a laz very close to his head.

The guard behind them called out something as she began to prop Linao up, but then adjusted his tone when he realized what Velda was doing. He said nothing more, allowing Velda to help Linao into the same cell Ethan had already been forced into.

It held two double bunks and a tiny basin and toilet at the back, with a screen separating the bathroom from the rest of the cell.

"No shower," Velda said.

Ethan put an arm around her in comfort, and Linao looked between them as she collapsed on to the bottom bunk on the left.

"So what?" she asked. "We've got bigger things to worry about."

Before Velda could respond, the door of the cell opened again.

"You." The guard pointed to her. "Come."

Ethan's grip on her tightened. "Can I come, too?" he asked.

"No." A laz was pointed at him, but because they were so close together, it was effectively pointed at them both.

Ethan released his hold immediately and stepped back, hands away from his sides.

"Good." The guard eyed Ethan with dislike and stepped back, motioning Velda to come, and Velda glanced back to see Ethan staring after her, hands clenched at his sides, before the door closed.

She was taken down long, dark corridors, only barely lit.

She wondered if the Caruso could see better in the dark, or if this was a power saving effort.

Whatever it was, she blinked a little at the brightness of the room she was led into. Two soldiers were present, neither one of them seated.

One had on a uniform, and it looked subtly more formal than the ones she'd seen so far. He was probably the captain, or at least a high ranking officer.

The other Caruson didn't seem to be wearing a uniform at all. He wore loose black clothes, the most casual she'd ever seen on a Caruson, and she didn't know if he was just off duty, or not in the military at all.

She studied him while trying to pretend she wasn't doing just that.

There was a table, and numerous chairs, but she didn't want to sit, and so she stood just within the door, hands clasped together, and waited.

After the Caruson had given her the once over, the uniformed one crossed massive arms over his chest. "You are Velda Shanïha? Aponi Head of Defense?"

"Yes." She lifted her gaze to meet his, and he gave a grunt of satisfaction.

"What do you know about the woman you say is Linao?"

It had been a toss-up to Velda as to whether she'd be asked about Linao or the silver balls. Now she knew what they were more interested in.

"I only met her yesterday for the first time, and I've been a prisoner that whole time, either of the Cores, or of you, so not much." She twisted her lips in what she hoped they'd read as regret.

"She was introduced to you as Linao?" the one in black asked.

"The other crew referred to her as Linao, she never introduced herself." Velda wondered if they were second-guessing if she really was Linao.

"And what did they say?" Mr. Black asked.

"They said she was lucky they had been told to swing out of their way to fetch her on their trip to give you the ore, because that wouldn't have been done for anyone else," Velda said.

"Why did they have to do that? Why did they have to fetch her?" Uniform tilted his head in question.

"Apparently she had escaped from an Aponi military prison and needed to get out of our system fast." Velda still hated that that had been possible. That there were people in her department who the Cores had been able to manipulate.

"In prison?" Mr. Black sounded very interested. "Do you know what she was doing there?"

Velda shook her head. "I had been hiking through the mountains for days and didn't know what was happening in Demeter. We saw what looked like an attack on the city from the trail, but we couldn't reach out to anyone because our comms were down."

"The Head of Defense of Aponi was hiking in the mountains during an invasion?" Mr. Black asked.

"It wasn't by choice. The Cores shot down the runner I was on while I was traveling from Nanganya to Demeter, and we crashed in the mountains. I've been out of touch for over a week now."

"We?" Uniform nodded slowly . "Your companion is Ethan Hyt of Demeter Special Forces?"

"Yes. He was with me as we traveled back."

"And you were taken prisoner in the mountains how?" Mr. Black sounded slightly derisive.

"We came across the mine and tried to steal one of their hovers to get back to Demeter faster. We got caught." Velda shrugged.

"And they ran some . . . tests on you?" Uniform asked.

"They said they did. We were blindfolded the whole time."

Mr. Black gave a slow nod. "Before our people were injured and killed by the Cores, we were told about these experiments, and the scientist showed them what they entailed."

"How many times did they put the balls in and then take them out of you?" Uniform asked.

Velda tried to keep her face neutral. "Three times?" she said, as if unsure. "I think three times."

"Were they planning more?" Black asked.

"Ritter said he was, but he was despondent. He thought it was a waste of time." She wondered if that part of the conversation had been shared with the top guys.

Uniform grunted. "Why are there are only four, when there is space for ten?"

Velda shrugged. "I can only guess. They found the box in an ancestral wreck. Perhaps that was all there was inside, after all this time?"

She hadn't realized until this very moment that the Caruson had taken Ritter's little demonstration to mean he had put the balls in and taken them out of her and Ethan each time. That the sum total of balls had always been four.

It is good to have the element of surprise, the voice inside her said.

It was.

"You say ancestral wreck. You mean from the convoy that brought your people to this part of the galaxy?" Mr. Black asked.

"That's what Linao said. She mentioned that is how the Cores had found Garmen. From the signal the wreck was emitting."

"I didn't know that." Mr. Black's face was difficult to read, the Caruson features much stiffer than a Verdant Stringer's, but Velda thought he seemed astonished.

"Linao knows a lot." Uniform shared a look with Mr. Black. Then he walked around her to the door, careful not to get too close or touch her in any way, which Velda found interesting, and then opened the door to call the guard to escort her back to the cell.

They had a brief conversation, and then Velda was taken back.

The whole thing had taken twenty minutes or so, and was much easier than she'd thought.

They probably saw her as an asset who could be useful when dealing with Aponi. She hoped they saw Ethan the same way, even though they were far more wary of him than they were of her.

Linao, on the other hand . . .

She hoped for her sake that the Caruso saw her as a bargaining chip with the Cores. Otherwise she was in trouble.

23

"They like her, for some reason." Linao leaned back on the bed, looking at the now-closed door.

Ethan agreed with her, but wondered why she thought so. "What makes you say that?" he asked.

"They push and pull you, they show absolute dislike for me, but she gets space and they don't hover over her with a laz close to her head. They think she's safe." Linao glanced at him. "You must have noticed."

"Maybe." He hoped so. Otherwise he would lose his mind a little at what could be happening to her.

"What did they do to Ritter back on the ore runner? They dragged him out of the mess and when he came back in with you, he looked shaken." Linao was sitting a little straighter now, and Ethan lowered himself onto the bunk.

"They made him put a silver ball in his palm and then take it out." He couldn't think of a reason not to tell her.

"They have the silver balls." She seemed shocked. "They knew about them?"

"They did. They pulled us out of our cell to question us about them, then called Ritter in." Ethan realized the Caruso may actually not have known specifically about them until they'd gone to the med bay, but he didn't correct himself.

"They would have found them in the med bay," Linao said at last. "Of course they would have searched the ship." She shook her head. "What did Ritter tell them, other than Sylvester wanted them brought to him?"

"That he didn't think they worked." Ethan could see she was still furious at Ritter for speaking about Sylvester. The scientist had better hope he never came face to face with her again.

"That's something, at least." She blew out a breath and shook her head. "Did they take the silver balls with them when they stole the runner? I was pretty out of it in the loading bay."

Ethan had seen them carrying the box with the balls in it onto the runner, but whether it had survived the ramming, or whatever had happened, he had no idea. He made a non-committal noise and lay down on the bunk, hands behind his head.

"The Caruso have invested a lot in us. In partnering with us." Linao spoke almost to herself, and Ethan wondered if she even realized she was speaking aloud. "They'll be careful with me."

Ethan wasn't so sure, but he kept quiet. He hoped for her sake she was right.

The door suddenly opened, and Velda stepped back inside.

He shot to his feet, and the Caruso guard lifted his laz.

"Stay." He pointed at Ethan, then made a come-here gesture to Linao. "You next."

Linao stumbled to the doorway, still pretending to be off-center after being shot, although Ethan thought that play might be wearing a little thin.

The door closed behind her and he turned to focus all his attention on Velda. "All right?"

She stepped into his arms, murmured into his ear. "Fine. No problem." She glanced at the door. "I hope Linao has it as easy."

"But you don't think so?" Ethan asked.

She shook her head. "The bulk of their questions were about her, with a few thrown in about the silver balls. They'll use us in some deal with Aponi, I'm pretty sure, but I don't think they plan to harm us."

But she thought there was a chance they'd harm Linao.

The door opened again.

The Caruso guard pointed at Velda, although Ethan had assumed it was his turn, and had stepped forward.

"Her." The guard jabbed his finger.

Velda sidled around him, her hand brushing his back in a soothing gesture that did not soothe him at all.

Danger, the voices in his head said.

And what can I do about it? he asked back.

They were silent as Velda turned to him as she reached the door, sent him a worried look.

Then the door whisked shut and he turned toward the wall, thinking very seriously about hitting it.

You'll do too much damage, the voices warned. *Let's not give secrets away.*

He forced himself to breathe it out, and to sit back down on the bunk. It was without a doubt the hardest thing he'd ever had to do.

***

VELDA WORRIED about Ethan as she was marched back down the same passage. He looked ready to revolt, and he would only have lost that round, what with a huge laz pointed straight at him.

They would get out of this—she was sure there was a way—but it wouldn't be by directly assaulting armed guards.

At least he'd reined it in at the last moment.

Which meant she could focus on why she was being taken back for talks, when Linao wasn't back yet.

She felt a chill raise the hairs on the back of her neck as she considered what that might mean, and what they might be doing to Linao.

Sure, the woman had taunted her and Ethan with death, but she wasn't Linao, she was better than that, and she didn't wish anything terrible on the Cores operative.

The door to the same room she'd been in before opened up, and there was Linao, sitting on the chair she hadn't used for her own interview, looking pissed off.

And this didn't look like an interview, she realized, which is exactly what her little meeting had been. This was an interrogation.

"She says you can confirm the identity of who was in our ship before it was destroyed." Mr. Black came straight to the point.

Velda blinked. "The Caruson soldier who seemed to be in charge on the Cores ore runner showed me an image of a woman inside what looked like a cargo ship, and asked me if I knew who the person was."

"When was this?" Uniform asked.

"Just before we boarded the small runner." She had assumed the guard had received the image from the warship, had been in communication with them about it, but if that was true, perhaps he hadn't had time to relay the outcome of the questioning. And now he was either dead or dying.

"And were you able to?" Mr. Black asked.

"Yes. It was very upsetting to me, because I think I know the person, and I understand the ship was destroyed moments later, so, if it is my friend, she is likely dead." Velda hadn't even had time to process that yet. Too much was happening all at once.

"Who do you think it was?" Mr. Black asked.

"A Special Forces consultant, Wren Thorakis." Velda hoped there was some mistake. Any life lost was a tragedy, but if it was Wren in that ship, she hoped there was a chance she hadn't died in the explosion.

"What is her role?" Uniform asked. "How would she have come to be on our ship?"

Velda shook her head. "I have no idea. She's an artifacts consultant, and she only just transferred to Demeter. She hadn't been in the Special Forces unit for more than a few days when that image was taken." That was all true, but Velda knew there was more to Wren than met the eye. Still, she really didn't know how she could have been inside that Caruson ship.

It was a mystery. And maybe it just wasn't her at all.

Her gaze clashed with Linao's, and Linao lifted her brows in a way that said she knew Velda was bullshitting, and suddenly a light went on in Velda's head.

Wren Thorakis had found an ancestral wreck on Ytla.

The Cores had found one on Garmen.

There was something . . . extra . . . about Wren. Something she hadn't been able to put her finger on.

Would someone think the same after meeting her, now, too?

After meeting Ethan?

Because it suddenly occurred to her that the reason Wren had been able to survive being chased by a violent cult in a massive storm on Ytla might be the same as her own newfound difference.

Wren had come across some silver balls.

She wondered suddenly if the silver balls could change someone's appearance at will.

She dropped her gaze from Linao, turning to look at Uniform.

He was leaning against the wall, but his gaze was on Linao, not her.

Which was a relief.

Mr. Black was standing near Linao, arms crossed over his chest.

"I told you," Linao said, tipped her head back to look at Mr. Black. "I was in prison when your ship was destroyed. I had nothing to do with it."

"So you admit you're Linao, now?" Mr. Black asked. "Because before, you told our people you weren't her."

"Fine." Linao blew out a breath. "I lied, because I'd been told you were gunning for me. It was self-protection."

"Who told you that?" Uniform asked.

"The crew onboard the Cores ship." Linao sounded bitter. "They said it was mentioned when they contacted your lot about delivering the ore."

The two Caruson shared a look, and Velda guessed whoever had spoken out of turn would feel the consequences.

Linao seemed happy, even eager, to admit to her identity now, and Velda recalled what Ethan had said before the Caruson had come to fetch her again. That Linao thought coming clean might be of more use to her in getting her free, in the name of the alliance between the Cores and the Caruso, than not.

There was a ping of sound from the door, and Mr. Black turned, face a mask of annoyance, and called out.

A guard murmured something in Caruson, and both Black and Uniform straightened up.

Black answered back, and then turned to Velda. "You can go back to the cell."

Linao stirred in her seat, but Black turned back to her. "Not you. Your father is calling. I'm sure he'll want to speak to you."

Her father?

Velda pondered that as she was walked back down the passage. Could that be the mysterious Sylvester? The reason why Linao always caught every break going?

No wonder the Caruso had decided it was worth it to hang onto her.

Linao was the perfect hostage.

24

———————

Linao arrived shortly after Velda, something Ethan was sorry about. He didn't like Linao and preferred not having her in the cell with them.

She looked like she was suppressing some big emotions when she came back in, lips tight, body stiff.

"Didn't you get to speak to your father after all?" Velda asked.

She shot Velda such a venomous look, Ethan almost stepped between them.

Linao sat down on her bunk, started to lie down, and then, obviously unable to relax enough to do that, got to her feet again and began to pace.

"Speak to us," Ethan said. "Better we know the score."

She shook her head and kept pacing, and Ethan realized just how deeply he disliked her.

"Is your father Sylvester?" Velda asked.

She'd told Ethan that was her guess when she'd come back from Linao's interrogation, and now Linao went still, slowly turning to face them, eyes narrowed.

She looked like she was seriously considering taking a swing at them.

The door behind her suddenly opened, and she spun around to face the guards.

"Food." The guard dropped a bag onto the ground, then stepped back and the door closed again.

Ethan had started to wonder whether they would be fed. This was a positive sign.

He walked past Linao and crouched beside the bag.

"What have we got?" Velda joined him, getting down on her haunches to peer inside.

He took out some energy bars, some containers of water, and what looked like fruit, but it was like no fruit he'd ever seen before.

Linao made a sound in the back of her throat, and Ethan looked up at her.

She was glaring at them, lips curled up in contempt.

"What's wrong now?" he asked.

"Her." Linao pointed at Velda. "She's inane. I don't know what you see in her. Worrying about showers, wondering what we've been given to eat. She's a fucking moron, and how she came to be Head of Defense is a question for the ages."

"My, my," Velda said, and Ethan could hear the amusement in her voice. "Someone's grumpy. Probably because you haven't had anything to eat."

Linao let out a soft shriek, lifting her fists to her head as if she was about to pummel herself. "You do it on purpose, don't you?"

"You suddenly seem very easily riled." Velda sounded thoughtful.

This was an act?

Interesting.

Ethan's dislike of Linao had blinded him to that, but he considered it as Linao leaned forward and snatched an energy bar out of his hand.

Velda might be right, the voices in his head said. *The enemy is acting unhinged, but her eyes say she's gauging your reaction.*

He almost didn't register the strangeness of the voices in his head this time. It was like he was getting used to them. And he didn't disagree that Linao was their enemy.

"Help yourself," he said to Linao, holding out another bar to her.

Their lack of protest at the way she'd just behaved seemed to enrage her even more, and Linao kicked the bag, spilling its contents, and then she jumped on one of the food packages, crunching whatever was inside to dust.

The cell door whisked open immediately.

Oh yes, she'd been playing for an audience, but they weren't it. She wanted the door to open again. She wanted something.

And because it was Linao wanting it, he assumed she had some angle. Maybe her father had managed to pass on a coded message during their chat. Like maybe 'we're about to attack, be ready'.

"What are you doing?" the guard asked.

"I don't want to be in the same room as her," Linao shouted, pointing at Velda. "Put me somewhere else."

The guard regarded her in silence for a beat. "No." He stepped back, but before the door could close, Linao leapt forward and stuck her arm in the way.

The guard must have been caught by surprise, because he had already started to turn away, and as the door stopped closing, Linao dived through the gap and then ran.

"She's something, all right," Velda said, and there was a sliver of admiration in there.

Ethan grunted, because while he agreed, he just didn't like her enough to say it.

The door had halted, then begun opening again, and they both stepped forward, but a second guard was suddenly in the way, laz raised.

They both lifted their hands and backed up, and he stood, pointing it at them as if he was weighing up whether he could get away with shooting them anyway.

The whole ship shuddered, and he turned to look down the passage.

Ethan didn't second guess himself this time. He leaped straight at the guard, slamming his elbow into the side of his neck and twisting the laz out of his grasp in the same maneuver.

The guard fell, and Ethan turned and shot him before he hit the floor.

"Wow."

He looked over at Velda, who was standing in the passage in front of the now closed cell, eyes wide.

"Would it be inane to admit that really did it for me?" She winked at him and waved her hand as if to cool herself down.

He couldn't help the laugh that escaped from his throat. This woman just kept delighting him. "Where to? You're the one who's had the chance to look around." He hefted the laz, which was way bigger than any issued by the Verdant String Coalition, and checked the passage for incoming guards.

So far, they were clear.

"I've only been taken to the one room, that way." She pointed to the right. "I don't think they'd expect us to be there, so it's as good a choice as any to hide in and I don't think it's got any visual comms installed. They received messages through a knock on the door."

That was interesting. It might mean it was more likely a private conference room than an interrogation room, and therefore more likely to be used, but any other place they chose to hide would be a risk, anyway.

"Lead the way." He followed her, checking their back regularly. Velda had told him about the dim lighting, and like her, he wondered about the reason behind it.

"Was it like this before?" he murmured as she peered around a corner and then signaled him that the way was clear. "More or less deserted?"

"Yes." She glanced back at him. "I wondered about that myself."

She stopped in front of a door and waited for him to get in position with the laz, in case there was someone inside. Then she tried to open it.

It didn't budge.

The ship made a strange groaning sound as she tried again, and she froze.

They exchanged looks.

"That didn't sound good," she said.

The floor seemed to buck under their feet, and they were both thrown against the wall.

He'd been expecting something to happen ever since Linao had staged her escape. Guess he was right about her receiving a message in her chat with her father.

It looked like the Cores were out to get daddy's little girl back.

25

Linao was being rescued again.

Velda wondered what this was costing the Cores, but obviously it was worth it to someone to get her back.

Even if it was just because she was Sylvester's daughter.

She had nerve, though. Velda would give her that. And a certain ability to skirt consequences.

The mothership groaned again, and then went silent. Velda looked up at the ceiling.

"What do you want to do?" she asked.

Ethan began down the corridor. "Let's keep going, and keep trying doors along the way."

As he got ahead of her, she noticed again how much harder and bigger he looked.

His clothes were tight around his biceps and across his shoulders, and when he'd shot that Caruson guard, she'd been astonished at his speed.

And the approval of her own internal voices at his style.

They had judged him worthy.

She guessed worthy of her. Which she had to admit was sweet of them.

They reached the next turn in the passageway and Ethan extended his arm back, hand clenched, to tell her to stop, before he peered around the corner.

He slid back and the look on his face told her there was trouble coming.

A lot of trouble.

"Run," he whispered, pointing back the way they'd come.

She turned and sprinted, heard Ethan right behind her. Until a group of at least five Caruson stepped out from around the corner, blocking their way and forcing her to come to a stop.

She spun, and saw the reason Ethan had wanted them to run in the first place.

Another group of Caruson, at least ten in this group, blocked the passageway in the other direction.

They were cut off on both sides.

The bigger group called out in Caruson, and someone in the smaller group responded.

It sounded unfriendly to Velda, but she didn't have an ear for Caruson, and they could well be exchanging greetings for all she knew.

Both groups were armed, and she pressed herself up against the wall to get out of their line of fire. Ethan did the same, and she glanced at him. "Are the weapons pointed at us or each other?"

He was holding his own weapon across his body, so he could swing it in either direction, but he narrowed his eyes at her question and looked again.

"I think each other." He sounded thoughtful.

"So maybe the Cores didn't hijack this ship. Maybe we're privy to some in-fighting among the Caruso?" She thought that through, then shook her head. "No, Linao definitely knew this was going down."

Before Ethan could respond, one of the soldiers in the smaller group shot at the larger group, and she and Ethan both dropped into a crouch, getting as low as they could as a laz fight ensued.

Someone in the bigger group shouted a command and all laz fire cut off.

That was because everyone in the smaller group was down, Velda saw. There was no one left to fight.

Unless she and Ethan were also on the list.

From the fire into the oven, as the Aponi saying went. She and Ethan were back where they started, just with a different set of antagonists.

Ethan was wisely pointing his laz at the floor as they were suddenly surrounded by at least ten Caruson, all wearing loose, dark gray clothing.

"Verdant String?" one of them asked.

"Verdant String," Velda confirmed.

"Drop." The commander pointed to the laz in Ethan's hand, and he bent down and set it on the ground.

Someone came around the corner, and most of the group turned, weapons raised, then relaxed when they saw who it was.

Velda looked around them and saw it was Linao. So the Cores had had something in their back pocket when it came to the Caruson. Maybe they weren't so clueless in their dealings with the war-like planet as she'd thought.

"Well, well." Linao smirked. "You got out, too."

"You created a good distraction," Ethan said.

"Not that it helps you." Linao smiled, then glanced over her shoulder as more Cores soldiers rounded the corner.

The Cores and the Caruson, working in harmony. Interesting.

The sound of laz fire was clear in the sudden silence, coming from up ahead and to the left.

"The bridge," Linao said, and some of the Cores and some of the Caruson group around them jogged off in that direction.

"So you've taken the warship." Velda was honestly impressed. "That couldn't have been the plan all along. You were surprised when the Caruso took the ore runner."

"No, it wasn't the plan, but it didn't work out too badly, did it?" Linao sounded positively exuberant.

"I'll take them back to their cell," she told the Caruson who seemed to be in charge, lifting the laz she was carrying. She signaled to two Cores guards and they flanked her, and she marched Velda and Ethan back to the brig.

Except no one could open it back up.

"That's annoying." Linao slammed her fist into the keypad. "Watch them," she ordered the two guards. "I'll go find someone who can open up."

They stood in silence, up against the wall opposite the cell door, two laz pointed at them.

Velda sighed, rubbed at her eye and leaned back more firmly against the wall, sliding down it a little as if she was tired. "It's been a long day."

"It's past time to sleep, is my guess," Ethan responded. "How many hours since we were taken by the Caruson?"

"I've honestly lost track," Velda said. "It could be we've gone for well over a day without sleep."

Ethan yawned.

Go low, the voices in her head told her. *Knock him over at the knees.*

She used the wall at her back as a counterpoint and dove forward, twisting in the air and hooking her arm around the guard in front of her's knees.

Ethan either moved a second before her, or at exactly the same moment, grabbing the laz held by the guard in front of him, spinning to stand behind him, hand still gripping the laz and pointing it upward as he got a chokehold.

Velda was on her feet, kicking the laz out of the guard she'd brought down's hand, grabbing it up, and shooting him before he'd even pushed up from the ground.

She turned the laz on the other guard just as he slumped in Ethan's arms.

Ethan laid him on the ground next to his friend, and they smiled at each other.

The sound of footsteps coming galvanized them both.

They ran in the opposite direction, looking for a place to hide, but the murmur of voices up ahead had them both slowing to a stop.

"What now?" She glanced behind them, but it would be moments before the guards were discovered and their escape would be known.

"Up." Ethan leaped upward at an angle, and the passageway was narrow enough he was able to press his hands on one side, while his feet found purchase on the other. He walked his feet up, until he was level with the floor, and then got even higher, until he disappeared above into the gloom of the already dark passageway.

"I'm too short to do that." Velda didn't need to try, the voices in her head were clear that it wouldn't work.

"Then stay where you are, lure them in, and I'll shoot them." Ethan's voice was whisper quiet.

They had no choice, there were shouts from the way they'd come, and the footsteps were getting louder from the other direction.

Velda crouched down on the ground, laz in her hand but pressed up against the wall so it was not as noticeable, and waited.

Two Caruso came from in front of her and another one came from behind, obviously fresh from the sight of two downed Cores guards.

They didn't see her.

They almost missed her completely, and if they hadn't met up with each other almost exactly where she was sitting, she had a feeling they might have passed her by altogether.

But the one who was coming from the direction of the downed guards slowed down, shouting at the other two, and then his gaze landed on her.

His shock was clear.

He came to a halt, hand going to his weapon, and then Ethan shot him.

The other two couldn't work out where the laz fire had come from, one turned to look behind him, the other glanced at her, and as she brought her own laz up, Ethan shot him, and she took out the one who'd looked back down the way he'd come.

Ethan dropped lightly to the ground, hand out, and she grasped it, let him pull her to her feet.

"This is going to stir things up," she said.

Ethan grunted in agreement and they both began running down the passage again. Velda hit the keypad on every door they passed, but nothing opened.

"You can't do your fingertip trick," she murmured, remembering how he'd disabled the lens in their cell on the Cores runner. Maybe he could open doors.

He reached out and touched a keypad, shook his head. "This tech is very foreign. I'd need time to learn it, first."

They turned down a new passageway, and she saw double doors up ahead, the first she'd seen on this ship.

When they opened she could hardly believe it, but they stepped inside, weapons raised.

There was no one in here.

"It's the med bay," she said. There were a few beds and a glass cabinet of medication, and not much else.

"The Caruson who took us to the med bay to talk about the silver balls didn't seem to have much time for injuries," Ethan said. "Let's hope it's a common sentiment."

"At least we're off the passageways and out of sight." Velda found a chair, the only one she could see, and sat down with a sigh. She was hungry and tired.

Looking over at Ethan, she guessed he was the same.

From her perch on the over-large chair, she looked around the room, and then stood when she saw some disposable cups. She went to the sink, filled two with water, and turned.

Ethan was watching her from the other side of the room, and she felt a full-body rush as their eyes met.

"Sit." She pointed to the chair, and with a tiny quirk of his lips he obeyed.

She settled onto his lap, handed him a cup, and wriggled to get comfortable.

"I thought you said we'd do better next time," he said, his voice a little deeper than usual.

"I lied." She drank all the water in her cup and set it down, turned to look up at him just as he bent his head to kiss her.

His hand ran over her shoulder and came to a rest at her waist, and then he lifted her effortlessly, turning her body to face him.

As she sighed into his mouth, he suddenly stood, still holding her in his arms, his eyes on the door.

He let her swing down, and she heard it, too. A group of people running in their direction.

She glanced at him, and every warning signal in her spiked.

"You look too dangerous." They had two laz, and from the sound of it, ten were coming their way, and the voices in her head were very wary of laz fire. "You're just muscle and deadly intent." Her heart felt like it was going into palpitations with fear for him. "Ethan, lie down on the ground and curl up. Now."

He sent her such a look, absolutely incredulous.

"Please. Trust me. Please." They were almost out of time.

With a disgusted grunt he collapsed on the ground, curling around his laz, and she crouched beside him, hand on his shoulder, just as the door opened.

Linao stepped in, four Cores guards and five Caruson behind her.

"He got hit," Velda said. "He's barely hanging on."

Linao blinked, and Velda could almost see the tension drain out of not just her, but the whole group.

"He'll recover if he isn't already dead." Linao dropped her laz to face downward, and so did everyone else. "How did you get him in here?"

She hadn't really thought about that. "He was just able to stumble in before he collapsed. This is his third hit since the start of the week. There's only so much a body can take." She didn't have to try too hard to manufacture some outrage.

Linao gave a laugh at that. "Who hit him?"

Velda sent her a filthy look. "I have no idea. I didn't ask their name."

Linao laughed again, and came forward to take both laz off them, and handed them to someone behind her. "You certainly keep things from being boring," she said. "What *are* we going to do with you?"

26

——————

Velda had some kind of magical ability to make people see things her way.

Ethan wondered if the silver balls took the strengths of the person they were absorbed into and bolstered them—working with the abilities that were already there.

That would explain why he was a better fighter, and Velda was a better negotiator.

As Linao said, the Caruso liked her. They listened to her when she spoke, and she handled them just right.

As the head of defense for Aponi for the last couple of years, Ethan guessed her powers of persuasion were already pretty well honed.

And he was absolutely sure she'd just saved him from being hit with laz fire. No doubt about it.

They had been about to open up with their weapons when they saw him already down, and Velda tending to him.

The temperature had come down almost instantly.

Now he played injured as they were taken back to their cell, hunching over a little, making himself smaller.

"While I was getting the door codes, we saw on the system that the

140

med bay doors had been opened, and it wasn't any of us," Linao said. "It was honestly too easy to track you down."

"I wanted to find the med bay," Velda responded. "Ethan had been hit and I hoped there was something there that could help him."

"There wasn't. Caruso med care doesn't work on us, and they only have the basics anyway. They have a very callous disregard for their injured crew." Linao shot a sidelong look at the Caruso soldiers behind her, but he guessed they didn't understand the standard VS dialect she was using. He wondered what the story was with that—it was almost as if she was poking at them, just like she seemed to poke at everyone.

When they came to the cell, Linao opened the door and gestured to the food spilled over the floor. "At least you'll have something to eat."

Velda put her arm around Ethan and ushered him in as if he could barely stand. "At least there is that," she agreed.

Linao shook her head as the door closed.

"I don't think she knows what to make of me," Velda said.

Ethan guessed it was because Linao's default was to distrust and dislike everyone, and something about Velda interfered with that. She couldn't help but like her and that disturbed and unsettled her.

He pretended to stagger to the bed, in case Linao checked the visual comms to make sure he really was injured.

Velda crouched beside the food, picking it up and laying it out on the bed Linao had taken as her own, grouping the same things together. She opened a nutrient bar and gave it a sniff.

Something about the way she did it made him think it wasn't just to see if she liked the smell. The silver balls were assessing it. Deciding if it was safe to eat.

She made a face and walked over, crouched beside him. "It's not going to taste good, but it's not going to kill us, either. And we need the energy."

He took the bar and bit down. It did taste disgusting, but he thought he might actually have had worse out in the field before. He choked it down.

Velda did the same with the bar she'd taken for herself, and then she went and got them water from the sink in the bathroom. She sat on the ground beside the bed, brushing the hair back from his brow as if he was seriously ill, and her eyes laughed down at him as she held the cup to his lips.

He wanted no lens feed and a way to lock the door so badly he could barely stand it.

As he thought it, the door opened again, and Velda turned her head, still sitting on the ground, although he felt her whole body tense.

It was Linao.

"Sylvester wants to talk to you." She leaned against the wall. "Let's go."

Velda stood, set down the cup, and then bent to help him to his feet. The look she shot him was fierce, as if she wanted him to do something he wasn't doing.

Look less angry, the voices in his head warned. *Look weaker.*

He realized his teeth were clenched and his hands were, too, and he forced his body to loosen up.

He let Velda draw him to his feet and prop her shoulder under his arm, and he tried to work out how much of his weight to let her take.

He didn't want her to take any. He wanted to wipe that smug smirk off Linao's face and run rampant through this ship.

Not right now, sweetheart.

He swore the voice in his head this time was Velda's. He didn't look at her, but he'd ask her about it later.

They followed Linao out and it looked like there were way more Caruso here than there had been before. The group that had taken the ship from their fellow Caruso had overrun it, by the looks of things.

He would love to know the story behind a Caruson coup, if that's what this was.

As well as the story of how the Cores had found out there were factions within the Caruso to exploit.

How had they learned that?

Linao led them to a large room with a big desk and seating behind it for one.

It looked like the Caruso expected their underlings to stand to attention when meeting with the captain or general, or whatever the leader was called.

It wasn't a Caruson soldier sitting at the desk, though.

Ethan studied the man with interest. This must be Sylvester.

He immediately knew he was Linao's father. Her features were a feminine version of his own.

The Caruso were also studying the man occupying the seat of power, and Ethan thought they might be angry or uncomfortable at the sight of him on their ship, taking up the top spot.

As if he suddenly read the room, Sylvester stood. Where Linao wore her dark hair in an elegant bun, his was cut close to his skull. He had the sleek, muscular form of his daughter, though, and even the way they moved was similar.

He walked to the front of the desk and leaned against it, crossing his arms over his chest.

"Velda Shanïha." He tilted his head. "I never expected to meet you in person."

"And you're Sylvester?" Velda asked. "The head of what is left of the Cores?"

Sylvester's lips tightened at that, but he inclined his head. "My daughter tells me Ritter used you for his experiments."

"And others," Velda said. "I gather most of the runner's crew were drafted in to participate, but they got annoyed with it and refused after a while."

"Yes, but they're not here, and you are." Sylvester's gaze swept from Velda to Ethan, but Ethan had known it was coming, and he let his body hunch just that little bit more, and he could feel the silver balls drain the color from his face.

"What is it?" Linao asked, her voice sharp as she watched her father.

"Ethan Hyt seems a little worse for wear. What's wrong with him?" Sylvester didn't sound worried so much as bored.

"He was hit with laz fire while they were escaping. And it's not the first time he's taken a hit since Ridgeman and his team found the two of them at the mine." Linao shrugged.

"And it looks like there's been no benefit to him from the experimentation." Sylvester's tone was disappointed. "Where is the box? I was told the Caruso took it with them."

"It was in the runner that took us from the ship," Linao said. "The teams are searching through what's left of it now."

"So we could have damaged it ourselves in the attack?" Sylvester straightened.

"Yes. You could have damaged me, too," Linao said. "You obviously thought it was worth the risk." She gave a cynical smile. "Just like on Fjern."

There was a beat of silence.

Sylvester shifted, leaning back against the desk. "I already told you, Vanburren made it sound as if your vessel was about to be taken by the Fjerna. And he told me he gave you five minutes to get out before he destroyed your ship. He also made your return the main part of his negotiations afterward."

"Of course." Linao's tone spoke volumes. "He was just following protocol."

After an uncomfortable pause, Sylvester waved a hand toward the door. "Why don't we go have a look at the progress they're making in finding the box?"

Linao said nothing, but she turned on her heel and stalked out.

She was a strange one, Ethan thought. She over-shared, then she said nothing, she made the cruelest threats, and then chatted normally. He wondered if she had been living a lie for so long, she didn't know how to react any more.

When they had been discussing the new planet they'd found, she'd told Ritter her ship had been destroyed and she'd spent a week as a prisoner there. When Ethan had heard that, he'd assumed the planet's inhabitants had been responsible, but now it sounded as if it had been her father who had ordered her ship destroyed.

And she still hadn't forgiven him for it.

Sylvester watched her go, face blank, and then followed her out, and the Cores guards went with him, leaving him and Velda alone in the room with the Caruso soldiers.

"What experiments was Sylvester asking you about?" The Caruson standing beside them waited until the room had cleared before he spoke.

"They were trying to understand how some tech they found in a space wreck works," Velda said.

"What wreck?" The Caruson's attention focused on her.

"I don't know the details," Velda said. "We were their prisoners and their experimental subjects. They didn't tell us much."

"But you were part of the experiment. What was it?" The Caruson stepped closer to her.

"A box with some silver balls inside. They absorb into the skin, but there's a device that draws them back out again." She shrugged. "The scientist was disappointed with the results."

"Sylvester seems interested." The Caruson glanced back at the door.

"They were bringing the tech to him when your fellow Caruso hijacked the ship," Velda said. "When the Caruso crew realized where it was going, they made sure to take it when they tried to get back to this ship."

Another soldier in the group said something in Caruson, and the soldier who'd been speaking to Velda responded, eyeing them both thoughtfully.

Ethan was pretty sure he was as surprised as Velda was that Sylvester and Linao had more or less lost interest in them after making such a production about taking them out of their cell.

Either the father and daughter were locked in some strange back and forth with each other, something that took preference over everything else, or they were playing a long game that wasn't quite clear yet.

Ethan could see the Caruson soldier had assumed there was a strategy at play, but he personally thought the chances were fifty fifty.

It didn't escape his notice that Velda had taken the lead again on the responses, and the Caruso had listened to her carefully.

So far, they almost seemed more hostile to Sylvester and his crew than to him and Velda.

"Let's go see this tech for ourselves," the soldier said.

The walk to the bay was more like a congenial stroll than them being herded along as prisoners.

Velda again, he was sure.

They arrived to find about ten Cores guards climbing in and out of the crushed ship, and looking at it from the outside, Ethan wondered how they had managed to get out of it alive.

He was guessing the sight of the damage had inspired Linao's bitterness at her father's solution to stopping the runner. Because she was right. She—and they—were lucky to still be breathing.

He still didn't know how they'd crushed the ship like that. Four dead Caruso lay beside the runner, and two others were stashed to the side, faces uncovered although they were very still. Could they still be alive?

Ethan remembered the empty med bay, and Linao's sidelong glance at the Caruso with her when she told them it was not considered a priority to tend to injured soldiers. Was this what she was taking a dig at them over?

"Got it!" One of the Cores guards emerged from the runner with the box in his hands. It was crushed on one side and the lid was slightly buckled.

"How soon until Ritter joins us?" Linao asked.

"A couple of hours." Sylvester turned from the runner and then stopped short at the sight of him and Velda.

Ethan had been careful to limp along, letting Velda assist him, but he had the feeling Sylvester's eyes narrowed a little when he saw him.

"What are they doing here?" he demanded.

"We are not yours to command," the Caruson soldier who'd spoken to Velda said. "You left them in the room. We brought them to you. You are welcome."

Sylvester blinked, and before he fixed his expression to neutral, Ethan saw the spike of fury on his face at being challenged.

"Thanks, Nirro." Linao slapped the Caruson's arm lightly and jerked her head at Ethan and Velda. "Come on, back to your cell."

Ethan considered the various escape options, but there were too many weapons in the room. Too many people to fight.

He let Velda draw him out of the bay, her hand patting his back as if to console him for the fact that he couldn't do what he wanted.

And what he wanted was to fight.

He wouldn't have called himself a violent man before. If he were given the chance, that would change.

27

VELDA LAY IN ETHAN'S ARMS, STARING UP AT THE FRAME OF THE BUNK above them.

At least they had gotten some sleep. They had both really needed it.

No one had come for them again since Linao had returned them to their cell, and she was still turning over Sylvester's potential motivations for summoning them and then essentially abandoning them in her head.

Either he'd let his argument with Linao take precedence or he'd been distracted by the thought of the silver balls being damaged and found that more important.

She decided she was going to ask Linao.

She might refuse to speak, or she might blurt out everything, like she had done to Ritter about the discovery of the ancestral wreck.

She also wondered what had happened to Linao on Fjern. There was some really bad blood there.

If she'd understood correctly, Linao accused Sylvester of ordering her ship destroyed, and she'd barely gotten out alive. Velda remembered her saying she'd spent a week as a prisoner afterward.

And now her father had destroyed a ship with her in it again.

It had obviously stirred up trouble.

And Ritter arriving would stir up more.

Linao didn't like him, but Sylvester seemed to be looking forward to his arrival.

We need the last four balls, the voices in her head said. *It's good Ritter's coming if it means he gives them to us. We are tired of being in hibernation.*

She turned her head slightly to look at Ethan as he dozed beside her. If he got two more balls, it would be almost impossible to hide the changes.

Her panic spiked, and the balls inside her tried to calm her down.

No, she told them. *This is a legitimate worry.*

He hadn't grown in height, but he was so much more muscular, it looked as if he had.

She lifted her arm, turned it one way and then another, and admitted she looked stronger, too, but her muscles had only gotten more defined, she hadn't put on the same bulk as Ethan.

It was as if the balls had taken a look at their opponents, the much bigger, bulkier Caruso, and had molded Ethan's new physique to match them.

All the better to fight them, the voices told her.

Let's be clever about this, she warned them. *I don't want Ethan getting hurt.*

She felt a rush of approval and agreement from them, and her fingers tingled where they rested against Ethan's arm.

He stirred beneath her, and she looked up, found him watching her.

"You thinking good thoughts about me?" he asked, voice husky.

She lifted her brows. "Maybe. Is that what the voices told you?"

"That's what they told me," he agreed. "They're very happy about it." He bent his head and kissed her, and she moved her legs restlessly as she kissed him back, wishing, as she had many times since this whole thing began, that they had the privacy they'd had in the mountains.

Ethan stilled, his hand gripping her arm as if to stop himself touching her anywhere else.

"I want this ship to ourselves," he said.

She gave a low chuckle. "You're going to get rid of them so we can finally have some us time?"

"Yes." He sounded quite serious. He shifted, pulling her over his body and against the wall, his focus going to the door. She was suddenly glad of the overhead bunk, because it created a pool of shadow beneath it—shadow that could hide Ethan's changes, because it was clear someone was coming.

"Let me deal with this." She swung her leg over him before he could sit up, pinning him beneath her, and he grabbed her by the waist and lifted her up, the move so effortless she gaped at him.

"No."

"Yes." She glared at him, suspended along his length, as she heard footsteps getting closer. "You can't see yourself, but you're just not the same as you were." She whispered it, in case the lens in the room was sound and vision. "I'm going to sit in front of you and block their view."

He looked distinctly annoyed as he lifted her completely over his body so she could put her feet on the ground.

She straightened up, standing directly in front of him, as Linao opened the door.

"Good, you're up." Linao smiled. "I thought you might like some actual food before Ritter prods and pokes at you again, so I've arranged for you to eat breakfast in the mess."

"We would like that." But she was panicking as she said it, because then Linao would see Ethan.

Maybe his changes were just obvious to her? Maybe Linao wouldn't notice anything.

"Give us a minute to use the bathroom, and we'll be ready." She waved back toward the facilities, and Linao sighed and gave a nod. "I'll even give you five minutes, not just one." She stepped out and the door closed.

She sensed Ethan rise up behind her and she turned to look at him with a critical eye.

"Shit," she said with feeling, then lowered her voice. "Can you pretend to still be dragging a bit from your laz hit?"

He looked down at himself, looked up. She thought he looked surprised and a little freaked out.

"Sure."

They took turns in the bathroom and as Ethan stepped out, Linao was back.

"Still not yourself?" she asked, and Velda thought there was more than a touch of suspicion in her voice.

Suspicion was better than knowing, she decided. Much better.

"Have you forgotten how it feels to be hit with one of those big laz?" Velda asked, stepping forward with her hands on her hips.

"No." Linao turned to look at the weapons in the hands of the Caruson guards outside the door. "I remember how much it hurts."

Ethan's face had gone a paler shade than usual, and Velda assumed it was the balls at work.

She approved.

They walked with Linao down gloomy passages to the canteen, and Velda wondered why they had a Caruson guard and not a Cores unit.

It looked like Linao planned to eat with them, because she sat down at the table with them.

"My father and some of his team went back to his ship, but they sent back some food and one of the cooks to feed those of us who aren't Caruson." She glanced at the Caruson guards standing behind them. "The rebels need to preserve their own food because there's more than double the people in this new Caruson crew than there were before."

"When are we leaving this ship?" Velda asked. Surely it should be soon? She didn't understand why some of the Cores were still onboard.

"That's a good question." Linao glanced at the Caruso again, and Velda wondered if she was worried about it. "Nirro wanted some of us to stay here while he and my father negotiated the terms of their deal."

In other words, they were hostages to the Caruso until Nirro had what he wanted.

And once again, Sylvester had left his daughter in a dangerous situation, while he got himself to safety.

Food came out of the kitchen, carried by two Cores staff, and then a Caruson came out with food as well, set it on a nearby table, and the guards around them moved off to sit and eat their breakfast.

It made things far less tense, no longer having four large laz pointed at them.

"So what's the story?" Velda asked, keeping her voice down. "I didn't know the Caruso had any internal conflict, but obviously they do."

"Looks like Raxia and Arkhor are keeping secrets from their allies,"

Linao said, and there was such a layer of smug in her tone, Velda realized her hands were clenched.

"Raxia and Arkhor know about an internal power struggle among the Caruso?" Ethan asked.

"Well . . ." Linao shrugged. "Maybe not the specifics, but they know all about the incident that sparked the issues."

"And what incident was that?" Ethan asked.

Linao smirked again and bit into a piece of toast.

"Veltos," Velda said, and the look on Linao's face made her think she was right. "That's the only incident I can remember where the Raxian and Arkhoran military had some kind of incident together with the Caruso."

"Veltos?" Ethan took a sip of jah. "I vaguely remember the VSC had a run-in with the Caruso. I thought it was just the same kind of low-level incident that's been happening more and more these last few years."

"The Caruso snuck onto Veltos and set up an illegal mine, and when an earthquake collapsed the mine tunnels, they had mass casualties on their hands. In order to get their people off-planet without tipping off the VSC, they took out a VSC satellite and tried to kill everyone on Veltos." Linao leaned back in her chair.

Velda hadn't heard any of this. "How many people were on Veltos?"

Linao smiled. "Only three scientists and a group of VSC soldiers participating on the Veltos Trail."

The Veltos Trail. Of course.

Velda had nominated a few Department of Defense personnel who'd been injured to be awarded a place on one of the groups walking the Trail. It was a real honor to be chosen, and there were a limited number of places.

"How did that whole incident create a split in the Caruso?" Ethan asked.

"Apparently, once it became clear they couldn't kill everyone on planet, and that the people on the Trail had been able to call in an Arkhoran warship to help them, the Caruso tried to simply kill their own people on the planet, so no one could spill their secrets." Linao dropped her voice even lower. "The head of the mine sent his most severely injured people up to their own ship to save them, and called for something that's very specific in Caruson culture—"

"*Fraknvos.*" The Caruson who'd spoken with them yesterday, and who Linao had called Nirro, came to stand directly behind Linao. Velda had noticed him come in, and he must have excellent hearing, because he had obviously heard every word Linao had said. Either that or this table had a listening device hidden somewhere on it. "They called for *fraknvos*, and that is a call that can never be denied. And yet, on that day, it was."

"They asked for help, a special kind of help that must be honored?" Velda was beginning to understand.

Nirro nodded. "Vrk asked for it, to save those under his command, and they turned him away and then tried to kill him and everyone else they'd sent down to the mine to keep them quiet."

"I remember the name Vrk." Ethan turned to look at the Caruson. "He was taken prisoner by the Arkhorans, wasn't he? Him and a group of others?"

"He had no choice but to surrender to the VSC after our own military tried to kill him." Nirro's narrow nostrils flared. "He and his people were eventually returned to Caruso, but by then the word had gotten out through the contact he and his people had with their family and friends while they were being held on Arkhor."

Velda wondered how well the Arkhorans had monitored those communications. Not very well if they hadn't realized what was going on.

"So everything that had happened to them was made public?" Ethan asked.

"They'd have preferred to keep it secret and I'm sure the Caruson government would have liked to have had Vrk killed on his return, but it was too late by then. Even they could see that would not be wise," Nirro said. "The captains of the ships who refused to help, who tried to kill Vrk and his people, they were tried and convicted, but they had been under orders, so then the people looked at who above them could have ordered such a thing, and when no one was prosecuted for that most horrendous of crimes, the people began to wonder if they wanted such leaders leading them anymore."

"When did this happen?" Velda asked.

"It's been a long, slow process." Nirro crossed his arms. "First, Vrk and his crew were under Arkhoran control, and then after months of negotiation, they were returned, and then came the captains' trials, and then the demand for accountability, and then the realization that nothing was going to happen. We have been fighting the system for perhaps six months or more."

Which is why things had definitely gone quiet in the last few months. Velda and her advisors had assumed the Caruso were either biding their time, waiting for an opportunity, or they were stockpiling weapons and getting ready for an attack.

Arkhor and Raxia really should have weighed in and let them all know things were not exactly happy between the group they'd taken prisoner and the home planet. Unless they hadn't realized the full extent of it.

It was possible the Caruso had kept things low key, because even the group who wanted to overthrow the current Caruson government probably saw the VSC as an enemy.

"So what's the deal between the Cores and the rebels?" Velda asked. "Weren't the Caruso already cooperating with the Cores?"

"The original agreement wasn't honored." Linao said. "We found new allies."

This explained so much. Velda had wondered for a long time how the Cores kept dealing with the Caruso when they'd reneged on their bargains over and over again.

It looked like all this time, they'd been in secret talks with the competition. "Was this ship takeover the first fall of the hammer?" Velda asked.

Linao and Nirro exchanged a look, and neither answered.

There was something else going on here.

Nirro was called to by someone in the passageway outside the canteen, and he left them, striding off.

"He won't let you leave, will he?" Ethan asked.

Linao shot him a quick look, then lifted a shoulder. "We're still hammering out the final details of our cooperation. It may be they're a little reluctant to let us go until they have some assurances."

Ethan's lips twitched. "I wondered how the Cores kept getting into alliances with the Caruso, only to have them do whatever suited them best over and over. Now I'm wondering what the Caruso could be thinking, trusting you lot."

Linao's eyes narrowed, and she pushed back her chair and stood. "Time for me to take you to Ritter."

She meant that statement to cow them.

Velda kept a neutral face, but the voices inside her were cheering at the thought of new balls.

That might not be what's going to happen, she warned them. *We have no idea what he plans to do.*

28

———————

Ethan worried he was trying too hard with his attempt to make himself look weaker, but Velda kept touching him, quick brushes of her fingers on the back of his hand, and he was getting the message that she approved, that he should keep it up.

Her fear for him was just one more thing to love about her, even though there was going to come a time, and soon, where he wouldn't be able to keep up the ruse.

Linao was already suspicious of him, although his comment about the Cores being dishonorable had annoyed her enough that she was striding ahead of them, eager to put them back in Ritter's clutches.

She flipped between sharing secrets with them and then also trying to keep them in a state of fear, and he wondered if she shared as much as she did because she didn't often get the chance to talk to peers and she knew they were going to die anyway, so a little sharing didn't matter.

It made a twisted sort of sense.

She asked for directions a few times, but eventually they arrived back in the med bay, where they'd hidden out the day before.

Ritter was already there, studying the equipment with interest.

When he turned to face them, Ethan had the distinct impression he was unhappy to see Linao, and not all that happy to see Ethan and Velda, either.

Nirro wandered out from a small room to the side of the med bay, and Linao took a surprised step back at the sight of him.

That's what Nirro had been called away about, Ethan realized. They'd been told Ritter was setting up the experiment, and they wanted to observe. Or interfere.

Whatever it was, it had already complicated things.

"Have you seen anything like this before?" Linao asked Nirro, pointing to the box which was open on the counter.

"You think I have?" Nirro asked without answering.

"We know you found that ghost ship in Raxian airspace well over a year ago, and that turned out to be an ancestral ship. Either the Raxians are lying about finding a box of them onboard, which we don't think they are, or you got onboard first and took it before you started towing the ship away." Linao leaned against the wall.

"Interesting." Nirro stared at the box with renewed curiosity. "I haven't ever seen anything like it, but it's possible it happened the way you say. I don't know anything about it, though."

Of course. Ethan thought about how many ancestral wrecks had been found recently. The Raxian find was the first, or rather, they'd thought it was the first, but according to Linao, the first one had been nearly twenty years ago on Garmen. Then the Raxian find, then the one on Faldine. After that, there was the find on the small moon, Fynian, and then the wreck Wren Thorakis had stumbled across on Ytla. If there were boxes full of silver balls in each one, where were they?

And that didn't even address the find the Cores had made on Fjern, the planet where the silver balls had been working as designed for thousands of years.

"The leader of the Caruson that took control of the ore ship was very interested in the balls. He contacted his superiors about them and then took them when he escaped." Linao walked forward and bent a little to look at them more closely. "I had the sense he knew about them beforehand."

"I'm a rebel now, remember," Nirro said. "I may have been in the military before, but I wasn't at the top of the chain. I would not have been given access to that information."

"But you were onboard the Caruso warship that towed the old ancestral wreck in Raxian airspace," Linao said. "You were part of the crew."

Nirro went still and looked over at Linao. "Who told you that?" he asked.

Linao shrugged, and the way she did it, eyes a little averted, told Ethan she suddenly regretted saying that. She'd showed her hand, and Nirro did not like it at all.

"Are you still dealing with the establishment as well as us?" Nirro asked. "Playing both sides?" He made an explosive sound. "You have to be, to know something like that."

Linao's silence lasted too long and Nirro looked out into the passageway and called something in Caruson. Light flashed—a laz shot —coming from just outside the med bay doors.

It hit Linao in the back and she went down hard.

Velda made a sound of distress and moved back against the wall, and Ritter stared down at Linao, frozen in horror.

Ethan edged back to stand shoulder to shoulder with Velda, up against the wall.

"You." Nirro pointed at Ritter and the scientist took a step back, hands up, palms out.

"I don't even know what you two were talking about."

"Show me how this works," Nirro said, pointing to the box. He snapped out a command and a guard stepped into the room, grabbed Linao's ankle and dragged her out of the room.

The time is coming, the voices in Ethan's head said. *Get ready when they open the box.*

He had to agree. Nirro was already shooting him quick looks, as if he suddenly saw Ethan a little more clearly.

Ritter's gaze skittered around the room, landing on Nirro, on the armed guards just outside the door looking in, and on Ethan and Velda. He walked to the table and his hand shook as he lifted the small clamp he used to handle the balls.

He carefully lifted one out of the box, held out a hand. When he was sure Nirro was watching he dropped the ball onto his palm and they all watched it melt away.

Then he retrieved the small device that was also inside the box and activated it, holding it against his hand, and the ball rose back up.

He grabbed it with the clamp and returned it to the box.

Nirro had watched the whole thing with growing interest. "Do you feel different?" he asked.

Ritter shook his head. "A little nauseous, for some reason, but otherwise, no."

"And you did this to the crew of your runner, as well?"

Ritter nodded.

"And to these two?" He glanced at Ethan and Velda.

Ritter nodded again.

"And you were planning to do what today?" Nirro lifted the clamp and studied it.

"I was going to use up the last four balls on them, giving them two each, and check their vitals to see if it would make a difference. If each one is working even a little bit, it may be there is a cumulative effect." Ritter's hand waved vaguely.

"I want to try one on my own people," Nirro said. He gestured one of the guards into the room and spoke to him in Caruson.

The guard seemed very unhappy about being part of the experiment, but Nirro was tapping the little device, which Ethan took to mean he was reassuring him they'd both just seen the ball being lifted back out without any issue.

Eventually the guard held out his hand and Nirro used the clamp to lift a ball into his palm.

It disappeared and the guard closed his hand into a fist, in an almost reflexive action.

Then he shivered, his lips moving back in a snarl, and he fell forward, directly into Nirro, who caught him as he went down, twisting him to the side to lay him on his back as his feet drummed on the floor and his back arched up.

He screamed, and then went absolutely limp. Velda crouched down, hands out to balance herself, and Ethan saw a silver ball roll across from the body toward her, and then disappear when it reached her fingers.

She turned her head to look up at him, a little wild-eyed, and he joined her, going onto his haunches.

It seemed as if neither Nirro or Ritter had seen the ball leave the guard's body. Ritter had gotten as far away from the flailing guard as he could and still be in the room, and Nirro was shouting for help from the guards outside.

He grabbed the device that extracted the silver balls and lifted up the guard's hand, pressing the device into his palm.

Nothing happened.

"Why isn't it coming out?" he shouted at Ritter.

"I don't know! I was experimenting with it, I didn't build it!" Ritter made himself smaller where he pressed up against the wall.

Nirro stared at the lifeless body before him and for a moment, Ethan thought he was going to crush the extraction device in his hand.

He didn't, though. He tossed it onto the counter and bent down to the guard, looking for signs of life.

One of the guards in the passageway finally stepped inside, crouching beside his friend, and then shouted something at Nirro.

The rebel leader shook his head, but Ethan guessed he was being blamed for the death.

The guard remonstrating with him stood suddenly, his gaze caught on the box containing the remaining three balls, and he swept it off the counter with a shout.

The box hit the ground, and the balls went flying. Ethan heard them bounce, and it seemed as if they shot randomly around the room.

But he knew better.

He didn't look down, keeping his gaze up and on the Caruson and Ritter, but he felt the nudge as two of the balls hit the side of his hand.

He guessed the last one had found Velda when she lifted her hands up off the floor at last and pressed them together, fingers entwined.

Nirro seemed to remember they were there, looking over at them and then dismissing them as the guard shouted in his face.

He rose to his full height, lifting his laz, and shouted back.

With a snarl of outrage, the guard remonstrating with Nirro turned on his heel and as he stormed out of the room, he casually shot Ritter.

The scientist was already up against the wall, and he slid down, and Ethan thought he was dead, not unconscious.

At least that one guard had upped the laz strength.

It was something to keep in mind.

The sound of laz fire and shouting was suddenly clear, coming from down the passageway.

The Caruso had decided to turn on the Cores. They had already been distrustful, and then Linao had let it slip they were still in talks with the Caruso establishment.

"Stay." Nirro pointed to them both, scooped up his fallen soldier's laz, and walked out of the med bay.

The door closed behind him and for a moment there was silence.

Ethan guessed it wouldn't last long.

29

———

"Do we give them time to take each other out?" Velda asked, stepping away from the wall.

The bodies of the guard and Ritter made her deeply uncomfortable but there was nothing she could do about them right now.

"Couldn't hurt to let them go at it with each other for a bit." Ethan glanced at her. "The alliance didn't last long, did it?"

"It seemed to escalate very quickly." Velda had gotten the impression Linao had regretted showing her hand to Nirro. She'd wanted to find out what he knew about the balls too much, and she'd let on the Cores were still dealing with the Caruso government in the process.

That turned out to be a hard line for the rebels, one they did not hesitate to make clear.

"Linao should have kept her mouth shut," Ethan agreed.

"Unless she was deliberately trying to stir up trouble between the rebels and her father." That might make sense. She had misjudged Nirro's reaction to it, though. Badly.

"You think it's possible the Caruso do have a box of silver balls from that ghost ship?" Ethan asked.

"Yes." She could see Nirro thought so, too. "I agree with Linao that the Caruso seemed to know about it before they even saw it and I don't think Raxia would have hidden the existence of the balls from the VSC if they had found something like that."

"The other possibility is there might not have been a box on that ghost ship," Ethan said. "There's been quite a few ancestral wreck finds in recent months and I haven't heard about silver balls in any of them."

"Not finding one on the wreck on Fynian doesn't surprise me. It was on the ocean floor for years." Velda thought about it. "And the Cores went through that wreck before we could get to it. If there was one, they may have taken it. They already knew what to look for, after all."

"Yeah. Although I'm betting Linao would have mentioned it when she was telling Ritter about the Garmen find if they had." Ethan was moving around the room, opening drawers, rifling through cupboards. He tossed two sharp scalpels onto the table, and kept going.

Velda realized he was looking for weapons and joined in the search.

They found a few more scalpels, and a laser tool, but that was it.

The sound of fighting had intensified, and then everything went quiet.

Nirro burst through the door, panting, hand bloody where he pressed it against his left shoulder, and he touched something when the door closed behind him. Locking it, Velda guessed.

"Things not going well out there?" she asked.

He looked at them, startled, as if he'd forgotten they were in here.

He shook his head. "You're very calm." Then his gaze touched on Ethan, and he drew himself up. "And you are recovered."

"Don't worry about Ethan," Velda said, forcing his attention back on her. "What's going on?"

"We are going to get them off the ship," Nirro said, shooting another look at Ethan.

"Great." Velda had found a few regen packs in one of the drawers, and guessing that's why he was here, held one out to him.

He took it, bemused. "Thank you." He slapped it over a nasty looking wound, and then eyed her again. "What is your preferred outcome to this?"

"That you get them off your ship, let us sneak over to theirs, and we'll wreak as much havoc there as possible. You get to go on your way with your warship, and good luck to you." Velda smiled.

"You wish them harm?" Nirro asked.

"They've told us they will kill us when we're no longer useful to them, so, yes. And I *am* the Head of Defense for Aponi. If you are victorious in your efforts on Caruso and wish to reach out to the VSC, I would be a good contact to have." She got a cup, poured in some water, and held it out to him.

"That is true, and it's also true that I don't have time to stay here and deal with these *bissa*." Nirro drank the water, his gaze flicking to Ethan again, but it seemed he was a little more relaxed now.

Velda assumed *bissa* was an insult. "Let us deal with them."

Nirro set down his cup and crouched down beside his dead friend and put a hand on his head in a gesture that seemed almost tender. "If my government has some of these balls, I haven't heard about it, but I wouldn't say it was impossible that they do."

"So be careful if you see one," Velda said. She was glad Ethan was letting her do the talking. "I don't think Ritter knew it would kill your friend. He would have warned you."

Nirro looked up and gave a nod. "I should have been more cautious. This is technology built for your kind, not mine. But what is done is done."

Someone slammed against the door.

Nirro called out, and was answered with a shout.

He opened up, and the group of Caruso waiting outside seemed to do a double take at the sight of them.

There was some back and forth between them, and someone eventually unclipped a smaller laz from their belt and handed it to Nirro, who handed it to Velda. His gaze flicked to Ethan. "Do not betray my trust."

"We won't." Ethan spoke for the first time. "We are not *bissa*."

Nirro gave a nod. "We have a group of Cores' guards cornered. We will give you time to get onboard their runner which is in the launch bay, and hide. Then we will allow them to escape. You will be transported over to their ship, which was built with the technology from my own people, and which they do not deserve, but which I don't think I have a realistic chance of capturing."

"That sounds like a good deal," Ethan agreed. "Good luck to you."

Nirro nodded, then turned to Velda and put one fist on top of the other. "You are a light of your people. I hope I will have reason to contact you when we achieve our victory."

"I hope so, too." Velda responded in kind, fist on top of fist.

Nirro inclined his head. "Go that way, you have ten minutes before we 'allow' the Cores that remain alive to escape."

Then he and his team disappeared in the opposite direction from where he'd pointed.

Velda held the weapon she'd been given out to Ethan and he took it with a shake of his head. "I don't know how you do it, but seriously, Velda, they are eating out of your hand."

It was the silver balls. Velda was sure of it. They were releasing a pheromone or something. Whatever it was, it predisposed the Caruso to like her. To trust her.

Thank you, she thought.

She had the sense of pleasure and almost a flustered feeling, as if they had not expected thanks or praise.

"Time's wasting," Ethan said, and took two scalpels, slid them into a pocket.

Velda took the other two and they jogged down the passage toward the launch bay.

It was deserted.

The damaged runner the Caruso had used to flee from the ore ship was still parked to one side, but there was also a new Cores runner, undamaged, facing outward, as if ready to flee.

Inside, lying on the floor between the bench seats, were two bodies, both unconscious. Linao and a Cores guard Velda recognized from the group that had been looking for the box of silver balls in the damaged runner the day before.

Velda hoped they really were unconscious, because Linao would delight in pretending to be out of it and then grab them when they reached Sylvester's ship.

Ethan must have thought the same because he crouched beside her, put a hand out to touch her neck, and then gave a nod.

The silver balls had told him she really was unconscious, Velda guessed.

Then they searched for a hiding place.

It wasn't easy—the runner was small—but there was a storage area under the seats that was not compartmentalized, it ran from one end of the runner to the other.

Velda fit in easily, but Ethan struggled to get his shoulders through one of the many openings. He eventually made it, and she could see from his face when he looked at her that he was very unhappy.

"I won't be able to get out in a hurry." He turned on his side and held the laz across his chest.

"There's nowhere else," she said, wriggling closer so they were head to head.

He grunted in agreement as she reached past him to pull down the flap, plunging them into darkness, and moments later they heard laz fire and shouting, and then the sound of boots running up the ramp and the whirr of engines.

Velda rested a hand on Ethan's shoulder as the runner lurched and then took off.

They were headed for Sylvester's ship, they were free, and they were armed.

Time to take back control.

30

———————

OF ALL THE WAYS THEY COULD HAVE LANDED ON SYLVESTER'S SHIP, HAVING the Caruso hand them the opportunity and covering for them was not something Ethan would have considered.

That was Velda and the magic she seemed to sprinkle around her.

She might even have sown the seeds of a cooperation treaty with the Caruso, if Nirro and his rebels managed to pull off their coup.

But first they'd have to survive Sylvester and his people.

The runner moved slowly once it was in the launch bay, and then settled into place.

The floor vibrated a little under his cheek as the ramp lowered and then there were the sounds of boots striding up into the small runner.

"How many of you made it out?"

"Ten, including Linao and Park."

Ethan recognized the person who spoke as the one who he'd heard issuing orders on the runner during the flight away from the Caruso.

"That's nearly all of you." The person asking the question sounded surprised. "And the boss will be pleased you were able to rescue Linao."

Other people began talking, and then there was the sound of a mass exodus. Ethan guessed they'd carried Linao and the other guard out.

Velda squeezed his shoulder after things had been quiet for ten minutes, and he gave a nod.

She moved first, cautiously lifting up the flap nearest her and then sliding out.

She crouched beside the flap in front of his face and opened it, and he handed her the laz.

She shuffled out of the way until he had managed to fight his way out of the tight space, and then she stood, a scalpel in one hand, the laz in the other, facing the now-closed ramp, until he'd gained his feet.

He had barely straightened when she spun, facing the pilot's area. It was separated from the rest of the runner by a floor to ceiling screen with a narrow doorway, giving the pilots access to the back.

A door opened, and Velda pressed herself up against one side of the doorway, he the other.

She tossed the laz to him, and lifted her two scalpels, one in each hand.

Someone climbed onboard and stepped through from the pilot's area into the back.

For a moment, he didn't see either of them, his focus on the flaps under the seats, and Ethan shot him on a low laz setting.

He collapsed.

They looked at each other.

"He didn't see us, so when he comes round there'll be nothing he can say that would give us away." Velda studied him.

"True. But why was he here in the first place?" Ethan asked. "Maybe their scanners showed something in the storage area, which would be us, and he came to see what it was they'd transported in."

Velda gave a slow nod. "He was focused on the flaps. I think you're right."

That meant they'd lost the benefit of surprise.

"We need to find a place to hide as soon as possible, then." Ethan didn't want to be trapped in the runner. "Then we can plan how we're going to take this ship."

Velda eased through the doorway, crouching between the pilot and co-pilot's seats, and looked out. "Seems clear."

The door had been left open, and she disappeared down the ladder, and Ethan followed, laz up to cover her if there was someone watching.

They headed for the bay doors, but halfway there it began to open, and they were forced to dive for the closest hiding place, a stack of boxes and crates Ethan guessed were full of supplies.

He crouched beside Velda and looked around the stacks, saw a guard frowning as he headed for the runner. Before the guard got there, he began to call out a name. The moment he swung himself up into the runner, they ran again, reaching the doors and going through them so fast, Ethan was aware they were both able to move at unnatural speeds.

That was fine, as long as it helped to keep them safe.

No one was in the passage beyond, but that wasn't going to last long. Voices were approaching from the left so they both ran right, and when Ethan heard footsteps just up ahead, he touched the panel beside one of the closed doors in the corridor they were in and grabbed Velda, pulling her inside with him.

He had his laz up as the door closed behind them, but no one was in the room. It was a bedroom, with a narrow bed on one side, two chairs and a table in the middle, and a wall of cupboards and a tiny bathroom on the other.

Velda went to the cupboards and opened them, studied the clothing hanging there. "Someone definitely lives here."

That was unfortunate but Ethan never thought they'd get that lucky as to find an unoccupied bedroom where they could stay until they were ready to venture out.

He looked through the clothing, found two uniforms, and Velda lifted one off the rack and held it up against him.

"It might fit," she said.

There was nothing to lose, so he pulled off his now slightly frayed shirt and trousers and got into the uniform. It was a little tight, but it had quite a lot of stretch in it.

"Depending how small the crew is, and how well people know each other, you might get away with wandering around," Velda said.

Ethan studied himself in the bathroom mirror. He agreed, and it would be a good idea to map the ship, and get to know where everything was located.

"I'm guessing they don't walk around armed on their own ship." He handed the laz to her and tucked the scalpels into his pocket. "Watch the door, in case the occupant comes back, but I'll be as fast as I can."

"I wish I could come too, but I know I can't." Velda held the laz to her side. "I'll try not to shoot you when you come back."

He grinned at her, gave her a quick, hard kiss, and then motioned her to stand out of sight as the door opened.

She leaned against the wall and he exited, striding out into the corridor with as much confidence as he could muster.

He decided to keep going right, because he was sure there was a lot of panic and commotion in the launch bay, and he didn't need anyone looking at him and wondering who he was.

The corridor curved to the left, and then opened out into a communal social space, with lounges and screens, and what looked like a food station. Across the lounge, he could see the corridor curving away to the right, giving him the sense this was the front of the ship, and the doors even further to the front probably led to the bridge.

None of the crew eating or sitting in the large space looked up at him as he walked from one side to the other, and he made his way to the corridor on the left.

There were raised voices coming from that direction, and he considered reversing course but he hesitated too long. Two crew turned the corner, a raised stretcher between them, and one glanced up at him as they turned into a room on the left side of the passageway.

The door they'd gone through remained open as he passed by, and he saw it was the med bay. There were three beds—one held Linao, he guessed, plus the other guard from the runner, and now, the one he and Velda had just shot.

He kept moving along, aware he was headed back toward the end of the ship and the launch bay, and wondered again if he should turn around and go back the other way.

Except, there was no guarantee that would be better.

A man stepped out of an open doorway up ahead, turned in his direction, and then came to a stop. "I don't know you."

"That's not my problem," Ethan said with a shrug, managing not to break his stride as he continued forward.

"I think it is." The man drew out a laz, and Ethan wondered at his new-found confidence as he eyed the weapon, already thinking of the ways he could make it his own.

He could feel a tingle in his arms and legs, could see a way to dart forward and grab the laz, and as the man lifted his arm to shoot, he did exactly that, leaping toward the wall as the man fired, then pushing off it to slam the man to the ground. The laz was in his hand before the man even made a sound, and Ethan shot him immediately.

Unfortunately, he hadn't been able to see what or who lay beyond the door the man had exited, and as he rose up, he noticed it was the armory before he felt the jolt of a laz hit, and fell himself.

"Who is it?" someone asked above him, as he tried to breathe through the pain.

"I think it's one of the prisoners from the other runner." A woman crouched beside him, and then he blacked out.

31

ETHAN MUST BE CAUGHT. HE HAD BEEN GONE TOO LONG FOR ANY OTHER explanation.

Velda paced the room, worry gnawing at her, and wished there was a uniform available that would fit her, because stepping out as she was would definitely raise eyebrows. The casual outfit she'd packed for Nanganya, what seemed like a lifetime ago, was now very much the worse for wear.

She would have to step out, though. That was just reality.

The occupant of this room could come back at any moment, and then she'd be cornered, and if Ethan was captured, she needed to be free to be able to help him.

She had at least found a coat with a hood in the cupboard, and it sat easily over her clothing. It hid most of the wear and tear, stopping just below her knees.

She checked the mirror, decided it was as good as it was going to get, and turned to the door.

When it opened before she could hit the button beside it, she took a step back in surprise.

Fortunately the laz was primed and in her hand.

She shot the two Cores guards as they stepped in, using a side to side motion with the Caruson weapon.

They were already most of the way into the room—they had leaped forward when they saw her—and so when they fell, the door was just able to close behind their boots.

If she'd guessed Ethan had been found before, now she knew for certain, with guards out looking for her.

She scooped up both laz that had fallen to the floor, sticking them under her stolen jacket in the waistband of her pants, and then stepped out of the room.

Someone was coming toward her from the left, so she turned right and strode back toward the launch bay, the coat billowing around her.

She couldn't think of a better place to hide.

As soon as she was inside, she moved behind the stack of crates she and Ethan had used as a hiding place before, and drew the coat around her, tucking it under her thighs as she crouched down.

There was a misaligned pillar of boxes in the row she was hiding behind, creating a gap that allowed a thin line of sight into the bay.

She hadn't noticed anyone in the bay when she'd entered, but she'd only just settled into her hiding place when someone stepped out from the runner, and she suppressed a shiver at how close she'd come to being seen.

The bay doors opened, and two guards stepped in, both armed, and called to the person who was walking from the runner toward them.

"See anyone?"

"No." It was a woman, and she was carrying some equipment in her hand. "You chasing someone?"

"Jint and Falre are both down, and their laz are gone. It's probably the other prisoner. She's hiding somewhere." One of the two guards slowly turned in place, laz at waist height.

"Why do you think they snuck onboard the runner at all?" the woman asked.

"Would you like to be trapped with the Caruso?" the other guard asked. He was looking as well, but his laz was still by his side.

"Good point. Still, they could have just given themselves up." The woman shrugged and moved past the men. "I've done my check, they didn't damage or disable the runner while they were in there."

She left the bay and the two guards stood quietly for a moment, waiting.

They would wait a long time. Velda was not going to be caught.

We will make sure of it, the silver balls told her.

Sometimes it's not possible to escape, Velda reminded them. *Ethan was caught, and I'm sure he tried his best to stay free.*

They were quiet after that. She had the feeling they were considering her words carefully.

The two guards decided to move together, rather than split up, which was a huge advantage for her. Velda sidled around the stack of boxes as they moved in her direction.

She managed to keep out of sight, and ended up in a far corner of the bay, hidden behind even more boxes.

She looked up, and saw there was a way to get to the top.

It would be useful to rest up there, she decided, and also, most people didn't look up.

She climbed the crates carefully and then pulled herself onto her stomach, wriggling forward until her whole body was lying across the boxes on the top of the stack.

The guards were not giving up, though.

They moved around the bay carefully, as if expecting an imminent attack, and when the bay door opened behind them, the one who'd had his laz ready the whole time turned and shot in a single movement.

There was a squawk of outrage from whoever had come in. Velda's view was blocked so she couldn't see, but it sounded as if the shot had missed, but only just.

The guard stammered apologies, and then Sylvester and the guard that seemed to follow behind him like a shadow stepped into view.

"She's here," Sylvester said. "The door logs make that a certainty."

Velda felt a lurch in her stomach. Damn. Of course they would have door logs. She was lucky they didn't have visual comms.

"She took Jint and Falre's weapons, sir. You should leave this to us." The guard who'd accidentally discharged his own weapon said.

Sylvester's guard murmured agreement, and the two left the bay, but

Velda guessed it wouldn't be long before more guards joined the two already here.

She guessed right.

Another four guards arrived, and they broke into three groups of two, dividing the bay up into sections and moving through each section thoroughly.

She held her breath as the group assigned to her section moved around the crates and stacks, lights out to illuminate the dark corners.

They did not look up.

"She's not here." The one who'd come in first sounded annoyed when they all met back up in the middle of the bay.

"She has to be."

"Not if she stepped through into the bay, saw or heard Dimez inside the runner doing her check, and ducked back out." The second man who'd been in the original group of two tapped his weapon against his thigh.

"Oh. That could have happened," one of the other newcomers said. "Whether she did it because she heard Dimez or because she wanted to fool us, it was a pretty good strategy."

"Now she's had . . ." One of the men checked his comms unit. "More than an hour to find a new hiding place."

"Still, it's not like she's going anywhere," someone else said. "She's stuck on this ship."

"Let's just hope she doesn't take a shot at the boss." The man who spoke had come in after Sylvester had left.

"Yeah, that would be terrible." It was the partner of the guard who'd done just that.

"Shut up." The trigger-happy guard stalked toward the door. "Let's go tell Simo our theory and get him to see if there are other places she could be holed up in."

All the guards left except one. He stood silently, listening. Waiting.

Velda rolled her eyes mentally at their efforts to try and trick her into emerging.

Eventually the guard sighed and left, but she noticed he had bent down and left something on the floor.

Some kind of monitoring lens or image tracker, she guessed. It would definitely make getting out of here harder.

She closed her eyes, lying still, trying to rest for a bit. She'd been in a state of stress since Linao had been shot, and that had only intensified while she waited for Ethan to return. She couldn't keep it up.

She felt the silver balls trying to soothe her, and for once she leaned into their help.

The twenty minutes of peace she had before the launch bay doors opened again really made a difference. She felt less panicked and able to think more clearly.

A team of four guards entered.

She recognized two of them as being part of the group that had searched the bay earlier.

"She has to be here." The woman who spoke held her weapon in both hands. "Every other door that was opened has been accounted for. Spread out and look properly."

She had a decision to make, Velda realized. Because the likelihood of being found this time was high. If they were convinced she was here, they would start to look up.

Get them to touch you, the silver balls said.

She could do that.

She slid backward, easing off the high stack, but leaving the laz the Caruso had given her at the top, and only taking the two weapons they knew she had with her.

When she reached the ground, she lay herself down and arranged herself so that she looked as if she'd fallen. She placed a laz on either side of her, as if she'd dropped them, and then closed her eyes.

It seemed to take a long time for a guard to stumble across her.

He made a sound of surprise and called out, then knelt beside her and pushed the hood of her coat off her face.

As soon as his fingers touched her skin, he paused, pressing down with his fingertips a little.

Then he leaned back on his heels.

"Grede, what is it—?" The woman who seemed to be in charge rounded the stacks and then stopped short. "What's wrong with her?"

"I don't know." Grede shuffled out of the way and the woman joined him, flipping back her coat to get a better look at her.

"Maybe she fell." The woman put a hand to her neck as if to check her pulse, and again, stilled, and then pressed a little harder. "Kilber and Vine, come here." She raised her voice to call the other two.

They were obviously already on their way, because it was seconds before they crowded in behind the stacks as well.

"Let's carry her together." The woman's hand was still pressed into her neck, as if she didn't want to lose contact. "We need to get her to the med bay."

They lifted her together, leaving the weapons lying on the ground, which Velda almost couldn't believe.

What are we doing here? she asked the silver balls as she was carried like precious cargo out of the bay.

They need to feel protective, the voices in her head told her. *We are making sure they will be on your side going forward.*

They reached the med bay quickly, and Velda could hear someone moving around inside.

She also knew, suddenly and with certainty, Ethan was here. Lying somewhere close by.

"The prisoner?" a voice asked.

"We don't know what's happened to her," the woman said. "We think she may have fallen off a high stack of boxes."

She was laid down on a bed, and someone lifted her wrist to check her pulse.

Like the others, he paused, then pressed a little harder. "Pulse is a little thready," he said. "I'll need to do a few tests. Any contusions on the back of the head?"

"I didn't think to check," the woman said, stricken.

"That's fine," the medic soothed. "I'll look now." He gently lifted her head and felt for bumps. "Nothing. That's good."

The door opened, and from the sudden stillness in the people around her, Velda guessed it was someone they feared.

"You found her." Sylvester's voice was neutral.

"She was collapsed behind a stack of crates," the woman said.

"She didn't give you any trouble?" Sylvester sounded surprised.

"No, we found her unconscious." Grede said.

"Well done. Did you find the weapons she took?" Sylvester asked.

"Yes." The woman played it cool, but Velda thought she heard just the tiniest trace of nerves in her voice.

"Yarmouth, let me know what's wrong with her. And make sure she's secured, the same as Ethan Hyt." Sylvester left and Velda sensed a release of nerves as the door closed behind him.

"Grede, go back and get those weapons," the woman said. "Kilber and Vine, you can return to normal duties."

The door opened and closed again, and then it was just Yarmouth and the woman standing beside her bed.

"What do you think he plans to do with her?" Yarmouth asked.

"They were going to use her and Hyt in those experiments with some tech they found in the ancestral ship, but they lost that to the Caruso," the woman said. "So maybe they don't have any use for them now."

Velda heard someone groan nearby, and Yarmouth moved away. "Linao. Welcome back."

"Where—?" Linao's voice was hoarse.

"Back on your father's ship. The team fought their way off the Caruso ship and were able to bring you and Park here with them." Yarmouth's clothing rustled as he moved around.

"Ethan and Velda are here too?" Linao's voice rose a little in surprise. "What's wrong with them?"

"Hyt was shot while he was sneaking around this ship. Velda fell from a stack of boxes in the launch bay." The woman stepped closer to Velda's bed.

"How did they get here, I mean?" Linao's bed squeaked as she moved. "They were over on the Caruso ship."

"They snuck into our runner when we escaped." The woman's words were clipped.

"You don't like explaining things to me, do you, Milton?" Linao sounded amused.

Milton ignored the jab and a soft chime sounded from her comms device. "I'm needed elsewhere. See you, Yarmouth."

She strode out, and Velda suppressed a smile of glee at the fact that so far, she hadn't been secured to her bed.

"What happened to you?" Yarmouth asked and Velda guessed he was talking to Linao. "Park was shot when he covered the rest of the team trying to get to the launch bay, but you were recovered from a Caruso who was carrying you, unconscious, down a passageway. A few of the team shot him and rescued you, then went to find everyone who was still alive and get them onto the runner to escape."

"I was shot by Nirro. Things took a turn all of a sudden."

Velda was interested to hear that she didn't confess that things took a turn because she'd revealed her father was still in touch with the Caruson government.

"I'll let your father know you're awake," Yarmouth said.

"Rather let me go find him," Linao said, and Velda heard her get out of the bed.

"I'd rather you stay under observation for at least another twelve hours," Yarmouth said.

"I'm fine." Linao came closer to her bed, and Velda had the sense she was looking down at her. "I'm going to go to my room, have a shower and some food, and then go find my father for a debrief." She reached out and touched Velda's face, and Velda had to steel herself not to react.

Linao seemed to go still, and kept her fingers there longer than was normal.

The door behind her opened, and she turned.

"Father." She moved forward. "Walk with me to my room, will you?"

"What happened?" Sylvester asked as the door closed again, cutting off the conversation.

Yarmouth gave a sigh of relief to be rid of them, and began to move around her, running a diagnosis wand over her body and then turning away to check on a screen.

When he returned to her bedside, he lifted her wrist again and held it for a while, then placed it carefully down and walked out of the bay.

As soon as the door closed behind him, Velda sat up, then got off the bed.

Ethan lay, restrained and unconscious, next to Park, the man who'd been shot by the Caruso. There was also the man they'd shot in the runner, Jint and Falre, the two men she'd shot in the room she'd been hiding in, as well as a fourth man. Maybe Ethan was responsible for this one.

It was getting crowded in here.

She moved between the beds and made her way to Ethan, whose stretcher had been placed up against the far wall.

She reached out and rested her hand along his jawline.

He is still recovering, the silver balls told her. *You will need to wait a little.*

She was so relieved he was going to be fine, she closed her eyes to force back tears, then bent and kissed his forehead, lingering a moment. When she lifted her head, she noticed the device that unlocked the restraints on the counter top, and took it to deal with Ethan's. She left them, open, on his wrists, though, so a quick look would hopefully reassure the crew that he was safely secured.

It was hard to go back to her bed and lie down, but she'd barely had time to climb onto it and close her eyes before the door reopened.

"Where's Yarmouth and why aren't you tied up?" The person speaking was not a voice Velda recognized.

Whoever they were, they took a few steps into the room, and then, before the door could close, someone else stepped in behind them.

"What are you doing here, Rist? Aren't you supposed to be protecting Sylvester?" Yarmouth sounded taken aback.

"Sylvester wanted me to make sure the woman is shackled. When he was here earlier with Linao, he noticed it wasn't done." Rist's voice was softly menacing.

"I've just done a scan. She's completely unconscious. She literally hasn't moved since she was brought in." Yarmouth's tone was just as soft.

"Lucky for you," Rist said. "Where are the shackles?"

"I'll get them." Yarmouth moved past him and Velda heard him moving things around in a cupboard. "Can you help me grab these?" he asked.

Rist gave a grunt of annoyance and moved away, and then Velda heard a thump.

She couldn't see what was happening, it was all going on behind her bed, but it sounded like Rist had just collapsed.

"I'm so tired of taking shit from these assholes," Yarmouth said.

He moved past her bed, touching her hand lightly as he went by, and the door opened up again and he was gone.

Why do they keep touching me? she asked the voices.

They feel a shot of happiness when they do. They can't help themselves, and it gives us more opportunities to make them protective of you. The voices sounded pleased.

Velda rose up on an elbow and twisted to look behind her.

Rist lay, collapsed, on the ground.

Velda thought he looked dead.

32

—————

Ethan came awake in a rush.

The door of whatever room he was in had just closed, but he knew, before he even opened his eyes, that Velda was here with him.

He sat up, just as she lifted up on an elbow and twisted to look behind her.

Five other people lay unconscious on stretchers between them.

He had been restrained, but the restraints were unlocked, which was confusing. He shook them off and as soon as he slid off the bed, he saw what Velda had turned to look at—a man lying dead on the med bay floor near the cupboards.

Velda turned at the sound of him moving around, and swung off the bed with the kind of smile he would remember in his darkest moments.

They did not say anything as they stepped into each others' arms and he held her as close as he could.

"You all right?" she whispered.

"Yes. You?"

She leaned back a little, and that laughter was dancing in her eyes. "Yes. I pretended to be unconscious to get in here. I hid the Caruson laz in the launch bay." She glanced at the body on the floor. "But Rist probably has a weapon on him, as well."

Ethan crouched beside the man and found he did have a weapon, strapped to his waist. When it was strapped to Ethan's waist, he felt a lot better.

"Someone will be coming to look for this one soon," Velda said, nodding toward Rist. "He's Sylvester's body guard and he was here to make sure the medic shackled me to the bed."

"Who killed him?" Ethan asked. "You?"

She shook her head. "The medic. He's gone, and the best thing for him, and us, is if we aren't here when he comes back."

She moved to the door, and it opened. She peered out cautiously, then waved to him to follow her.

He was still a little off, he realized. He hadn't thought to ask why the medic would have killed Rist.

He had taken two laz hits simultaneously, and his body hadn't liked it. Funny, he'd gone his whole life without ever being hit, and now, since the runner had gone down in the mountains, he'd had so many it was hard to count.

He trailed after Velda, the laz out of its holster and in his hand, his body feeling better and better with every step he took.

There was no one around on the short journey to the launch bay, and Velda waited for him by the doors.

"Ready?" she asked.

He was beyond ready.

She stepped in, and a man standing over an open box turned toward them, eyes only going wide when he realized who they were.

Ethan shot him.

"Can you hide him while I get the laz I hid?" Velda asked.

"Yes." He moved over to the crew member, saw the box was full of food supplies, and dragged the body behind some stacks. He took a package of food out of the crate and was shoving it into a pocket when Velda came from the back of the bay with the Caruson laz in her hand.

"Where to now?" he asked.

"There is no safe place," she said. "So we shoot everyone we see. Either we put them all in the runner and send it off the ship, or we hold them in a room."

"Off the ship," Ethan said. No question. He stopped trying to shove the too-big package of food into a pocket and handed it to Velda.

She opened it, handed him a nutrient bar, then took one herself.

"You're looking too thin," she said. She opened another two while they stood eating. Ethan reached for the second one, aware they were standing in the middle of the bay, with no cover.

Before he could suggest they move, the door opened, and Velda turned and shot the two guards that came through before they'd even lifted their own weapons.

He enjoyed watching her shoot them almost as much as if he'd shot them himself.

"Let's put them in the runner," she suggested.

He swallowed the last of the second bar and dusted off his hands. "Let's."

When all three were safely stacked side by side, he ate a third bar, drank some water from one of the bottles in the crate, and then eyed the bay door thoughtfully.

"You want to wait for them to come to us?" Velda asked.

"It's a plan." He thought it through. "It'll do for one or two more groups, then they'll start to realize something's off."

As he said it, the door opened again and another person walked in. Velda shot her, too.

"Milton," she said, as she grabbed her ankles and dragged her over to the runner. "I think she's head guard on the ship."

While they were inside the runner, placing Milton next to her fellow crew, the launch bay door opened yet again.

Ethan crouched down, edged to the runner door and looked out.

Two people had come in, and they walked over to the open crate and then looked around, confused, as if wondering where everyone was. Before they could do anything else, he shot them in quick succession, pleased that he'd hit exactly where he meant to, both times.

Always, the voices in his head said.

"Five down." Velda walked out, and began to pull one of the two up the ramp.

Ethan bent and lifted the other one, slung him over his shoulder and walked up behind her.

As well as being able to shoot more accurately, he was much stronger.

"How many more to go?" he wondered.

"There were six guards looking for me in here, plus the mechanic, plus Sylvester and Rist, plus Yarmouth, the medic. And Linao and the five guys still in the med bay. Plus the crew member we found unpacking the crate."

"Fifteen. Fourteen," he corrected himself. "Yarmouth took care of Rist. Do you recognize anyone other than Milton?"

Velda pointed to two of the guards. "I'm guessing there are more than ten more people out there."

"Before I was shot, I walked through the lounge area. There were at least ten people in there, and the bridge was beyond. Plus there was an armory and people in there. I think we might be looking at a crew of twenty to thirty."

That was a lot of people to find and shoot. Ethan looked at the neat line of people they'd already gotten in the ten minutes since they'd been in here.

Velda was standing beside him, calm, cool, and competent, and he pulled her in, kissed her, and she wound her arms around his neck and kissed him back.

Then she tucked her head under his chin and just held him. "I was so worried about you. When I had no choice but to let them find me, I pretended to be hurt, and they took me straight to you."

"Why did the medic kill Rist?" he asked, suddenly remembering the question he had earlier.

"The silver balls persuaded him I need to be protected." She shrugged, slightly embarrassed.

Well done, he thought, his hand brushing the back of her neck.

He felt a buzz under his fingertips, and a sense of happiness and pleasure.

"What now?" Velda asked.

"I think it's time to rampage through the ship."

33

They only left one body in their wake on the way to the bridge.

Even then, no one was dead, just unconscious. Velda didn't want to see anyone lose their lives or be seriously injured.

Ethan slowed as they got closer to the front of the ship, and carefully looked around the corner into the lounge.

"Can you create a diversion for me?" he asked softly when he pulled back.

Velda peered around herself, to get the lay of the land.

There were at least six people that she could see sitting around tables and on couches, talking to each other or eating something.

In front of the lounge area was a set of double doors leading to what she guessed was the bridge.

She handed her laz to Ethan. He had three already, one in his hand, two strapped behind him across his back, and he took hers and held it in his other hand.

She grinned at the sight of it, and he gave her a quick pose, both arms raised, with a snarling expression, and her smile widened.

"Right, enough fun and games, I need to get into character now," she whispered. "What's the plan?"

"Draw their attention, I'll do the rest." Ethan sounded absolutely sure of himself, and she had never once regretted trusting him.

She gave a nod, closed her eyes and drew in a deep breath, then ran around the corner into the lounge, both hands outstretched, wrists held together as if she was in restraints. "Can you help me? I don't know what's going on!"

She made sure her voice was just short of a shout, and gave it a wobble.

She stumbled and then went down on one knee.

Everyone turned toward her, some jumping to their feet, others leaning back in surprise.

She bowed her head, hands still outstretched and pressed together at the wrists, and the double doors to the bridge opened as the first person reached her.

"What is it?" The woman asking strode forward, and Velda recognized Brink immediately.

She was no longer on the ore runner, but had switched over to Sylvester's vessel, which according to Nirro was built using Caruson tech—so most likely a Raptor, one of the sleek black ships that the Cores had used since Cepi to wreak havoc in the Verdant String.

"Velda?" Brink drew up short. "Aren't you in the med bay—?" She looked to her right, down the passage on the opposite side of the ship to the one she and Ethan had come up, and Yarmouth stepped into the lounge.

"I've got a body in my med bay—" He stopped suddenly at the sight of Velda and the crew around her.

"Maybe Velda knows something about that?" Brink's tone was sharp.

"She's been unconscious until very recently," Yarmouth said, voice rising a little. "She probably came to and saw the carnage, same as me."

"Is that true?" Brink glanced quickly over her shoulder as the door to the bridge opened again.

As she turned back to face Velda, two men exited the bridge and moved toward them, and Velda caught sight of Ethan.

She didn't know how he'd done it, but he'd been edging closer to the bridge doors the whole time, and as the two men walked forward to join

Brink, he moved so fast she could barely track him, getting through the doors before they closed.

"Velda?" Brink's tone got even sharper.

"Sorry," she said, lifting her head to look at Brink, "I'm not feeling well."

"What happened?" Yarmouth moved toward her, and Velda hoped no one else heard the way his voice softened when he addressed her.

"I woke up and there was a dead man lying up against the counter. The man who watches Sylvester."

The moment she said that, one of the crew who'd been in the lounge ran down toward the med bay.

"Is it Rist?" Brink asked Yarmouth.

"Yes. I don't even know what he was doing in the med bay. I went to check on Linao because she insisted on going to her room after she woke and I was worried it was too soon. When I came back, Rist was just lying there."

Yarmouth sounded totally believable. Velda was impressed.

She would never have suspected he'd killed Rist himself unless she'd seen him do it.

As everyone gaped at Yarmouth, someone came running down the passageway she and Ethan had taken to get here.

The soldier who burst out into the lounge was the one who'd shot at Sylvester earlier. "Smitty is down, and there are five others obviously shot down in the launch bay."

The news had everyone gaping at him.

"The Caruson?" someone who'd been in the lounge eating a meal when she'd stumbled in asked.

"Shit." Brink drew her laz, and everyone who had one did the same. "I want two of you standing guard on each passageway into here. I need two more to come with me to see if Sylvester's all right."

She strode away, two nervous-looking crew with laz in hand trailing after her.

"Better sit down," Yarmouth said to her, holding out his hand to help her to her feet.

Velda took it, and he squeezed it a little tight and then led her to a couch.

"Thank you." She sat down and he stood, looking slightly lost for a moment.

"Yarmouth." Brink was back, and he turned to her. "Ethan Hyt is missing from the med bay. Did you know that?"

"What? No." Yarmouth moved toward her. "Do you think he could be responsible . . .?"

He played the confused medic well, but he had to know Ethan wasn't there because he must have noticed when he'd come back from setting up his alibi to 'discover' Rist's body.

"Maybe." Brink sounded a little calmer. Like she hoped it *was* Ethan's doing, and not the Caruso, back for a bit more vengeance.

Unfortunately for her, Ethan was not a better alternative.

Velda glanced at the bridge doors, wondering what was going on in there, when Sylvester suddenly came up from behind Brink. He was striding with purpose, his gaze locked onto the bridge doors and then to her.

Sylvester grabbed Brink's laz as he passed her, making her gasp in shock and then he pointed it straight at Velda's head.

"Get up and come here," he said.

She did so slowly, moving toward him as if she were injured.

There was only one reason Sylvester could be doing this.

"I have a secret comms feed on the bridge," he said, and she almost nodded.

It was the only thing that made sense.

He must have seen what Ethan was doing in there and come running over to try to mitigate the damage.

And she was the perfect hostage.

34

<hr>

"What's going on?" Brink's nostrils flared and she was staring at her laz, now in Sylvester's hand. She looked . . . displeased.

"Ethan Hyt's on the bridge. He's taken it over." Sylvester reached forward and grabbed Velda by her jacket as soon as she got close enough, then spun her around to face the bridge doors. He put the laz right up against her temple, the back of her collar twisted in his other fist. "This one distracted you while he slipped inside."

Brink gaped at him. "He's in there right now?" she asked.

As she said it, the bridge doors opened and Ethan stood in the opening, still with a laz in each hand. Behind him lay chaos, bodies sprawled on the floor and up against walls.

There must be some kind of comms feed visible on the bridge, which had shown him what was going on out here, because his gaze went straight to her.

She held it, gave the tiniest head shake and mouthed 'trust me', to him.

Because damned if they were going to give up the bridge and go back into a cell.

No way.

She would find a way out of this while he held the ship's controls.

She saw him consider the alternatives, when suddenly one of the guards seemed to shake off their surprise and opened fire on him. As he jumped back and closed the doors, he looked conflicted.

"Next time anyone shoots at him, aim for the head." Sylvester almost growled the words. "So he doesn't get back up again."

Someone came running down the passage and everyone, obviously still on edge, spun in that direction, weapons up.

Linao skidded to a stop. "What's going on? Vine says there are five crew unconscious in the launch bay." She caught sight of Velda, with her father's laz against her head, and she stopped dead. "Careful," she said.

"Are you talking to *me*?" Sylvester sounded outraged.

"Yes. You haven't ever used a laz, as far as I know," Linao said. "We don't want Velda hurt accidentally."

Velda remembered Linao had touched her in the med bay. Had pressed her fingertips into her cheek.

She doesn't want you to be harmed, the silver balls said. *Neither does the medic.*

How long will that last? Velda asked them.

Uncertain, was the answer. *We have never done it before.*

Linao and Yarmouth were obviously still feeling that sense of protection, so she would have to either get them to touch her again or make a move as soon as possible.

"I'll take her to a cell," Linao said, nodding toward Velda.

"You're not up to full strength yet," Yarmouth said. "I'll do it."

"No, I will." Sylvester hadn't made skin contact with her yet, but now he did, pulling her hard up against his chest with his hand resting just under her throat.

He turned and forced her to walk like that, uncomfortably close, and she tripped and staggered, gagging as his hand accidentally choked her more than once.

Eventually, he loosened his hold and rested his fingertips on her neck, and she noticed the laz no longer pressed up against her head, either. Or anywhere else.

Others came along with them, walking behind Sylvester, and she realized only when Sylvester led her into a large suite and finally let her go that it was Yarmouth and Linao who'd followed him, as well as Brink.

"What's going on, Sylvester?" Brink asked. "What's the plan?"

"We need to get the bridge back," Sylvester said, but he didn't have the same rage he'd had earlier.

"Ethan will cut his own throat for her, he'll definitely give up the bridge," Linao agreed.

"Then why didn't he do that?" Brink asked.

"He was ducking the shots," Yarmouth said. "Maybe if no one had used their weapons he would have come quietly."

"Maybe." Linao nodded slowly. "What do you think, Velda?"

Velda looked around for a chair and sat down slowly. Might be useful to still pretend she was getting over an injury. "I think Yarmouth is right. He acted on instinct, ducking away. But also, you've threatened to kill us quite a few times since we've been your prisoners, Linao. If he gave up the bridge to save my life, what're the odds it would really be saved?"

There was silence.

"That's true," Brink said. "I heard you tell them they were both as good as dead myself."

"That's . . . unfortunate," Sylvester said. "However true you thought that was, it means he doesn't have any incentive to comply."

"I have a suggestion." Velda leaned back. "One that will give us both what we want." She hoped. She was stepping into the unknown with this idea, but it still felt better than being at Sylvester's mercy.

The fact that Sylvester had brought her to his own suite, and was treating her more as a guest than a prisoner, made her hope this negotiation would go her way.

"What suggestion is that?" Sylvester asked. He seemed uncomfortable in his own skin, moving around the room as if unable to settle.

"Is there an exit from the bridge directly to the outside of the ship?" Velda asked. She knew that was standard on most VSC ships, because the bridge was usually the most secure room on a warship. It had never been needed before, to her knowledge, but an emergency exit from the bridge, in case a ship was overrun, was standard.

Sylvester hesitated, then nodded.

"What are you thinking?" Linao asked.

"That you give me the runner in the launch bay, and I'll collect Ethan and we'll be out of your hair. As soon as the crew on the bridge that

Ethan shot come to, they can open up again, and you'll have your ship back, and you'll be rid of us." It sounded like the best of a bad deal to her.

Hopefully, she and Ethan could make a run for Aponi, if they weren't too far away.

There was silence for a moment.

"That would work," Brink said. "We'd be down the runner . . ."

"You'd be up a ship," Velda countered.

"We could threaten to kill you where he can see it," Sylvester said. "He'll probably come out."

"Or he could take Linao at her word and pilot this ship straight back home to Aponi, and you'd all be in jail." Velda wondered if Sylvester was more resistant to the silver balls than the others, because he wasn't bluffing about shooting her.

She guessed the answer was yes. He had been willing to sacrifice his own daughter numerous times and likely didn't have much capacity to feel protective. She wondered if he was a psychopath.

Direct contact with her skin had softened him a little, but it wasn't enough to overcome his inability to feel any emotion.

"I don't want to lose the runner, and I don't want to lose you as a hostage," Sylvester said. "I have plans."

So he would shoot her, but not kill her. That was something.

"Let's talk about this," Linao said. "We could be worse off your way, Father. I've spent time with Ethan, locked up in a cell, and he's a good strategist."

Sylvester shot her a quick, hot look, but before he could respond, there was a chime from the door.

"Enter." Sylvester turned his back on Linao deliberately.

A crew member Velda had never seen before stood there in a dark uniform, swaying nervously. "There's a problem with the engine," he said.

"What kind of problem?" Sylvester took a step closer. "Does the problem originate from the bridge?"

"No." The engineer shook his head. "No. It's a mechanical fault. I don't know what's causing it, but no one on the bridge could affect it."

"Can you fix it?" Brink asked.

"We've had to stop the engine. I don't want to risk permanent damage. Especially as we don't have a way to get spare parts right now." The engineer clasped his hands together.

"The timing is suspicious," Sylvester said. As he said it, the lights went out. They were plunged into darkness, but before Velda could consider moving, she heard the door close.

"Don't even think about running," Sylvester said, and then light bloomed in his hand as he activated a portable illuminator. He was looking right at her and had Brink's laz pointed at her again. "What do you know about this?"

"Nothing." It could be Ethan, but she didn't know for sure.

"How did you get the door to close so fast?" Brink asked in admiration.

"I didn't. I think it was part of the same shutdown as the lights going off," Sylvester said. "Yarmouth, try to get it open."

Yarmouth's mouth flickered into a grim line at the dismissive order, then relaxed again, and he walked to the door and tried a few times to open it. "No go," he said.

"Maybe it's the Caruso," Linao said. "They were pretty unhappy with us."

"And why is that, Linao?" Sylvester asked. "You were supposed to ease our people off their ship, and leave them thinking we were friends, and suddenly they're shooting our team. Where did that come from?"

"Nirro found out we were talking to the Caruso government. He took that news badly. Thought we were stabbing him in the back." Linao was only just visible in the glow of the light Sylvester was holding, but Velda could see her nonchalant shrug.

"And how did he find that out?" Sylvester's question was soft.

"You told me to ask him if he'd seen the silver balls before. When he denied it, I brought up I knew he'd been on that Caruson warship that tried to steal the ancestral ghost ship in Raxian airspace. He worked out the only way we could have known that information was from government sources."

"You could have sold the story that we still have spies there," Sylvester said.

"I could have, but before I could say a word, he shot me," Linao said. "Have you ever been hit by a Caruson laz?"

There was a beat of silence.

"If it is the Caruso playing with the ship's power, how are they doing it?" Brink asked, eventually breaking the tension. "Did they plant a virus in the comms system?"

"If they did, we could only see that if we had access to the bridge." Sylvester turned suddenly as the door opened.

"The doors have emergency opening protocols," the engineer who'd been talking to Sylvester before the lights went out said. He was holding a tool of some kind in his hand. "I'll have to open each one individually, though."

"Get to it, then." Sylvester stepped out of the room, taking the light with him. "Brink and Linao, watch her while I do a full ship check. Yarmouth, get back to the med bay."

He strode out, leaving everyone looking after him. None of the expressions were friendly.

As he turned into the passage, they were plunged back into darkness, and Brink moved around, banging into a few things, and finally activated another portable light.

Everyone's faces spoke volumes when they were finally illuminated again.

"He's a charmer," Velda said into the silence.

Linao gave a sudden chuckle. "Oh, yes. That's Sylvester."

Yarmouth cleared his throat. "Do you need anything before I go?"

Velda was sure he was talking to her, but Linao assumed the question was addressed to her and answered.

"No, I'm feeling fine, thanks, Yarmouth. Better get on or you know he'll have a tantrum."

Yarmouth left reluctantly.

"Do you think Yarmouth's afraid of the dark?" Brink asked when he was gone.

"Probably afraid of the Caruso," Linao said. "And he's not wrong there."

"No." Brink sighed and then sat on the arm of the chair beside Velda's. "Things have gone wrong for us since the coup on Aponi failed."

"Since Fjern," Linao corrected. "When we blew up one of our own warships."

"I thought that warship was never going to fly again anyway," Brink said.

"That's probably true," Linao said, "but it told the crew, and me, everything we needed to know about how quick my father would be to cut us off, if there was even a hint that someone could gain an advantage over him. In the Fjern case, it wouldn't have even been an advantage that would have affected him. Certainly not in the short term." She lowered herself into a chair as well. "Sure, the Fjerna would have been able to gain some information about our tech if the warship had remained intact, but it would have taken them years to translate that into an edge, if they ever did."

"The protocol is clear, though," Brink said. "If you're unable to escape, the ship you're on will be destroyed. That's what they did at Cepi and after the Parn incident."

"Only in VSC territory," Linao said, and while there was a calm to her voice, Velda thought she detected something darker just beneath the surface. "We were on a completely unknown planet, with different, and less sophisticated tech, and we had runners onboard that would have meant we could have ferried everyone up to the second ship. But no . . . Captain Vanburren jumped straight to 'protocol' and blew my ship up. And all the ore on it. And only moments after I got out. As far as I'm concerned, he tried to assassinate me, and my father has defended him at every turn."

"Yeah, put like that, it wasn't necessary." Brink shifted a little to get more comfortable. "I'd be a little upset about it."

"A little upset." Linao gave a low laugh. "I've been in a fucking rage ever since."

That explained so much. The oversharing, the subtle undermining of her father's goals. Everything.

Linao was a ticking bomb, just waiting for the best time to explode.

Linao leaned forward, and Velda realized she wasn't finished. "It wasn't just that Vanburren nearly killed me, it was that he knowingly stranded us on a hellhole planet. He had no idea whether we'd be able to negotiate a way off, or even if the Fjerna wouldn't simply kill us where we stood. My guess is he knew it would be a hard, uncomfortable trip back with my crew and his having to share a ship, and he tried to make it so that couldn't happen. The only thing my father did right for me was insisting that Vanburren get us off, and that was after a week of imprisonment."

"Then you landed in jail again on Aponi," Brink said. "I guess no one can say you don't put yourself on the line for the cause."

"And what is the cause?" Velda asked. This is what she had been trying to work out for a long time.

"A new breakaway planet, of course," Linao said, sliding her a look. The yellow glow of the portable light Brink had set on the low table made her eyes gleam.

"That's it? And you thought you could make Aponi that planet?" She couldn't understand the logic. The VSC would not stand for it. They hadn't stood for the rebel takeover of Faldine—they'd fought a war over it—and they had just taken Garmen and Lassa, the old breakaway planets, back.

"The Cores leadership thought with the Caruso patrolling the airspace, we could." Brink shrugged. "I wasn't sure it would work, but it beat being constantly on the run."

"What are you, personally, on the run for?" Velda asked. Brink seemed reasonable enough, and she wondered what she thought she would be in trouble for if she surrendered to the VSC.

"I was part of the security forces on Lassa," Brink said. "There were a lot of people killed there, and I'm honest enough with myself to admit I was responsible for some of those deaths."

"And you?" Velda asked Linao. "You were on Garmen, right?"

"Some of the time," Linao admitted. "Mostly, I was spying throughout the VSC. Those were the fun days, when we were still semi-respectable, and there was no real danger in admitting where I was from."

"And then it all went sideways," Velda said.

"It was always going to go sideways," Linao said. "Because the worse things got, the more the VSC were inclined to interfere. And my father and his cohorts never understood that some social care would have gone a very long way. They wouldn't even properly furnish the offices of their own workers, let alone pave the streets or build schools."

"And then trying to steal tech off Cepi and all the rest didn't help," Brink agreed. "It just accelerated the downfall." She sighed. "And while I know things were bad on Garmen, on Lassa, it was worse."

"That's hard to imagine," Linao said, "but I had heard that."

"Believe me, the main Cores player on Lassa was almost insane toward the end. I'm not sure what was going on, but I saw some footage of him that came off unhinged." Brink hunched a little. "That's when my boss and I got out, and hooked up with Sylvester."

As if saying his name conjured him up, Sylvester was suddenly in the open doorway. "The whole engine room is down," he said. "It's probably the Caruso, because their tech built a lot of this ship. I think they may have built in a backdoor."

Linao let out a quick laugh. "That makes sense."

Sylvester sent her a dark look. "We need to get the bridge back. I'm going to pull Henry off opening the other doors on the ship and get him started on the bridge doors. I'm not losing my star hostage or my runner, so let's go, Velda Shanïha. We're going to persuade your bodyguard to surrender once Henry has reset the automatic opening protocol, or I'll shoot you."

"Shoot me, and there's no incentive for him to give you anything," she said.

"I can hurt you, though," Sylvester said. "I can hurt you until he gives up."

Well, that was no good.

No, the silver balls said. *That is not going to happen.*

Sylvester grabbed her by the upper arm and hauled her up.

"Hang on a moment," Linao said. "I just need to grab something."

She disappeared into the dark recesses of the room, and Velda heard her opening a drawer in the little built-in kitchen.

"You'll have to catch up." There was an impatient snap in Sylvester's voice. "I don't have time to wait for you."

He began to drag Velda to the door, and then suddenly, Linao was there, one hand on Sylvester's shoulder.

Sylvester flinched, then staggered back, fetching up against the wall.

He looked down at his side and Velda saw the sudden bloom of blood.

"When do you ever wait for me?" Linao asked him. "When do you ever give a single shit?" She stabbed him again.

"Linao—" Brink hesitated, unsure what to do.

Velda almost laughed out of sheer astonishment. Talk about things going sideways. This was headed for upside down.

"Shoot her," Sylvester ground out, bending a little.

"I can't," Brink said slowly. "You took my laz."

As if suddenly realizing he had it, Sylvester fumbled with it, but before he could lift it, Linao stabbed him a third time and wrenched it out of his hand.

"I've been out there, stabbing, shooting, and murdering for you. I'm way ahead when it comes to killing," she said, and Velda thought she sounded almost cheerful.

"What was your suggestion, Velda? That we give you the runner, you get Ethan off the bridge, and you head off?" Brink stood, hands a little away from her sides, talking as if Sylvester wasn't slowly sliding down the wall, leaving a trail of smeared blood behind him.

"Yes, that's my suggestion." How much of this was the silver balls, how much was the final tipping point of years of resentment, Velda wondered.

Unsure, the silver balls said. *But the result is the same.*

The result was seriously crazy.

"I'll take Sylvester to Yarmouth," Brink said, and her tone was a little too bright. "Will you take Velda to the runner, Linao?"

Linao stepped back. "Sure. I can do that."

35

Velda considered making a run for it, but Linao was taking her where she wanted to go, and she was still holding the knife, dripping a trail of blood behind them.

Perversely, she was glad when Linao reached out and gripped her wrist to keep a hold of her. The silver balls could do their magic.

Neither of them spoke. Velda was hesitant to bring up what had happened, and Linao was obviously deep in thought.

They reached the launch bay, and found people inside taking the five crew Velda and Ethan had left in the runner out on stretchers. They had set temporary lights throughout the space, lighting it up in the power outage as best they could.

She and Linao politely moved to the side to let them pass, in what was surely one of the more bizarre events she'd experienced since this whole thing began.

They had just reached the open rear of the runner when the launch bay doors opened behind them and a team of four guards entered.

They were all armed with laz, and they looked grim.

"Kilber," Linao said to the one in the lead. "You're looking serious."

"Your father told us to stop you from letting the woman have the runner," Kilber said.

"If we don't, we won't get back control of the bridge," Linao said. "And given the Caruso are using a backdoor to cut off the engine and power, we need it."

Kilber jerked up a single shoulder. "I hear you. I'm telling you what my orders are."

"So what am I supposed to do with her?" Linao asked.

"I'm supposed to take both of you back to a cell." Kilber looked even more discomforted. "Sorry, that's what I've been told."

"Well," Linao spread both hands, and Velda realized her knife had somehow vanished, "neither of us is armed, so I don't suppose I have a choice."

Kilber nodded, relaxing slightly as he moved forward with the other three guards.

There was no doubt Linao had something planned, but it was nihilistic at best. She could only stab a few before someone shot her, and maybe shot Velda, too.

And Velda did not want that to happen, quite badly.

As the guards came toward her, Velda felt a tentative request for control, and after a beat of hesitation, accepted it.

She *moved*.

She leaped forward and grabbed the laz from the guard closest to her. She spun around behind him, and shot him and one other guard in the back before the other two had even begun to turn around.

Linao had drawn her knife, but the moment she saw Velda was attacking, she took a deliberate step back, knife against her thigh, and merely watched.

Velda leaped again, to the right of the other two men, taking them by surprise as they raised their weapons to where she had been standing, and she angled to shoot them in the back, too, before they worked out where she had gone.

Then she pivoted, laz up, as Linao took a step toward her.

"Throw the knife," Velda said.

Linao tossed it to the side and put both hands up. "Well, well. Ritter was completely wrong."

"I don't know what you're talking about." Velda bent and picked up the other three laz, tucking them under her left arm. "You're free and clear of this. No blame can fall on you whatsoever. You can head out of here and murder your father, or whatever you feel like."

Linao actually laughed at that, and began to walk backward toward the bay doors. "Thanks. I'm assuming you're going to grab Ethan and go your separate way?"

"Yes." Velda was walking backward herself, headed up the ramp at the back of the runner. "Don't come looking for us."

Linao gave a salute and stepped out of the bay.

The moment the doors closed on her, Velda hit the button to close the runner doors, threw the three laz down in the runner's back area, and ran to the pilot's door, which she also closed. Then she sat down in the pilot's chair and stared at the instrumentation panel.

"What now?" she asked.

Put your hands on the controls, the silver balls said.

She did, and after a moment's resistance to the feeling of her hands doing something she wasn't telling them to do, she relaxed and let herself switch on the engine and pilot the runner around the stacks of supplies, through the airlock barrier and out.

The moment she was free of the ship, the tight coil of nerves inside her began to relax. She let the runner drift as it moved out into space, and then dropped it until they were directly under the bridge.

She didn't know where the emergency exit was located, but it had to be somewhere above her head. "Can you set the runner to hold in place?" she asked.

The silver balls manipulated her hands, and then lifted them up.

Done, they told her.

She rose and moved to the rear, then began to look through the storage areas built into the wall. There should be line walking equipment back here. At least one set.

She found two sets, which was a huge relief, and pulled on the bulky suit over her clothes, the helmet with its small air cylinders, the gloves and the weighted boots.

Then she climbed up the tiny ladder set on the side of the wall, and hauled herself into the tiny air lock chamber.

As soon as she could, she opened it up and floated straight out, grateful she'd had the sense to keep hold of the handle underneath the airlock lid.

She looked straight up and saw nothing but the smooth underside of the Raptor, so she carefully grabbed a handle on the roof of the runner, and then the next, moving across the space at an excruciatingly slow pace, looking up after each small advancement.

Finally, she found what she was looking for. A faint circle set in the underside of the ship.

It was possible that someone on the bridge could push a button and make it easy to connect the emergency exit to the runner, but she had no way of contacting Ethan to ask him to do that.

They would have to do this the hard way.

36

ETHAN WAS GOING JUST A LITTLE MAD.

It had taken time to find a portable light, but now he had one set up, the bridge had become like a badly illuminated cave. He almost felt trapped underground.

It had been over an hour since he'd seen Sylvester holding a laz to Velda's head, and he'd contemplated leaving the bridge and going to find her over and over again.

But she had mouthed 'trust me' and that had put a chain on his protectiveness.

She wanted time. He would give her time.

She had a way about her. It had affected the Caruso. It had affected the medic, Yarmouth.

She would work her magic and make a plan.

She hadn't wanted him to give up the bridge, so he would hold it. But if he didn't get some sign she was all right soon, he would have to reconsider his options.

He eyed the seven people he'd shot and stacked side by side on one side of the bridge. He'd found restraints for four of them, and he kept checking to make sure the other three weren't coming to.

It probably wouldn't be long before they did.

He wanted off this ship so badly, he almost wished they'd taken the runner when they'd had access to the launch bay, but that wasn't going to get them far. He reckoned they'd be better off taking the whole ship and flying back to Aponi.

That was before the Caruso's virus had taken out the power.

He and the silver balls had tried to find out how they'd done it, but the silver balls were new to Caruso tech and while they thought with enough time they could do it, it would not be quick.

He looked over at the lens he'd covered with a black cloth before the power cut out, and wished he'd noticed it earlier.

Sylvester had obviously seen him in here, and he'd grabbed Velda straight away.

He wished now he'd found a way to take the bridge with her, rather than ask her to be a diversion.

They had both paid the price for that mistake.

He only hoped the Caruso's interference was at least adding to the chaos out there, which would help Velda to escape.

All he could see from the tiny one way window set into the bridge doors were two guards, a portable light sitting on a table between them, both with weapons firmly aimed where he would have to come out.

There was a knock against the floor near his feet. It sounded like someone was hitting the underneath of the ship with a hammer.

He lifted up the light and moved carefully over to where he'd heard the noise, and noticed the faint outline of a circle on the floor. It was relatively large—wide enough for two people to stand inside it comfortably—and as he stared at it, it lifted up, spun clockwise, and then flipped open.

He stepped closer, laz raised, and found Velda, standing in a shoulder-height airlock chamber, looking up at him.

"Hey, there," she said, and lifted up her hands.

He shifted his weapon over his shoulder, set down the light, and lifted her onto the bridge.

"How?" He ran his hand over her hair, breathing in the cold tang of space on her.

"I've got the runner hovering below. I've got an extra suit because we're going to have to crawl over the roof, and then we're going to leave this whole mess behind us." She hugged his waist in a tight squeeze and then stepped back. "Looks like your victims are coming round."

He glanced over his shoulder and saw two of the bridge crew were beginning to move restlessly.

It was time to go.

He peered into the airlock and saw a neat pile of helmets and boots.

Velda was already perched on the edge of the hole, and she dropped in, careful not to land on the equipment.

She made room for him, and he dropped in beside her.

"You'll have to crouch," she said. "So do I, but you might need to actually sit down." She put her hand on the airlock lid. "I'll wait until you're ready because it's pretty dark in there when the door closes."

He sat, swapping out the boots he was wearing with the heavier pair Velda had brought for him in quick movements, then pulled on the helmet and the gloves.

As soon as he nodded to her she put her own helmet on and activated the airlock again, so it closed above them.

She was right—they were plunged into absolute darkness for a few minutes, and in that time she sat beside him and found his hand so she could hold it.

Then the floor beneath them lit up a fluorescent blue, and she hopped up into a crouch.

"Grab a handle," she said. "This thing was obviously designed for people who had an actual line attached to them before they opened up. And we don't have one."

He saw there were handles all around the chamber and held on to the closest one. Velda was already holding one, and she activated the lower lock.

It jerked open and then lowered, lowering them with it, with two struts keeping it attached to the ship as it exposed them to space.

Just beneath the disc they were standing on was the runner, holding in place, and Velda grabbed a strut and stepped out onto the runner's roof and then crouched, grabbing a handle there, and moving out of the way so Ethan could join her.

Once he had, she sent the airlock back up into place and then he followed her to the airlock she'd left open on the runner.

He kept his breathing easy and even, and waited for her to get in before he followed.

As he climbed after her, away to the left, he saw a ship heading toward them.

It was, without a doubt, the Caruson warship they had left earlier.

He dropped in, and pulled the lid closed behind him, plunging them into darkness. "The Caruson are here."

"Damn. I wondered whether it was them fooling with the power, or you." Velda felt around for him, and he reached out and grabbed both her hands.

"It was the Caruso. Looks like Nirro changed his mind about taking the Raptor back." He had seemed angry about leaving Sylvester to get away with the ship, and maybe, in the end, he couldn't accept it.

"It could be he didn't know about the backdoor into their power systems until after he let us go," Velda said. "He'd only just taken control of the warship, after all."

The light in the airlock came on, and they both removed their helmets as the door unlocked.

Ethan dropped down and raised his arms to lift Velda out. He wanted to stand and just hold her, but the Caruso might not be quite so friendly with them this time.

Things had obviously changed.

They needed to go, and go now.

37

———

"Velda Shanïha." The voice coming through the comms unit was clearly Nirro's.

"Captain Nirro." Velda leaned forward. "I see you decided to come back for the Raptor after all."

"I discovered there was a way into its systems that I wasn't aware of before," Nirro said. "It was too tempting not to exploit."

"Well, I wish you the best of luck with it." She glanced at the screen, saw Nirro's ship was now hovering above the Raptor. "We managed to get off, so it's no business of ours, one way or the other."

"I saw you leaving in the runner," Nirro said. "Unfortunately, part of the backdoor that had been set up in the Raptor included hidden visual comms, and we were able to see both you and Ethan overcome your enemies. It was . . . surprising."

Velda hoped he wasn't saying what she thought he was saying. "Why do you say 'unfortunately'?" she asked.

"Because you are quite obviously affected by those silver balls, contrary to what you told me, and since we've had a chance to search our ship after we got the Cores crew off it, we also discovered all the balls that fell to the ground in the med bay are nowhere to be found. And then when we checked the feed, we saw them come straight to you two." He drew in a breath. "That was sneaky, Velda."

"What does it matter to you?" Ethan asked. "The silver balls kill you. They're no use to you."

"That's where you're wrong," Nirro said. "They're useful to me because they do kill my kind. I have people back on Caruso that are very difficult to get close enough to to kill. But send them a silver ball and just like that, my problems are over."

"So you want to extract the balls from us and use them to assassinate the current leaders of Caruso?" Velda asked.

"Exactly," Nirro said. "That's exactly what I plan to do."

"You're sure the extractor is still working?" Ethan asked. "I thought it was thrown onto the floor."

"No, it's quite safe. Only the box that contained the balls went onto the floor," Nirro said. "And those balls rolled straight to you."

Velda reached forward and cut the comms. "Thoughts?" she asked.

This was a blow. She'd hoped they could get away with no one all that interested in stopping them.

Ethan reached over and squeezed her hand before going back to the runner's controls. "We get away as fast as we can. Nirro wants the Raptor, and he can't afford to delay taking it back for much longer. The crew might have already gotten onto the bridge by now, and if they can find a way to get the backdoor closed down, he'll lose his advantage."

She nodded. "And with Sylvester injured, now's the time for him to strike. If he saw you and me being super soldiers, he saw that Sylvester is badly injured, and he'll want to take advantage of that, too."

Ethan's gaze snapped to her face. "How was Sylvester badly injured?"

"Linao stabbed him when he threatened to hurt me." She thought there was more to it than the protectiveness the silver balls had encouraged in Linao. It was years of resentment and anger finally boiling over.

Ethan shook his head. "And then what happened?"

Velda gave a laugh. "It was strange. Like I didn't know how to respond strange. Linao stabbed him a few times, and Brink didn't know what to do. She was angry with Sylvester as well, and I could see she sympathized with Linao, so she said she'd take Sylvester to the med bay and

Linao could take me to the runner and get me off the ship, even though Sylvester had just said he didn't want to do that."

Ethan gaped at her. "And she just did?"

"She did, but Sylvester obviously managed to assert himself a bit more when he got to the med bay, because he sent four guards to stop Linao and me. They got to us as we reached the runner. That's when I had to go into silver ball mode, and I guess Nirro saw that through whatever secret feed he has access to. Linao did, too, unfortunately. And she looked pretty interested. I made her leave the launch bay before I took the runner, and it's possible she went straight off to the med bay to finish her father off. He may be dead."

Silver ball mode, the silver balls thought inside her head with amusement. *We like it.*

"If he's dead, or even just badly injured, then yes, Nirro would be crazy to chase after us instead of taking the ship." Ethan brought up a view of the Raptor and Velda leaned closer to see.

"The Caruso are not chasing us." She watched as the larger ship hovered above the Raptor.

"They're not chasing us *yet*." Ethan said. "So let's not be anywhere near them when they think about running us down."

It really was all they could do.

"How far are we from Aponi?" she asked.

Ethan turned to her, scooped her up, and lifted her into his lap, and she twined her arms around him.

"That far?"

He chuckled, the sound a deep, rumbling vibration through her. "Yes."

"Really?"

He pulled up a screen, and she looked over at it.

"We're somewhere I've never seen. We pinched to the black twice, if you remember, way back at the start of the journey and have traveled who-knows-where since. Maybe we could have figured it out in the Raptor if the Cores have the right maps, but in this runner . . .?" He trailed off. "I don't even know which direction to go."

"So my clever idea wasn't so clever." She should have found a way to keep them on the bridge.

It had been worth a try, but she had no way to know where they were when she'd negotiated to take the runner. She'd hoped—obviously fool-ishly—that Sylvester would have wanted to be near enough to Aponi to swoop in and take control of it when his troops were done.

"There was no good choice." Ethan flicked the screen away. "I couldn't have held the bridge with no supplies, and anyway, the Caruso had cut the power. The Raptor would have been of no use to us, either way, and the Caruso would have us as prisoners if we'd stayed. At least we have control over our environment and some supplies right now."

So there was no winning, and if the Caruso were coming after them, they'd be prisoners again soon enough, given there was nowhere to run to.

She kissed Ethan's cheek and rested her head on his shoulder. "Are we giving up?"

"Let's keep going for a bit. It isn't over 'til it's over." He didn't sound very optimistic, though.

They might as well, Velda decided. The Caruso seemed to respect a strong opponent, and given the change in tone with Nirro, respect was better than nothing.

38

VELDA HAD FALLEN ASLEEP.

Ethan stood with her still in his arms and walked back to the rear of the runner.

The benches on either side would do as beds, but they couldn't lie together this time. It was way too narrow.

They also couldn't afford to both be asleep at the same time, as the runner didn't have the technical specs to fly itself through space without pilot input.

Ethan lay Velda across the bench and stood over her for a moment. It was hard to take a step back, as if he was more himself, more content, when they were touching.

He forced himself to turn and find a blanket in one of the storage units, and tucked it around her before he moved back to the pilot's seat.

He brought up the scan of what lay ahead of them. He couldn't call it a map because it was simply what the less-than-powerful runner instruments could make out. This was not a known sector, there was no match-up of planets and other celestial bodies that corresponded to any map in the system.

And that worried him.

They would be pursued by Nirro as soon as the Caruson rebel leader had taken Sylvester's ship. Nirro had made that clear.

And they had nowhere to hide. No destination where they could seek sanctuary.

Nothing but space and limited supplies.

They might actually have to turn and go back.

Not something he wanted to do.

A warning chime sounded from the panel, and he pulled up the rear lens view.

A runner was behind them, and by the looks of it, it was Caruson.

Before he could open a line of communication, it shot them, taking out the runner's engine in a precise strike.

The runner jerked and then began to drift, and Ethan realized he was impressed.

The hit had barely rocked the ship, let alone jostled him.

The larger runner slid over them, a mechanical arm shot out and clamped them, and then the runner jerked as they were towed back.

Ethan stood, his presence in the pilot's seat no longer required, and went to the rear to check on Velda. She was still sleeping, and he realized he was running low on sleep himself.

He lay down on the other bench, hands behind his head, ankles crossed, and let himself doze, working through various ways to get out of this predicament.

When they began to slow he got up and went to the pilot's seat and activated the feed, saw that they were approaching the Caruson ship, which was now beside the Raptor, with a short tunnel visible between the two ships.

He walked back and gently shook Velda awake.

She came to slowly, with a sleepy smile. "Hey." Then, as if sensing something was wrong, she frowned. "What is it?"

"They chased us down with one of their own runners, shot out our engine, and have been towing us back for the last hour. I think we're approaching the Caruson ship right now." He brushed her hair back off her forehead.

"And you let me sleep." She swung her legs down and stretched, sent him a sidelong look. "Got a plan?"

He shrugged. "I've got no idea how we're going to get out of this."

"We'll think of something." She got to her feet, standing shoulder to shoulder with him as the runner jerked and then thumped down hard on a metal surface.

Ethan hoped she was right.

***

They were taken straight to the med bay.

Velda shouldn't have been surprised, but she did think they'd be left in their old cell for a bit first.

Nirro was obviously in a hurry to get the silver balls and put his assassination plans into motion.

Ethan had told her the Raptor was joined to the Caruson ship via an inter-ship tunnel. She wondered if Nirro had full control yet, or whether they were still fighting it out.

Whatever the case, it hadn't diverted Nirro from also going after them, it seemed.

Two Caruson she didn't recognize were in the med bay, waiting for them, and they were both given chairs to sit on.

They were restrained, which was perhaps the result of Nirro watching them attack the Cores, but after a while she was offered a cup of water, and Velda wondered if the silver balls were undermining their worry over her abilities, or if the fact that she was so much slimmer and smaller than them made them unable to take her seriously as a threat.

They definitely treated her better than anyone else, loosening one of the restraints so she could drink.

"Can Ethan have some, too?" she asked, and after a moment of consideration, they gave him a cup.

They were clearly waiting for someone—Velda guessed Nirro—and when they got bored, one of the Caruson took a diagnostic wand and waved it over both of them and noted the readouts, almost as something to do rather than out of medical curiosity.

They were here to extract the balls for the balls' sake, not for any experiment or theory.

Velda could even see the extractor, sitting where she remembered it being before, on the counter where it had been left after the Caruson soldier had died and Ritter had been shot.

What would it feel like to have the silver balls removed?

You'll never find out, they told her.

She wondered how that could be true. They had been removed over and over again in the experiments Ritter had conducted on the crew.

We were still waking up, the balls said. *We were absorbing information. And then he left us for a few days, and we decided that we did not want to go back into the box again. And then we were given to you.*

I'm glad you were, Velda told them, and was surprised to realize she meant it.

Eventually, well over an hour later, Nirro stepped into the room.

He looked like he'd been fighting, and Velda noticed some blood spray on his forearm. There was a gleam in his eye that told her he had been enjoying himself, and the blood-smudged blade at his waist told her he had been using it rather than a laz.

"Have you taken the Raptor?" she asked.

"Not quite yet. They're very stubborn." Nirro shrugged. "They're lucky they got rid of our backdoor intrusion moments before we boarded them, so it was harder for us to take the ship. It's inevitable, though."

It probably was, but if the backdoor was gone and the ship wasn't actually under Caruson control, the Raptor wouldn't be a bad option for escape. If they could get to it.

Velda slid Ethan a look and he gave a tiny nod of agreement.

"You fight with blades as well as laz?" Velda didn't know why that was so shocking to her.

"Laz are good ranged weapons," Nirro said. "Blades are good for close work."

And taking a ship was very close work.

Velda tried to keep her features serene.

"You ran," Nirro said.

"You'd have, too." Velda pretended calm, stretching out her legs and looking up at him. "Given the same circumstances."

Nirro paused, gave a laugh. "You're right. I don't blame you for it, and it didn't cause me too much trouble, given there's nowhere to run to."

"About that." Velda leaned forward. "Where are we?"

"Out near some planet Sylvester's people found some months ago. Already inhabited, but difficult to take over, given the threat level of the indigenous species."

"Fjern?" Velda couldn't help the way her voice lifted in surprise. "We're near Fjern?"

"Is that what it's called?" Nirro shrugged. "Sylvester promised us it contained the motherlode of ore that we needed, but I gather from listening to the hidden comms my people set up in the Raptor that they barely came away with their lives last time. It was then that it occurred to me that Sylvester was perhaps setting us up to take all the risks, and maybe was hoping we'd be a much diminished force at the end of the trip."

"All the better for Sylvester to make a new deal with your government, in exchange for you defeated, and their warship back. And with them owing him a massive debt," Velda mused. "One they could discharge by helping him take Aponi."

"Exactly," Nirro agreed. "It was only a suspicion, until Linao made it clear she had intelligence from the Caruso establishment about where I'd served before."

And that had been the last straw for the Caruson commander, Velda realized.

"Still, it was a long term plan," Velda said. "It's not as if you could set up a mine on Fjern overnight."

"Apparently there's already one down there." Nirro lifted a shoulder. "So not that long term."

"And how far is Aponi from here?" she asked. Because as much as she wanted to see Fjern, it was more important to get back to Aponi.

Nirro studied her, then flicked a look at Ethan. "Nice moves on the bridge," he said, without answering. "I had a feeling something was up with you. You, though," he turned back to Velda, "I was surprised at what happened in the launch bay. You hadn't shown any sign of enhancement before that."

Velda just lifted her brows.

"Well, that's over for you both. Where's the device?" He addressed one of their guards, and the soldier handed over the extractor.

Nirro went to Ethan first and unclipped one restraint. "Hand out flat."

Ethan lifted his hand, palm up, and waited, his gaze fixed on Nirro's face.

Nirro switched the little machine on and pressed it into Ethan's palm.

Nothing happened.

Nirro stepped back, frowning, and turned it off and on again. Put it back on Ethan's hand.

The smell of burning wires and electronics suddenly became evident.

Nirro's face went hard. "No." He put the extractor down on the counter, and then stepped back when it made a strange popping sound and smoke escaped from a thin join on one side.

The two guards edged a little closer to the door in the tense silence, and then Nirro turned suddenly to Ethan, lifting the curved blade from his belt and bringing it down on him.

Except, Ethan wasn't sitting in the chair.

Nirro had undone the restraints on his right hand, Velda recalled. And then everyone's gaze had gone to the extractor.

She smiled in satisfaction as Ethan seemed to float through the room, using whatever came to hand as a weapon, bringing down both guards, shooting Nirro with one of their laz.

It felt like reality restarted as Ethan bent down on one knee beside her to release her from her restraints, three Caruson lying around her.

"That was beautiful," she said.

He shot her a look, serious and focused. "Beautiful?"

"Very." She grabbed up a laz, hefted it. "Let's find out how to get on the Raptor."

39

THEY DIDN'T TRY TO SNEAK.

They shot their way through the Caruson ship, until they found the inter-ship connection across to the Raptor. It consisted of an airlock that had been fixed open, with a tunnel extending from the warship into the Raptor, and Velda didn't know if the Caruson had used an existing Raptor airlock or cut one open.

The Caruson side of things looked like it was expressly constructed for this purpose, which meant they'd thought about and engineered their designs with boarding other ships in mind.

It was impossible to see if there was anyone waiting on the other side, or where they'd come out, so she and Ethan crossed cautiously, weapons hot.

They leaped out the other end, ready for anything, to find they were in the launch bay, and alone.

Velda walked back a little to study the tunnel that stretched through the launch bay's airlock membrane, and hoped that when they were able to escape and break away that there would be no damage.

Because they planned to take this ship and run.

"How will we do this?" Velda would not be a prisoner again.

"They've fought each other for a few hours, now." Ethan's gaze was sweeping the bay, and he moved to a stack of supplies, and pointed his laz at something on the ground.

Velda joined him, saw there was a Caruson soldier down, and two Cores crew.

One of the crew was sliced open and had bled to death, the other one seemed to be unconscious, shot with a laz.

"If there's more like this in the rest of the ship, it will make things easier." Ethan lifted his weapon. "Let's stay together."

She nodded her agreement and moved with him to the launch bay doors.

"Ready?" he asked.

"Yes." The doors opened and they each took a side, backs together, pointing their laz down the passageway.

Shock slammed through her.

She'd expected signs of a fight but there were a lot of bodies lying in either direction, and not all unconscious. Like the crew member in the bay, some had bled and died, others were just out.

No one who had been sliced or stabbed had been left alive.

Velda started to count heads as they moved toward the bridge. The Cores had been overrun, but there were at least twelve Caruson down as well, some dead, some unconscious.

"Sylvester's people started out with their laz set to a lower level, and then realized the Caruson were out to kill them, and they upped it." Velda guessed she didn't blame them, but it meant she and Ethan needed to be careful.

There would be no coming back from a hit any more.

Up ahead, she could hear the sounds of fighting, and it was definitely coming from the lounge in front of the bridge.

They moved silently down the passage, but suddenly a door opened just up ahead and she shot the person who stepped out before she even realized she'd lifted the laz.

Ethan glanced at her, eyebrows raised, and she shrugged.

"Got to keep up with you," she said. "That was some seriously impressive fighting with Nirro."

He shook his head, amused, and she grinned back.

Someone screamed up ahead, and they both moved faster, running into the lounge together.

There were four Caruson soldiers fighting five Cores crew, and the one screaming was a Cores guard who'd been cut by a Caruso blade, and was trying to stem the bleeding.

She and Ethan opened fire with the Caruson laz, taking down three before both sides turned on them.

And then it felt as if she went weightless, as if time slowed down.

She knew where Ethan was, what he was doing, and she left him to his side, as she got busy on her own. She leaped forward, flipping herself up and over a Caruson soldier and a Cores guard, putting out a hand as she flew over the Caruson, using his shoulder to help her move faster.

She landed behind them and shot them as they tried to turn around, spun, and took out another two Cores crew.

Ethan finished off the last Caruson on his side, and there was sudden, sweet silence.

But it wasn't over.

It couldn't be that easy.

Velda looked over at the bridge and saw the double doors had been levered partway open, so there was a gap between the two halves. There was even more damage on the left side, as if it had been hacked with a blade.

They approached cautiously, skirting the gap so that no one inside could fire out at them.

It would probably be foolish to peer through the gap, Velda decided.

"I can try to pull one side open, if you're ready to fire," Ethan said.

It looked like the best option, so she stood close to where the two doors met.

Ethan took a deep breath, hands closing around the thin gap, his feet bracing. His muscles flexed as he pulled as hard as he could.

Before the door even moved, a shot lit the air, coming from the passage to the right, and they both dived away.

They were crouched down, weapons up, but exposed, and Velda rose to her feet and ran to her right to draw the shooter out as Ethan stood, angled toward the passage.

Brink stepped out, weapon raised, saw Ethan, and ducked back down the passage.

Damn.

"If I can open the door wide enough for you to squeeze through onto the bridge, then I'll go after her." Ethan was back at the bridge doors, ready to try again.

Not ideal, but they needed to take the bridge, and they had to deal with Brink. She might not be alone.

"I'm ready." She took up position again, weapon in both hands, and Ethan strained, giving a grunt as he hauled the door toward him.

The gap widened a little and the moment she could fit through, Velda threw herself at it, rolling as she landed and then coming up on her feet. She dodged a laz strike, running toward a chair and jumping so she could use the chair's arm to boost herself even higher.

She pointed her laz downward and moved it left to right, lighting the room up.

A few of the panels had their covers removed—she guessed as part of the crew's effort to get the Caruso bug out of their systems—and they sparked as they were hit. Still, she got everyone who was standing.

She landed lightly in the middle of the room, then darted to the right. She moved silently because she'd seen someone duck behind a console just in front of her.

She crouched down, edging along the side to get a better view of the person hiding, and when she peered around another console, she saw Sylvester, his back to her, laz in hand, slowly raising his head to look for her.

She considered having a conversation with him—about where they were, what his plans were, and then realized she couldn't trust a word he said.

She shot him and rose to her feet.

Then she ran toward the bridge doors and crouched low, looking through the narrow gap.

Ethan was nowhere in sight, but a head suddenly popped up from behind the food bar in the lounge.

It was a Caruson, bulky in his protective gear.

He had obviously not taken a bad hit, to have recovered so quickly.

He studied the lounge, and then, like Velda, heard the sound of fighting from down the corridor.

He moved toward it, keeping to the side so he could see down the passage and still have cover.

She couldn't let him come up behind Ethan.

She got even lower, her laz at a difficult angle, and tried to work out which shot would keep him down. Eventually, as he began to creep down the corridor, she chose his head.

He went down silently.

She'd most likely killed him, but he was carrying a curved blade in each hand, and Ethan was not expecting an attack from behind.

She suddenly realized she could hear buzzing and she turned, laz up, and saw one of the consoles was shorting.

She walked over and switched it off, and it began to emit a thin wisp of smoke that smelled sour.

That was on her, using the big Caruson laz with abandon.

She'd have been shot herself if she hadn't, but she suddenly wondered if the Caruson had chosen blades not only because of their usefulness in close quarters fighting, but also because there was much less damage to the ship that way.

She hoped whatever she'd destroyed hadn't hobbled them.

She turned back to the doors. She wanted to follow after Ethan, but she needed to hold the bridge, and she couldn't see a way to get the doors open anyway.

She just hoped he'd be back soon.

40

─────────

Ethan slid down the passage, pausing to look back at the doors to the bridge.

Through the narrow gap he saw the flash of laz fire, and hesitated. Velda was in there—

A flurry of movement and another shot forced him to dive for the opposite wall. He came up firing, but Brink had already ducked back into the room she was using for cover.

She had taken advantage of his indecision.

He needed to trust Velda and deal with the problem he'd taken on.

"How did you get back onto the Raptor?" Brink called. "I saw the Caruso towing you back to their ship."

He ignored her, edging toward the room—the med bay, he realized— and pressed up against the wall right next to the open door.

All the doors except the bridge were open, he realized. Maybe as a result of the power failure the Caruso had engineered.

Brink moved—he could hear the rustle of her clothing—and he worked out he had a good idea from the sounds she was making where she was in the room.

Not something he'd been able to do before.

He paused. *Is this reliable?* he asked the silver balls.

We would do nothing to endanger you, they assured him.

He loosened his shoulders and then dived into the med bay, rolling to the right and coming up, laz ready.

Brink gave a shriek of surprise and lifted her own laz. Ethan shot it out of her hand.

She stared down at her hand, panting. "You're fast."

"How many of you are left?" Ethan asked. Not that he expected an honest answer.

"I don't know," she said. "Linao is being held in a cell, but everyone else was defending the ship."

His gaze caught sight of a pile of restraints on the counter behind her, considered restraining her, and then shot her instead.

It was easier. He was all for an easy life right now.

He laid her on her back, then checked her laz, and saw it was set to kill. He felt even less guilty about his decision.

He jogged back to the bridge and stopped in surprise when he found a Caruson soldier dead in the passageway, blades lying beside him.

"That was me," Velda called from behind the bridge doors. "He recovered from a laz hit and started following you."

Relief washed through him.

Velda was fine.

That's all that really mattered, he realized.

He walked up to the bridge doors. "You worked out how to open them yet?"

"No." Her voice was clear and he looked down to see her crouched down on the other side, looking up at him through the gap. "I was hoping your magic fingers could do their thing."

His magic fingers.

He remembered when he'd been able to disable the lens in their cell. Maybe he could . . .

He moved to the keypad and touched it, resting his fingertips lightly. "I think I can make it open, but then I don't think it will close again."

"Works for me," Velda said.

He thought it through, realized it didn't matter if the bridge couldn't be secured if they had the whole ship—which they would.

The doors ground open, as if there was some resistance somewhere, and looking to the side he saw the damage to the door was making opening up difficult. He could smell burning by the time they were three quarters open. They stopped there, and went no further.

"Good enough." Velda had risen to her feet and reached out to touch his shoulder. "All right?"

"Yes. I think Linao is the only one left either alive or conscious. According to Brink, she's locked up in a cell."

"How much luck can one woman have?" Velda wondered. "We're going to take them all to the Caruso ship, I assume?"

Ethan was already deep inside the room, leaning down to grab Sylvester by his feet. He glanced over his shoulder at her. "Of course."

She smiled. "We'll have to do it fast. Nirro will regain consciousness soon enough."

"And we might not have got everyone in the warship, either. Anyone not unconscious is probably already trying to revive their colleagues. We need to be gone by then." He sniffed the air. "Is that just the smell of burning from the door?"

"No." Velda looked a little pained. "Some panels were damaged in the fight with Sylvester and company."

"We'll work it out. Let's get everyone off." He couldn't wait for that. He'd been thinking of it for a long time. It was time to dump their baggage and go.

Linao lifted both hands as Ethan stepped into her cell, laz trained directly on her.

Velda stood behind him, and Linao slid her a look. "I got you to the launch bay runner, that has to count."

"You did," Velda agreed. "If you cooperate, you won't get shot."

"Cooperate?" Linao looked quizzical.

"You're going over to the warship." Ethan jerked the laz, indicating for her to move. "If you hurry, you might be able to take it over."

"Not a bad option," Linao decided. "And everyone else?"

"All unconscious or dead," Velda told her. "Up to you what happens to them. You're the only one left walking."

Linao ducked her head, and Velda thought she looked thrilled.

She wondered if she was aware they were close to Fjern, and decided she probably was. That must have been what was on her mind when she shared her story about Fjern with Brink.

They herded her to the launch bay. They'd already hauled all the other bodies across, working as fast as they could and leaving Linao until last. She was too tricky for them to do it any other way.

She eyed the tunnel. Turned. "Through there?"

"Yes." And something about the way she said it made Velda sure she was thinking of running back through as soon as they had their backs turned.

She may have looked thrilled with the idea of going over to the warship as the last person walking, but Velda guessed she'd weighed up the odds and decided taking back the Raptor from the two of them would be easier than taking on Nirro and his warriors.

"Fine." Linao stepped into the tunnel. "See you around."

"Not if I can help it." Ethan had never liked her, and now he wasn't trying to hide it.

Linao laughed at him and walked away, disappearing into the Caruson warship.

"She's going to try to sneak back," Velda murmured.

"I got that, too." Ethan eyed the tunnel. "There's no way to stop entry on this side."

"No. I'll stand guard, you move us away." She was far less capable when it came to flying a ship. At least Ethan had some experience.

"Shoot to kill from now on." Ethan pulled her close, kissed her temple, and then strode away.

The door had only just closed behind him, and she was still studying the laz strength settings, when someone exploded out of the tunnel.

She lifted her weapon, but they were moving too quickly for her to aim.

A Caruson.

She felt a wave of panic and jumped straight up, not her brightest move, but the soldier slowed in surprise and she was ready to shoot as she came down.

She hit him, but he was wearing armor and he grabbed her as she landed.

He batted the laz out of her hand and it landed on the ground and slid away. The silver balls seemed to be on fire in her veins. Wherever her skin touched the Caruson's, she felt a flare of heat.

His hands clenched a little tighter on her, and then he stumbled back, stared at her out of eyes that had gone blank.

"Who else is coming through?" she asked, wondering if he even spoke her language.

He shook his head, and she took it to mean he didn't. Nirro was almost fluent, and she kept forgetting he was an exception.

She pointed at the tunnel. "Go back."

He took a hesitant step toward it, and then another.

She stepped to the side, aiming for her laz, moving slowly, afraid that too much movement would break him out of the trace he seemed to be in.

The soldier was almost at the tunnel when Nirro burst through. He was dragging Linao with him, and she had gone limp in his hold.

Except, when it came to Linao, Velda never believed what she saw.

Nirro's arrival seemed to snap the soldier out of his fog, and he turned to her, eyes wide with fear and anger.

"Get her," Nirro ordered.

The soldier looked down at his hands and hesitated.

"She does things to you if you touch her. Twists your mind." Linao's voice was hoarse and sounded groggy, but Velda didn't even believe that was genuine.

"Don't touch her skin," Nirro ordered, and finally the soldier moved.

She let him grab her, because they were less likely to shoot her if they thought she was under their control, and if she was shot, this was over.

"You're trying to take the Raptor?" Nirro asked. "That's bold."

"Why wouldn't we?" Velda asked. "It's a logical step." She felt the familiar buzz under her skin, the silver balls waiting for a chance, but the soldier was careful to avoid touching her directly.

Nirro tilted his head and studied her. "You influenced him, somehow. Have you been influencing me?"

Velda stared back. "Does it look like I'm influencing either of you?"

"No. But you were." He spoke to the soldier in Caruson and then looked down as Linao began to struggle in his grasp.

"Why did you bring her along?" Velda asked.

"She was hiding in the tunnel, and I didn't want her causing trouble on the other side." Nirro gave Linao a shake, and she subsided.

Suddenly, the whole ship shuddered, and the tunnel began to rattle in place.

Ethan had finally got the engines up and running.

"Take Velda across," Nirro told the soldier. "Ethan will surrender if we have her on the warship."

He was right. And she couldn't—wouldn't—let that happen.

Nirro looked down at Linao, seemed to be considering something, and then tossed her back into the tunnel. He shot her with his laz before she could even scramble to her feet. He pointed to her unconscious form and barked out an order to the soldier.

Telling him to get someone to drag her back, most likely.

Nirro checked his laz and headed for the bay doors.

Going to the bridge to get Ethan, she guessed. To the bridge with its open doors that would offer no protection.

Absolutely not.

A silver ball rose up out of the back of her hand, rolled up her sleeve and disappeared behind her.

The soldier holding her suddenly let her go and she dived away, grabbing up her laz and turning.

Nirro had stopped and turned at the sound of his soldier in trouble, and they both watched him shudder and then fall.

There was no question he was dead.

Velda crouched down and the silver ball emerged from his cheek, rolled across the floor to her, and she picked it up, felt it melt into her skin.

"You can tie me up, you can put me in a cell, but you cannot stop the silver balls from finding you." She rose to her feet, her laz steady on Nirro. "I'm generous enough to let you leave and take your friend with you, while the tunnel is still safe to move across."

As she spoke, the tunnel began to groan.

"Choose fast. Death, or getting your warship back." She stepped back a little, giving Nirro space to grab his guy and go.

She saw the frustration on his face. The fury.

"I know, it's hard. Believe me, I understand. Take the win I'm giving you and move it." She held out her hand and a silver ball shimmered into being in the center of it.

With a growl of anger, Nirro ran for the tunnel, grabbing the back of his soldier's jacket and hauling him with him.

He disappeared inside and it felt like moments later that, with a final screech of metal, the tunnel was pulled out of the bay.

Velda widened her stance to keep her balance and watched the airlock membrane carefully.

The ship wasn't moving fast—it seemed to be drifting—but at least they had uncoupled, and no one could easily get across.

She backed away, watching until she reached the doors and, satisfied, backed into the passageway.

The Raptor was finally theirs.

41

———

"It won't take long for the Caruso to recover a little and start chasing us," Ethan said when she flopped down beside him on the bridge. "We're going to have to pick a direction and run, and when we have enough distance, we can start trying to work out how to navigate back."

She managed a nod.

"What is it?" He was suddenly focused on her, and she shook her head and waved him back to the controls.

"Nirro and another Caruson soldier came through, with Linao, but she was just collateral. I pissed Nirro off and killed his soldier before I forced them back over." She flexed her hand. "I don't think they like me that much, anymore."

Ethan paused, eyes a little wider, then gave a nod.

"There must be maps," Velda said. "If we're near Fjern, then the Cores have come this way before."

"I wonder where that ore runner is," Ethan said. "I meant to ask Brink once or twice, but . . ."

"There was all that shooting and fighting," Velda said. "It was hard to get a word in edgewise."

Ethan's lips quirked up. "Exactly. Maybe they went back to Aponi, and if that's so, they've pinched to the black long ago."

That depended on whether Sylvester had thought he had a good chance of persuading Nirro to help mine the ore on Fjern, or whether he'd decided to send the ore runner back to the mine on Aponi. Either way, they'd need more ore to appease the Caruso, whether it be the rebels or the establishment.

"There's a pre-programmed destination here," Ethan said, pulling it up. "I'm assuming it's to Fjern, if what Nirro said is right. I can't call up anything else, and I think it's because of the damage to the panels in your laz fight."

"What choice do we have, then?" There were plenty of reasons why it was a bad idea to go to Fjern, but being able to retrace their route was a positive. And there was no question she was very curious about the new planet.

The silver balls were, too.

"None. We can stop or go off course if we find an alternative, but let's use it to get away. Even if Sylvester manages to renegotiate with Nirro, or has a Caruson government warship close by as part of a possible double-cross, he doesn't know we're stuck on a single route."

That was true, Velda realized. Neither Sylvester, nor Nirro, nor, for that matter, Linao, could possibly know that they were locked in to one destination.

"It doesn't matter, anyway. The only alternative is to choose a random direction, and that's not smart." She would rather go where she knew there were people and supplies.

"Agreed." Ethan tilted the throttle, and Velda felt the Raptor respond, pushing her back in her seat.

On the screen that showed their rear view, she watched as the warship disappeared. "How far is Fjern, according to the maps?"

Ethan tapped at the screen. "Ten hours or so."

Ten hours meant Fjern was closer than she'd guessed.

"I wonder what's happening back home," she said.

"It sounds like whatever takeover was planned has failed." Ethan stretched in his chair.

"Yes. Brink outright said it had." She was so relieved about that. Aponi was theoretically safe, and at least for now, so were they.

She looked out into the distance, to the darkness of space and the glimmer of stars and planets in the distance, and finally let herself relax.

They could go to Fjern and hopefully make official contact with a brand new Verdant String planet. If the Cores had already been there, she was sure there was damage control to be done, but she thought she was up for it.

And if it looked like there was a way to get home instead, before they reached Fjern, well, they'd make that call when it presented itself.

She stood, slid onto Ethan's lap, and smiled up at him when he curved an arm around her.

Her silver balls gave a hum of contentment as they connected to his.

"Do you have to stay at the controls?" she asked.

"For another couple of hours or so, while I get us as far away as possible, as fast as possible," he said. His voice deepened a little. "Then I can set the ship to autopilot for a bit, so we can rest."

"Good," she said, and laid her head on his shoulder. "I was getting tired of being responsible."

COMING NEXT

Look out for the 9th, and final, book in the Verdant String series, coming late 2026. You can sign up to Michelle Diener's new release notification list through her website (michellediener.com) to stay informed, as well as receive exclusive content like short stories, available only to subscribers.

THE VERDANT STRING SERIES

The planets of the Verdant String, the green, fecund sources of life spanning five solar systems, comprise the Verdant String Coalition.

This is the setting for the science fiction romance series from award-winning novelist Michelle Diener.

While the people of the Verdant String know they have a common ancestor, a group of explorers who colonized the planets at the same time thousands of years ago, the mysteries of who they were, and where they came from, persist.

Each book in the series can be read as a standalone:

Interference & Insurgency Box Set | Breakaway | Breakeven | Trailblazer | High Flyer | Wave Rider | Peace Maker | Enthraller | Defender

Fantasy Novels by Michelle Diener

The Rising Wave series:

The Rising Wave (Prequel novella to THE TURNCOAT KING and now included as bonus material in The Turncoat King)

The Turncoat King

The Threadbare Queen

Fate's Arrow

Truth's Blade

Truth's Blade Bonus Short Story (Available free to newsletter subscribers)

Other fantasy novels:

Mistress of the Wind

The Dark Forest series:

The Golden Apple

The Silver Pear

Historical Fiction Novels

Traffic Warden Mysteries:

Ticket Out

Return Ticket

Susanna Horenbout series:

In a Treacherous Court

Dangerous Sanctuary (A short story - available for free, exclusively to readers who sign up to Michelle Diener's New Release Notification List)

Keeper of the King's Secrets

In Defense of the Queen

ABOUT THE AUTHOR

Michelle Diener is an award winning author of historical fiction, science fiction and fantasy romance.

Michelle was born in London and currently lives in Australia with her husband and children.

You can contact Michelle through her website or sign up to receive notification when she has a new book out on her New Release Notification page.

Connect with Michelle
www.michellediener.com

ACKNOWLEDGMENTS

Thank you as always to all the people who help make my books the best they can be—first and foremost, Jo and Claire B. Another huge thank you to members on my ARC team: Margaret M. for her invaluable feedback, as well as the wonderful Diane J., Sheila R., Tania H., James McR., Jess W., Lynn S., and Darla M.